HERO

The Horse That Rescued Me

Camilla Kattell

Light Horse Publishing
Santa Fe, NM

Hero: The Horse That Rescued Me
Camilla Kattell

Light Horse Publishing
Santa Fe, New Mexico
www.lighthorsepublishing.com

ISBN 978-09966754-6-8 (paperback)

ISBN 978-0-9966754-7-5 (epub)

ISBN 978-0-9966754-8-2 (mobi)

Library of Congress Control Number: 2019909946

Printed in the United States of America

First Edition

Front cover picture: *Cimarron*
Permission from The Horse Shelter, Los Cerrillos, NM
The Horse Shelter serves as a sanctuary for New Mexico's abandoned, abused and neglected horses. Rescued horses will be rehabilitated and adopted out whenever possible to environments that support their well-being and future long-term care.
http://www.thehorseshelter.org

Dedicated to my family:
Chris, Doug, Trish, Sam, and Jake

CHAPTER 1

As I APPROACH my sixteenth birthday, the events of the past year force their way into my awareness. They demand that I do some revisiting in an effort to find understanding and closure. They come back to me in my dreams. It has been a difficult year with many ups and downs, but in the end it has been a year of growth and mostly happy endings. It all started the day Black Diamond was born.

I was alone that day and my first thought was, this can't be happening!

Bess, our mare, was restlessly pacing in her stall and she was sweating. I knew those were signs of impending birth. My parents were out of town and had left me home for the first time. I found Bess like that shortly after our ranch hands, Miguel and Andy, my helpers, had left for a square dance. I ran to the house to call Doc Mason, our vet, but he was still out working on a ranch and not expected home soon.

Feeling a bit panicky I returned to the barn and sat down outside Bess's stall to collect myself. Maybe I could get Mom and Dad's friend and our neighbor, John Winslow, to help. Then I remembered that the Winslows were on a packing trip this week. Luke Winslow, my best friend, was like a brother to me, but that wouldn't help tonight.

I knew I must calm down. It sure looked like I was on my own.

The timing was totally unexpected and worrisome. Bess wasn't expected to foal until Dad was home. She seemed to have progressed very fast all of a sudden. My dad, Colin, planned to let me watch and learn when the foal was born, because I want to be a veterinarian, but it was never intended that I would deliver the foal.

I was jerked back into the moment when I heard rustling in the straw. I got up to check Bess. She was down. Was she was going into labor? Again I ran to the house for a bucket of warm water. We had a bundle of clean towels already in the supply cabinet of the tack room and I got those.

I told myself I was about to do my first serious vet work. In my head that sounded much more confident than I felt. My knees were shaking.

When I got back to the stall, Bess was standing up and started to pace again. I felt relieved. Maybe this wasn't going to happen before Miguel and Andy returned later in the evening.

Doc Mason had loaned me a book about foaling, so I knew what signs to watch for and Bess's behavior matched all the symptoms. The two most important things to watch for were that the foal was born front legs first and then, when it arrived, to make sure its nose was clear so it could breathe. I even remembered Dad talking about how important it would be to clean the foal's face and nose.

Okay, after my review of the steps, I felt a bit more confident that I knew how this was supposed to go. I crossed my fingers and hoped it would go according to Doc's book.

I told myself Bess was good at this and would probably do fine mostly on her own. She has had several foals without any trouble. However, try as I might to reassure myself, I still felt panicky. I'll turn fifteen when my parents return and I've been around the horses with Dad all my life, but I'm not ready for this responsibility. I did know it was important to stand by to help, just in case there was a problem. But what would I do if there was a problem?

I eased into the stall and slowly used a pitch fork to make sure all the straw was clean. Bess seemed calmer now and she nosed around for a treat. Maybe this won't happen so fast, I thought optimistically. I kept looking for a reprieve.

"Sorry Bess. No treat. This is a time when you need to focus on the job ahead. I'll stay by you, but I hope you are ready to handle this pretty much on your own, if the time has come," I said to her as I stroked her neck, wondering if it was Bess or me who needed the most calming. Then Bess lay down again and sort of groaned. Gosh, this must be it after all!

And then it happened. Bess had several large contractions and I could see the foal was coming. Then there were more strong contractions and, before I knew it, the new foal was laying on the clean straw. Why, that wasn't so bad! I would make a vet after all, I congratulated myself.

I moved in quickly to towel off the foal's head and make sure the nostrils were clear of mucous. The foal sort of snorted and took a deep breath.

"Oh, Bess, we did it. We have a live foal. Well, I guess you really did it. What an amazing miracle," I said to Bess, so proud, relieved, and moved by what I had just witnessed. I just sat there for several minutes watching the foal breathe.

But then I felt an uneasy sense that something was wrong. Something just didn't seem right. I looked at the foal very closely and it appeared to be just fine. Then I realized that Bess was still lying out flat. She hadn't even lifted her head to look at the foal.

I was really scared. It seemed like she should be showing some sign of movement. Going to her head I sat down beside her and stroked her neck. She was breathing heavily and quivering. "I guess you are very tired, Bess," I tried to comfort myself into thinking all was right.

Bess opened her eyes and looked up at me. She nickered very softly and took a deep breath and then she lay still. Had she just quit breathing? I was stunned. What should I do? And then I realized Bess was no longer with me. Her heart must have failed!

I put my head on Bess's neck and cried. My heart felt like it would burst. Our dear, sweet Bess was gone. She had been my friend for as long as I could remember.

Then rustling in the straw jolted me back to the moment and I remembered the foal. Without a mother would the beautiful black foal die? I put my head on Bess again and thanked her for the gift she had just given us. I promised her I would do everything I could to save her son or daughter. I stroked her silky neck one last time and turned my attention to my new problem.

To my delight I saw we had a filly. She was black, like her sire, with three white feet and a white star on her forehead. She looked perfect.

I hated that the filly was lying close to her dead mother. I knew nature would soon urge the foal to find her dam. It wouldn't be long until she would stand and search for her first meal. I knew those instincts were strong and I realized I needed help.

Afraid to leave the foal alone, once again I ran like a mad woman to the house and called our neighbor, Mrs. Swenson.

"Mrs. Swenson, Mom and Dad are away and I'm here alone. Our mare Bess just foaled, but she died in the process. Can I get one of your nursing bottles that you use to feed orphan calves? I've got to try to save this foal," I rushed to explain.

"Calm down, dear," Mrs. Swenson said in a composed voice. "I'm on my way and I'll bring the bottles. Keep the foal warm and quiet," she hurriedly told me, as she picked up on my anxiety. "I've saved a few orphans in my day. We'll do our best to save your foal." Thank goodness calling for help got the experienced voice of Mrs. Swenson.

I ran back to the barn and made sure another stall had a deep bed of clean straw so we could move the filly away from Bess.

Mrs. Swenson, the miracle lady, arrived very soon and I met her coming to the barn with the bottles. She gave me a crushing hug. Mrs. Swenson was a large, competent woman who raised three sons on a cattle ranch. She and Mr. Swenson are good, worthy people and I was so relieved to feel her confidence.

I was afraid the foal's instincts would soon drive her to try to stand and find food while we were getting organized. Nature prepared foals to stand, feed, and be able to run in only a few hours. In the wild they are flight animals and they had to be ready very quickly to escape danger.

Mrs. Swenson assessed the situation quickly.

"I have another stall for the filly if we can move her," I said, hoping that the filly wouldn't be confronted with a non-responsive mother.

"Good idea. I'll lift around her girth and you lift her hind quarter. She will be heavy, but we can sort of drag her feet," Mrs. Swenson said, leaping into action.

We managed to get the move completed, though not gracefully, with no harm to the filly. Phew, she must weigh a hundred pounds.

Bess never had a chance to perform the ritual of greeting that a mare gives her foal, welcoming it into the world. They should have been sniffing each other all over and getting acquainted. The mare would clean the foal. The filly would have explored until she found her mother's udder and would have drunk her fill. Sure enough instinct for that process kicked in and the filly started trying to stand.

"I'll go to the house and warm some milk. You keep massaging her with a towel to help her circulation," Mrs. Swenson instructed. "If she wants to stand just stay by her and make sure she doesn't crash into anything." Mrs. Swenson moved her sturdy bulk with amazing speed toward the house.

Right on schedule the filly began her first struggles to get up. With a new born foal it was quite entertaining to watch how they learned to manage their long legs. Soon she got up with her four legs spread in four opposing directions. But she was up and balancing. She took a few wobbly steps and fell back down into the soft straw. Presently, she was struggling again and she gained her feet. The filly plopped down into the straw once more, but after a little rest she began to get the hang of getting up and standing.

Then nature triggered her first realization that she had another job to undertake. She had to find where her first meal would come from. Fortunately, Mrs. Swenson made her appearance with a bottle of nice warm milk.

I held the bottle in a position that would keep the filly from choking and offered her the nipple. At first, she wasn't getting the idea and I was terrified that she wouldn't learn to use the bottle. I knew it would be a death knell for her if she wouldn't accept this less-than-perfect substitute.

I put some milk on her lips and let her suckle some on my fingers. Finally, she got the idea and she drank enough that she was out of danger for the moment. Unfortunately, we could not duplicate the nutritious value of the mother's natural milk.

"Good job," Mrs. Swenson said. "You are a natural. But how in the world are you going to save this filly until your parents get here. This is an around the clock job. I can come over and give you some relief a couple times a day, but you are going to need more help."

"I think I should take her into the mud room that we added to our house. It is roomy and I can cover the floor. I'll need to feed her often and check on her through the night. I could set up a cot in there," I thought on my feet about how to do this. "Miguel and Andy will be home later and they'll help. We'll manage. I sure appreciate your help now, though. I was a bit panicked."

"I think you have a cool head on you. You have probably saved this foal. However, I can't imagine that Anna would approve of a horse in the house," Mrs. Swenson gave voice to reason, thinking of my mother. "A cot in the barn would be better. You could catch time in the house when the men are here to spell you. Why, Anna would never forgive me if I let you take a horse in the house. That's just too much for her to face when she comes home."

"I guess you're right. I'm not thinking too clearly. I'll bring a cot down here. It will just be very sad to be here until we can move Bess," I told her.

"Don't you fret. I'll have Mr. Swenson come over early tomorrow morning and take care of that issue. You go up to the house and get something to eat and then bring your cot and blankets down. I'll watch the foal until you get back." Relief and gratitude flowed through me at the kindness of our friends the Swensons. Mrs. Swenson's logic made sense.

"Thanks, Mrs. Swenson, you've been a life saver. I think I feel a little like I'm in shock at this point," I confessed.

"Go on now. Everything will be okay. Don't forget to call Doc Mason first thing in the morning," Mrs. Swenson said.

I gratefully went to the house to prepare myself for a long night. When I got into the house the phone was ringing.

"Hello," I answered, wishing it would be my parents.

"This is Doc Mason. I just got home and Lizzy said you had a foal born, but the mare died," Doc Mason said.

"Oh, I'm so glad you called back. Mrs. Swenson is here helping me with the foal. Bess quit breathing right after the foal was born. We are feeding the filly from a bottle. She is standing now and has nursed some," I reported to the Doc.

"Well, I'm sorry to hear about Bess. I'll come out in the morning first thing to check the foal. Mrs. Swenson has a lot of experience and she'll be good help. Just feed the foal each time she seems to be searching," he instructed.

When I returned to the barn with my cot and sleeping bag, Mrs. Swenson was dutifully watching the filly. "I think I have a plan, if it works for you," she said.

"What's your plan?" I asked.

"Until your parents return, I'll stay here at night in the house. About every three hours I'll warm some milk and bring it to the barn. You must stay near the filly to keep an eye on her. She needs to be watched," Mrs. Swenson explained. "I'll go home during the day and Miguel and Andy can help you."

"Are you sure that isn't too much?" I worried.

"No, my dear. It is a very tricky business to save an orphan horse and we have to get her a good start," she said.

"Doc called back and he'll come out early in the morning, which isn't long from now," I said with a yawn.

"Good. It's okay to sleep some if you can. I'll wake you when I come out. I imagine you'll hear the foal getting up or down and just keep a close eye on her," Mrs. Swenson said as she left for the house.

I set up my cot in a corner of the stall and left a light on in the barn. The filly was stretched out sleeping, which was a good sign. I got into my sleeping bag, but as tired as I was, I couldn't sleep. I was too excited.

My thoughts wandered. This was a special foal for us. Bess is . . . was a Quarter Horse that had produced consistently nice foals. She had been given to Dad by a grateful client who wanted a good home for her. Dad splurged for this breeding and paid for a top Quarter Horse sire, Diablo. He was a coal black stallion and had been siring successful offspring in the show ring.

I was pleased we got a filly. All the other horses on the ranch are geldings because they made good workers on the trails. Having Bess around had given us a chance every few years to have a foal. I love playing with the foals and teaching them to lead. When they become well accustomed to people, they make better partners.

Very late I heard the pickup truck drive in and stop by the barn. My thoughts returned to the present. I jumped from the cot and ran to meet Miguel and Andy.

Andy staggered and almost fell from the truck. "Well, hello beautiful. What'cha been doin'," Andy greeted. I stood staring at his uncharacteristic behavior.

"What's wrong with Andy?" I asked Miguel.

"Nothing that a good sleep won't fix. I'm afraid he had a bit too much beer. He met some of his old rodeo buddies and they celebrated a little too much," Miguel explained. He came around the truck and pulled Andy's arm over his shoulder and started leading him toward the bunk house.

"Well, I got news for you. He better be sharp tomorrow because he's going to be doing some extra work," I told Miguel. "I didn't know Andy was a drunk."

"He's not a drunk. He just had a few too many beers. What happens tomorrow?" Miguel asked.

"We have a new foal in the barn and a dead mother," I blurted out through my haze of fatigue. "I need help and I was counting on you two."

"What happened? When I left Bess looked okay," Miguel said.

"I think her heart must have failed. The foal was born okay, but Bess never got up. Mrs. Swenson came and helped me move the foal. She set me up with bottles for feeding. Mrs. Swenson is in the house and will warm milk through the night."

"Let me dump Andy in his bunk and I'll come help you," Miguel said, as he half dragged Andy toward the bunk house.

"I'm okay for tonight. Mrs. Swenson will help. But you guys may have to spell me some during the day until Mom and Dad get home. I'm hoping you guys will take care of all the chores while I stay with the filly," I told Miguel.

"A filly. That's good. I'll be back to look in on you when I get rid of this bum. Your dad will be so pleased if you are able to save the filly," Miguel said as he moved with his charge on to the bunk house.

Back in the barn I couldn't quit watching the filly. It seemed like no time at all when Mrs. Swenson came into the barn again.

"Have you slept any dear?" she asked.

"I don't think so. I've been so worried. The filly got up once and I went to her to make sure she felt warm. I stroked her and talked to her. I expect she was looking for her mother," I said.

The foal raised her head and studied us. Then she got to her feet and I thought she nickered very softly.

"Maybe she'll think I'm her mom," I told Mrs. Swenson.

I went to her and stroked her neck. Then I offered her the bottle again and she took it quickly this time.

"That is a good sign," Mrs. Swenson said. "I think she is going to be a strong filly and will thrive with your care."

I smiled my thanks to my helpful angel.

Early the next morning while I was once again feeding the filly and Mrs. Swenson was leaving, Doc Mason arrived as promised.

"Oh my, look at this beauty," he said when he saw her. She was standing tall like she had been on her legs for weeks and thoroughly working on a bottle of milk. "Looks like you have done an amazing job of getting her started without poor Bess."

"I hope so. Mrs. Swenson has been a life saver. I have to admit, though, that I'm dead on my feet. Miguel and Andy will take turns today watching over her while I get some sleep between feedings," I said, wondering if I was making any sense."

Doc Mason came in the stall where the filly was alertly watching him. I put one arm around her chest and the other around her rump to hold her while the Doc checked her temperature and heart rate. He looked into her mouth for healthy gum color and a clear throat passage. Doc determined that she seemed in fine condition. He gave her shots in her rump muscle. She jumped a little at that but, didn't really seem distressed by it.

"I have what I hope will be good news. After I talked to you last night about the foal, the foreman of the Horseshoe Ranch called and said he had a mare that had just lost a foal. He said she is a gentle mare that has always been a good mother. He wondered if I might know anyone in need of a nurse mare for an orphan foal. I told him about our conversation and said I would ask you," Doc said.

"What would that mean?" I asked. "Would the mare accept a strange foal?"

"I don't know for sure. It would be tricky. Since this foal is so new and the mare just lost her foal yesterday, it might work. Do you want to try?" Doc asked.

"Gee, I don't know. I wish Dad was here to decide something like that. But if you think it might work, it seems worth a try. I think the filly would have a much better chance to thrive if she had a mother," I said.

"I'll call Alonzo back right away. He would have to bring the mare over right now. We would put her in the next stall, then bring her closer to the foal, and gradually see if the mare would accept the filly and let her nurse," Doc explained further.

As we were talking Miguel walked in. "I've seen a mare adopt several times and they were very successful. It sounds like it would be worth a try Emily."

"Okay. Let's see if we can make it work," I decided, feeling very grown up making such an important decision. I just felt Dad would expect me to take the responsibility and give this a try. It could make all the difference for our little one.

Chapter 2

Soon Doc came back from the house. "I was able to get hold of Alonzo and he was delighted that we had a foal that his mare might be able to help. I gave him the directions and he said he would bring her right over. He'll be here in about a half hour."

While the Doc and I waited, I went in to call Mrs. Swenson to let her know what was in the works. If this mare would accept the foal it would make a lot of difference in the work load for her and me.

Back at the barn Doc asked, "What are you going to call her?"

"I thought about Black Beauty, but that has been taken," I said.

The doc laughed good-naturedly. "Yes, that one is taken," he said.

"How about Black Diamond?" I asked. "She has a star, but my buckskin is named Falling Star so I won't use star in her name. The white on her forehead is diamond shaped. I think that will be her name. Black Diamond."

"That sounds like a great name," Doc replied.

When Alonzo arrived he led a nice paint mare from his trailer. She was medium size and had produced many foals. It was easy to see that she had lots of milk as a result of foaling yesterday.

Doc greeted Alonzo and introduced me and Miguel.

"Well, Emily, I hope this works for your foal. I'm not sure how this mare will react, but she has always been an attentive dam and I wouldn't be surprised if she would adopt your foal," Alonzo said.

We led the mare into the stall next to Diamond and let them put their noses together through the gap in the boards. The mare nickered softly to the foal and Diamond showed interest, but she didn't really seem to understand what the mare could mean to her.

Since there were no fireworks from the mare, we brought her around to Diamond's stall door and opened the door. Again the mare showed interest in Diamond and didn't display any hostility. Soon Diamond walked over and they sniffed each other.

"Emily, go in and hold Diamond against the far wall. I'll bring the mare gradually closer. We want to make sure she doesn't want to kick," Alonzo instructed. I was learning a lot that would help me to become a vet.

The paint mare, named Magpie, eased into the stall. She sniffed Diamond all over and they seemed fine together.

"Okay, Emily, so far so good," Alonzo said. "Now, keeping your body between the mare and foal, but close to the front of the mare, move Diamond toward Magpie's udder and see if she allows the foal near her."

I did as Alonzo told me. Diamond was a bit slow getting the idea that her breakfast might not be coming from the bottle. Soon she reached for the udder and Magpie snorted and moved away. My heart sank. I realized how much I was hoping this would work.

"That's okay. This might take a few tries," Alonzo said. "Magpie isn't acting hostile to Diamond and that's a good sign.

I glanced up at Miguel standing in the door and he gave me a thumbs- up to encourage me.

After the third try Magpie allowed Diamond to nurse. It was a lovely sight. She turned her head and nuzzled Diamond, a sure sign of acceptance.

Doc exhaled a big sigh as though he had been holding his breath. "This will make a big difference for this filly. The dam's milk has colostrum, an antibiotic like substance, which will protect the foal from infection and will help start her digestive system."

We quietly moved out of the stall to watch and see how this bond developed. Since Magpie accepted the foal and showed no hostility, it should be safe. Diamond was sniffing around Magpie and Magpie stood very quietly. It was like she was handling Diamond with kid gloves.

"I believe we have a match," Alonzo said with a big smile.

"I'm very grateful," I told him. "I wasn't looking forward to having to feed her every couple hours. I'm a bit punchy just from being out here all night. Can Dad talk about the arrangements for using Magpie when he gets back in a couple days?"

"Sure, that will be fine. I'm really glad that the timing worked like it did. Thanks Doc for getting us together so quickly. The timing was key to success," Alonzo said.

We all watched for a while and Magpie seemed quite at home looking after Diamond. Soon Diamond was stretched out in the straw taking one of her many naps. She would grow much better in this natural situation than she would have with bottle feeding.

Alonzo said he needed to get on. We would be in touch and I wrote down all his contact information. Doc said he had calls to make, but he would come by when he finished in the afternoon to check on us.

I placed my cot right outside the stall of my new little family, determined to keep an eye on them. I fervently hoped Magpie would continue to look after our orphan, but I wanted to make sure there was no trouble. I lay down on the cot and was out like a light.

About four hours later I woke up startled. Where was I? And then it hit me that I was asleep in the barn with a new foal and a mare that I didn't know. What a shameful lapse! I jumped up to see if anything horrible had happened while I so carelessly slept.

To my great relief, Diamond was stretched out in the straw sleeping and Magpie was standing with her head hanging, dozing. She seemed quite happy to watch over this orphan. They made quite the scene of contentment.

When I moved to the stall door, Diamond raised her head to see what was going on. Magpie nuzzled her. Diamond blinked at this new world, and struggled to her feet. Magpie nickered softly to her.

They nosed each other and seemed to be expressing their new found affection. Then Diamond started searching under Magpie until she found that warm, full udder that provided so much good health for her. Magpie patiently let Diamond nurse, even when Diamond was a little rough.

Since I didn't really know Magpie, nor she me, I spoke to her and slowly went into the stall. Since she was facing me I was able to go to her head and let her sniff my hand. I talked quietly to her and stroked her head and neck. I wanted her to decide she could trust me.

I got some hay and put in Magpie's feeder. It had to be some time since she had eaten, but I only gave her a small feeding. She'll need to get used to our hay. I don't want her change in diet to upset her milk. I'll give her several small feedings of hay and start her on a small amount of grain tonight. While she was in my charge, I didn't want her losing weight.

When Diamond was done nursing, Magpie ate peacefully. She seemed comfortable with my presence. Some mares with foals can be aggressive and touchy, but this mare trusted the situation.

Diamond was looking at me curiously. I think she had it sorted out by now that I wasn't her mother despite the bottle feedings. She took a couple tentative steps toward me. I held my hand out so she could begin to recognize me by my scent. I was able to walk up to her and gently pet her neck. She seemed rather bold, which was a good sign. If we're lucky she'll have Bess's good nature.

Miguel came into the barn. "Sleeping Beauty, you're up! I think you were really tuckered out," he said. Miguel bantered with me a lot, but today he was speaking tenderly to me. Sometimes he treated me like a daughter. "I came in a couple times and the new mare was doing fine. Once the filly was nursing and once she was sleeping. I think you could leave them for a while."

"Thanks. I'm glad you were watching while I got my beauty sleep. The mare is called Magpie and I'm just calling the filly Diamond, short for Black Diamond. It looks like Magpie will make a very good stand-in for Bess. I sure wonder what Mom and Dad are going to say about what has happened."

"They'll be in for several surprises. While you were asleep we were able to remove Bess. We buried her on the small hill at the back of the big pasture. I hope that was okay," Miguel told me.

"It's good that her stall was far enough from where I was that I missed that. I think watching her be buried would have been too much for me. Thanks to you and Mr. Swenson for taking care of that," I said sadly. I'll visit her in a day or so, when the shock of her being gone diminishes a little.

"The mare and foal are doing well enough that you could go get a shower and something to eat. You'll probably want to sleep out here again tonight, just to make sure that nothing outside disturbs them," Miguel said as he helped me close up my cot. "I'll feed the mare some more hay and some grain when Andy and I feed the string tonight. Get some rest."

"I'm sure glad you are here to step up and take care of everything on the ranch with Dad gone. By the way, did Andy live?" I asked.

"He's alive, but not very pleasant. I'd stay away from him. I'll back you up here in the barn and keep him working by himself until his headache is better," Miguel laughed.

"Well, don't baby him," I too laughed. "He needs to sweat it out."

I checked my charges again and then went to the house. A long hot shower helped revive me.

The phone rang and it was Mrs. Swenson.

"I owe you so much for all the help you gave me last night," I told her. Then I gave her the details about Magpie and how well she seems to be working out.

"That's wonderful. Your foal will prosper with a substitute mother. The mare will help teach her how to be a horse, too, once you can start putting them out on pasture. I'm so glad for you. You did a marvelous job last night and your parents will be very pleased. Do you have anything to eat?" the 'in-charge type,' Mrs. Swenson, asked.

I laughed. "You are like a substitute mother yourself. There is a steak in the frig I'll put on the fire and Mom left some potato salad and one of her pies. I got some sleep while Miguel checked on things. Say thanks for me to Mr. Swenson for taking care of Bess."

"You're welcome. What are neighbors for? Let me know if you need anything else," Mrs. Swenson offered and then hung up.

After a good meal with lots of iced tea, I fell asleep again. I realized that until Mom and Dad got home this would be the kind of schedule I'd be living. I could count on Miguel to cover for me anytime. We're a team.

About 3:00 o'clock Doc Mason stopped by again on his way home. He stood with me and observed the foal and dam for a while. He could learn a lot about their condition by observing their behavior.

"That looks like a fine, strong foal," he said. "The mare looks like she is doing her job. Why don't you put a halter on Magpie and face her toward me. She knows you and won't be alarmed by you entering the stall. Then I'll come in."

Doc Mason came in the stall and petted Magpie, talking quietly to her all the time and reassuring her with his non-threatening movements. He checked Magpie's temperature and heart rate.

"She looks fine," he said. "She isn't showing any sign of discomfort or fever since her foaling yesterday. She seems to have adapted to the new situation."

Then he turned to Diamond. She was alertly peeking at him from behind Magpie. He walked to her and put one arm around her rump and one around her chest and eased her to the front of Magpie. Magpie watched alertly, but didn't show any unease.

Doc checked Diamond's temperature and heart rate again. He looked her all over and determined that she seemed to be doing fine.

Then Doc and I moved out of the stall to watch them again. As Doc left the barn he said, "When your dad gets home, tell him he has a fine healthy filly. I'll come by again in a couple days to check Diamond, but I think with Magpie's help, she'll do fine. You've done a good job saving this foal."

"Thanks Doc," I said. "Dad will be delighted with Diamond. Until he gets home, I'll stay in the barn at night. Miguel helps with them during the day."

"Well, get some rest and let me know if you need anything," Doc said as he got into his truck.

CHAPTER 3

THE NEXT TWO days are a blur in my memory. I spent nights on the cot in the barn and the days mixing some rest with helping Miguel and Andy with our usual chores and watching over Diamond.

I found Diamond to be a laugh a minute. Foals are fascinating as they discover their world. Diamond was curious and showed a lot of boldness for her age. She recognized me and when I went into her stall she would come right to me. When I was cleaning the stall or putting out feed for Magpie she stuck her nose into everything. I loved it.

I missed Bess, but I truly appreciated Magpie. Diamond was really doing well under Magpie's watch. She was visibly filling out, and her coat was growing sleek. I could hardly wait for Dad to see her. She was definitely the best foal we had bred and I knew he would be pleased.

Miguel and Andy were working hard to pick up the extra work in Dad's absence. Andy, after apologizing for his drinking folly, was shyly sorry.

I spent a lot of time watching Diamond and had time to think about how lucky I was to have been born into the beautiful mountain country of Colorado. With Dad running his own adventure trips in the mountains we lived a quiet, but contented, life on our ranch. I felt very happy. I felt proud of my accomplishment with Diamond.

Since I was little, my dad had let me tag along with him whenever I could and he had taught me so much about the skills needed to get around in these mountains. My lessons had been about things like handling horses, cooking on an open fire, packing a mule, handling a raft, making sure not to be caught by a lightning storm above tree line, and setting up a tent. As you have no doubt guessed, I loved the outdoor life.

Mom worked in Alton at Samaritan Hospital as a physician's assistant. It wasn't a bad commute and she was really good with patients. She had a great bedside manner and was a compassionate caregiver. She even had enough patience to teach me a lot of first aid skills that I might need in the wilderness.

My dad had proudly told me the story about the name Campbell, which means "crooked mouth." To Dad a crooked mouth must be a "smiling mouth" so he creatively named the ranch "Campbell Ranch." My parents named me Emily because they liked it and it meant "industrious and striving." For some reason, they believed that was the way I would be and, sure enough, I was energetic and always working toward some goal. Life on a ranch was geared to the ebb and flow of daylight hours and the needs of jobs and livestock. My parents said I had limitless energy and enthusiasm for our ranching life style. And they are right.

Dad grew up around here and when he graduated from high school all he wanted to do was be a guide and work in the mountains. However, his parents were insistent that he go to college and expose himself to other places and ideas. So he dutifully went off to Colorado State and studied literature and husbandry. He was very smart in college and graduated with honors. He was no slouch.

Mom and Dad met in college while my mom was studying medicine. I guess it must have been love at first sight because they dated all through college and then married.

Mom supported Dad in his dream of working outside. She agreed to come to the mountains so he could build his business. They bought several hundred acres of valley grassland and built a roomy, log style home. Mom worked to support things until Dad could get his business off the ground. My dad was a hard worker and he always did right by his clients, so he built up a good business.

When I came along Mom wanted to continue working, but she stayed home until I was two, when Maria came to live with us to keep house and look after me. As soon as I could toddle after my dad, I was with him as much as I could be.

As I grew I was good with the horses and enjoyed work around the ranch. I didn't have any sisters or brothers. I believe it was decided that, with two careers in the family, one busy little one was enough to keep everyone occupied.

We had Miguel and Andy year around to help Dad with the upkeep of the ranch and at least one of them always went along when Dad was guiding. Guiding was a lot of work. Horses have to be cared for, camps set up, food packed and cooked, and the visitors kept happy.

Miguel used to seem to me to be about a hundred years old, but judging from the amount of work he did, I've figured out that he wasn't that old. He had been with Dad since the early days and they worked as though they were four hands with one brain.

Andy came to us about five years ago. He was down on his luck and really needing a job. He had been riding the rodeo circuit, but that was a rough way to try to make a living. He grew up on a ranch in Nebraska, so he knew how to do everything we needed. Andy was especially good with maintaining the rafts and the equipment that goes with them. He liked the white water rafting, too, so he usually went along on those trips.

Finally, it was time for Mom and Dad to come home. I was so excited, with so many things to tell them and, of course, show them. I was proud of our success with Diamond and felt very grown up after being in charge.

At 5:00, as Miguel and I were feeding the horses, I heard them drive in. I ran to greet them. I flung myself into Mom's arms.

"Wow, I've missed you guys. I have lots of news," I burst out.

Dad gave me a bear hug. "Have you enjoyed being in charge?"

"Well, it has been interesting. More than I expected. I'm glad you guys are back to take over the responsibility," I laughed. "Come with me. I have something to show you."

My parents looked puzzled, but smiled and indulged me. They followed me to the barn. I opened the stall door. Diamond was lying down as usual. But as soon as she saw company she got to her feet. Magpie moved to be between Diamond and all the excitement, but Diamond peeked around her.

"Wow. Where did they come from?" Dad exclaimed. "Where did you get these horses?"

"Dad, when the foal came, I was here alone. I couldn't find Doc, and Miguel and Andy had gone to a dance. I had to deliver the foal alone," I explained, recalling my fears at the time.

"That doesn't explain who these horses are," Dad said with puzzlement.

"I'm sorry. I'm too excited to make sense. Dad, this is our foal. Bess did all the work and delivered her. I'm afraid she died after the foal was born. It was awful. I was scared to death that Diamond would die, too. Mrs. Swenson came and helped me. She knows how to care for orphans. And then Miguel and Andy helped all week and I slept here in the barn. Doc found Magpie and she has served as a surrogate mother to our orphan. I'm calling the filly Black Diamond. Diamond for short." I explained everything in one breath.

Mom put her arm around me and said, "Emily, how in the world did you do everything?"

"I'm so sorry about Bess, but finding this mare sounds like a god send," Dad said. "I take it she is Magpie."

"Yes," I said, regaining my composure.

"It sounds like you thought of a perfect name for the filly," Mom said. Dad nodded. After petting Magpie and letting her sniff him, Dad moved around to where he could look Diamond over with his trained eye.

"She's a fine looking filly. I'm so glad we got a filly. She will be fun for you to train. I think Magpie and Diablo were a good nick," Dad said. His pleasure showed in his smile. "Emily, you've done an amazing job here. I'm very pleased. You'll make a fine vet."

Those words are all the reward I would ever need for the stressful week I had just lived through.

"Mr. Swenson and Miguel buried Bess on the hill in the pasture," I told them, feeling the sadness again. "She did a good job delivering Diamond."

"Well, we owe the Swensons a debt of gratitude. I'll invite them over for your birthday celebration tomorrow," Mom said.

Miguel came in and welcomed my parents. They thanked him for helping me so much this week. They would do the same for Andy later.

"Let's get unpacked and get some dinner," Dad said. "I'm anxious to get back to normal."

Mom agreed and gave me another hug. It felt good to be a happy family together again.

When we were finally able to sit down to a light dinner I inquired about Mom and Dad's time away from the ranch.

"How was it to not have to get up with the sun to start working?" I asked.

"Just marvelous," Mom said. "Though your dad, a man of habit, was still up making coffee before sunrise. You can't take the rancher out of the boy."

"I hate to admit it, but I missed the place. This ranch and YOU are our lives. I'm glad to be home. And I don't even have to worry about going through a foaling. I seem to have left things in very good hands," Dad said with a big smile for me.

"You can say that again," chimed in Mom. "You are an amazing young woman. I hope your birthday present will seem like a worthy reward."

"Don't tease me, Mom. That is cruel. Just exactly when will I be receiving this present?" I inquired.

"We'll have the Swensons over and Miguel, Andy, and Maria will join us for dinner tomorrow night. You will wait until then," Mom cheerfully proclaimed.

"Mom had time to do some dress shopping for you in Denver. I hope you'll like the colors she chose," Dad said seriously.

"I'll run away from home if my fifteenth birthday is cerebrated with a new dress. Where would I wear it anyway?" I mock pouted.

"Well, Luke Winslow will probably be asking you to dances after you enter high school. We'll want you spiffed up fine for that," Dad continued teasing.

"I'm not going to any ole' dance with Luke. I'd rather stay home and ride Star," I said.

Mom laughed. "Oh honey, that will all change in time."

After dinner Dad and I walked to the barn for a last check on Magpie and Diamond. We decided that Magpie was very competent to care for Diamond.

It was the first night that I got to sleep in my bed since Diamond arrived. I looked forward to clean, cool sheets and a firm mattress. I didn't know if I could sleep because I was so excited about my birthday tomorrow, but I was asleep when my head hit the pillow. It was 6:00 AM when I next opened my eyes.

Chapter 4

I WAS PRETTY sure that I knew what my birthday present would be. I rode and worked with all of our saddle horses and I loved them dearly. Each horse had a saddle and bridle that fit them specifically.

Our trail horses were all pretty big for hauling dudes into the mountains. To my delight Dad bought a smaller, Buckskin gelding a couple months ago for my personal mount. His name was Bucky, but I thought that was very un-literary, so I called him Falling Star—Star for short. I thought that was more romantic, poetic, and even Indian. I was delighted to have my own horse that fit me. He was well trained and I spent many happy hours with him, but we only had an old saddle that would fit him.

I was pretty sure Mom and Dad were going to give me my own saddle for the first time. I knew they had been saving some money in our "special things" jar and doing a lot of whispering. Since they knew I dreamed about having my own saddle, I was sure that was what they were working on.

When I asked Miguel if he knew what I was getting for my birthday he just frowned at me and said, "Now what makes you think you are getting anything for your birthday?" He never told me any secrets.

Andy was more talkative and tried to make me feel grown up and important, but I didn't think he was in on any secrets. Anyway, he had avoided the subject.

When I woke up on June 1st, my birthday, I was out of bed pronto. I dressed to help do the feeding and whizzed to the corrals. Miguel was loading hay on the wagon. He drove around the corrals so I could throw the hay from the wagon into the feeders. He said "Happy Birthday" to me, but it was in Miguel's usual pre-coffee mumble.

As soon as we finished feeding I ran to the house. Luckily it was Saturday and Mom didn't have to work, and Dad wouldn't be leaving on a guided trip until Monday.

I dashed into the kitchen and Dad was already at the table and Mom was serving up the eggs and pancakes. They both wished me a warm Happy Birthday with lots of hugs and kisses. There was some of the usual reminiscing about the day I was born. Ugh! That was always embarrassing for some reason. I scanned the kitchen for any sight of a present, but Mom and Dad were playing it cool. They loved to torture me, like all parents I suppose.

"How did the horses look this morning?" Dad asked.

"They all look fine, but I think Lady Bug has loosened a shoe. Diamond was tearing around the stall. I think she may be ready for a trip out into the pasture for an hour or two," I reported.

"Aren't you glad you are out of school for your birthday every year?" Mom asked. "It shows good planning on the part of your dad and me," she teased. "You should get your report cards in the mail this next week. Then we'll know if you will be headed into high school next year."

"Is there truly any doubt?" I asked cocking my head and putting my fists on my hips. "Really!" Dad gave me a loving punch.

"Better come off your high horse lil' girl," he said.

"Actually, some of the science final questions were tough, but you had me well prepared," I assured Mom. "I have to get an A in science to get into advanced science next year. I think that is a must for vet school."

For as long as I could remember I'd wanted to be an equine or horse veterinarian. I knew it would take a lot of study, especially in science, and lots of money for tuition. In high school I would have to work hard to keep my grades up so that I'd qualify for college and I would have to try to win a scholarship to pay for it.

"You just aren't giving up on the idea of vet school, are you?" Dad said. "I think you should just plan to marry Luke Winslow when you graduate. His dad owns two thousand acres of prime cattle grazing land. I'd love to have my daughter married to a cattle baron."

"Geez, Dad, you know I'm going to be too busy doctoring horses to be a cattle baron's wife," I reminded him disgustedly.

"I have to run into town this morning to get some groceries and I'll pick up your cake for supper tonight. We'll celebrate then. Miguel, Andy, and Maria will eat with us. I think the Swensons are coming over, too. I thought we would cook some buffalo burgers and have your favorite corn-on-the-cob and baked potatoes. Mrs. Swenson said she would bring some of her fresh strawberries," Mom informed me. "She also told me that you saved Diamond."

"I'm glad you were quick thinking. I'm sorry it was hard to find help. We sure didn't plan it that way, but calling Mrs. Swenson was a good answer. You did a great job," Dad said.

"Thanks, Dad. I guess looking back it was a good experience for me, but I sure was scared at the time. I didn't want to disappoint you," I told him.

"Well, you never have," Dad assured me. He really did spoil me. In his eyes I could do no wrong. Mom took care of any necessary discipline and she was good at it.

I kept wondering if they were going to make me wait until evening to find out if that new saddle of my dreams was going to materialize. And talk about that Luke Winslow was enough to make me feel pukey. I remembered he tried to kiss me on the bus the last day of school. What a slime ball, though he was my best friend. I didn't know what had come over him.

It was a long day for me. Mom went to town and I helped Dad and Andy organize the tack for Dad's trip. Six clients were coming from the east and they wanted to go up in the mountains for five days. That took a lot of preparation. Fortunately, once Maria didn't have to watch me, she became our head cook and house keeper. She helped prepare the food and pack it. She had been busy at that all week. Much of the food had to be dehydrated.

About four o'clock we knocked off work early to clean up for the evening cook out and birthday bash. Well, not really a bash, but it felt like one to me. By six o'clock we were all ready. The barbeque fire was heating, the food was laid out, and we were set up to eat outside under the covered patio. Later in the evening we would have a bonfire and sit under the stars. That was always my favorite time at our cook outs.

Andy and Miguel arrived all cleaned up and there were the usual jokes about how well they looked and what a good clean up could do for such wretched looking fellows. Miguel was even jovial. Of course, Andy was shy, but he enjoyed the attention. The Swensons arrived right on time. Orrville Swenson was a fifth generation rancher. Mrs. Swenson was a transplanted New Yorker. They were a perfect match.

When everyone had gathered, my parents decided not to torture me any longer. They told me to shut my eyes and there were sounds of people moving about and a door opening and closing in the toolshed, a place where I never go.

"Okay, honey, you can open your eyes," Dad said.

And there it was—the most beautiful saddle, breast plate, and bridle I had ever seen. I was stunned for a minute for I never expected all that. Then I whooped and rushed over to hug both of my parents, Maria, Miguel, Andy, and both of the Swensens.

Then I moved over to the saddle and began to take in every detail. It was a dark brown with burgundy tones. There was some tooling on the back skirt, the stirrup fenders, and the leather bound stirrups, but it was only a small amount. The tooling was enough for decoration, but not so much that cleaning all the grooving would be a huge chore. I had cleaned enough saddles to appreciate smooth leather. The seat was a stitched cushioned seat of an even darker brown. I was just sure it was the most beautiful saddle ever a girl owned.

It was on a new saddle rack that Andy had made, so I could sit on it to see how it fit and it was perfect. I guess Andy was pretty good at keeping secrets, after all. I gave him a kiss, making him blush. I could hardly wait to see how it looked on Star.

We had a wonderful evening with good food and good company. Being fifteen was going to be splendid, I was sure. I sat on my saddle all evening, even while eating, until the stars came out and we all moved away from the house to lose all ambient light and to enjoy the beautiful night sky.

My mom called out, "Look, a falling star!"

"Well that is a sign of good luck for you Emily. You will have a good life for sure," my dad said softly to me.

Later when the guests had left, and I was saying thanks and good night to Mom and Dad, my dad said to me, "This week was proof of how you can step up to hard work around here and take responsibility. We truly feel you earned the saddle of your dreams. You show good common sense around the horses and help a lot with the outfitting. Mom and I have decided that, if you want to, you can go along on the trip this week and help as a crewmember. I think you are ready to do that."

My heart leaped. Two dreams coming true in one day. That was almost too much.

"You mean it? I have really wanted to go with you. Maybe I can help with all the trips this summer. I know Star and I are ready to do this," I replied with enthusiasm.

"Well that just might work out," Dad said. "We'll see."

Mom gave me a big hug and I noticed tears in her eyes. "Don't worry Mom. I'll be helpful and observe all the safety rules I've learned. It will be a wonderful trip. Thanks for letting me go," I told her.

"You will do just fine, as you always have." Mom hugged me again. It had been a very "huggy" day.

It was a perfect birthday, a perfect evening, and now I had the trip to anticipate.

CHAPTER 5

THE NEXT AFTERNOON I was working where I could keep an eye on Black Diamond. She was mostly sleeping, but periodically she got up long enough to nurse and do some exploring.

Mom came running out of the house looking for Dad.

I asked her, "What's the matter," and she said, "Come along so I only have to tell this once. Where is Dad?"

"He's down at the corral shoeing Lady Bug," I told her. We hustled down to the corral.

"Colin," Mom called, "Tom Norton, from animal rescue, just called. They picked up a couple horses that have been neglected and were starving. They were out near the old Wheeler place. He said one of them, an old one, didn't make it, but one is a young gelding that he thinks, with some very good care, should recover. They have him out of danger, but now the horse needs a home and building up. If they can't find a home for him he'll go to the action block, probably for meat. He says the horse looks like a pretty good horse and would be worth saving. He wants to know if you can take him." Mom explained.

"Oh boy, I don't know." Dad replied. "We can always use a good horse, but we have so much work around here that, with a new foal and Emily and me leaving, I don't know that we can handle more. What do you think honey?" he asked.

"I don't know either. I just hate to see the animal not given a chance. With your business growing we're probably going to need more stock and this horse is free. Tom said Doc Mason will donate the shots and the supplements it will take to bring the horse back to good health. So the cost would be right. It is just a matter of doing the work, I guess," Mom said.

"If Emily was going to be around to care for the horse next week it might work, but I really wanted her help on this trip. What do you think, Emily?" he asked.

"Dad I know I could take good care of him. I would like to do that, but I have been very excited about this trip and using my new saddle and all." Mom and Dad let me have a few minutes to think.

"I suppose it would be good experience for me to learn about this poor horse's care with the proper feed, medicines, shots and all. I guess I would do whatever you and Mom think is best. Maybe Luke Winslow would go with you to help. He has wanted to go on a trip with you and he is good with horses. I think they got back from their trip yesterday. I suppose I'll have plenty of chances to go with you this summer," I thought out loud.

My heart sank at the thought of missing this trip into the mountains, but I also felt flattered that Dad thought I could take care of a horse that was such a special case. I knew that doing the right thing wasn't always the thing I wanted to do. I felt that adding a free horse to our herd would be a big help to Dad.

"Well, that might work. Miguel will be here to help, too. Anna, before we make a decision, would you see if you can get hold of Luke to see if he would be available next week. I really need a third person to help Andy and me with the livestock and all the camp work. We'll see about the horse when you find out if he can do it," Dad decided.

Mom was able to get hold of Luke and she quickly reported that he would love to help out and it was okay with his dad for him to take the week off from work at home. So Dad sat down on the old stump we used as a seat by the corral and looked very thoughtful.

"Emily," he said, "I really hate for you to miss this trip, but it looks like I need to depend on you to look after some things here while I'm gone. We'll plan better for the next trip and have more help available if we need it. How do you feel about that?"

"Dad, I will honestly be disappointed to not go. You know I love going into the high country and I want to learn how to do everything to run a trip. But I do agree with you—there are things that need to be looked after around here and it is too much for Miguel alone. Andy is a good help for you. Luke won't be as good as I would be, but he's okay. I'll stay here and work with Miguel. Promise you'll take me on the next trip?" I asked.

"How about you, Anna, what do you think?" Dad always wanted us all to have a say and hopefully concur on decisions, though he makes the final decision. We operated as a team and that always made me feel good.

Mom thought a little and then she said, "I think that would be a good choice for this trip. There will be plenty of times when Emily can go and help you. She already knows how to do everything required on a trip, but she'll need to work with you on how to put it all together. We know that she and Miguel can take good care of the horses that will still be here. Plus, I hope we can save the horse that sounds like it needs a lot of help."

And so the fateful decision was made. I would stay and help Miguel. I would focus on caring for the horses that would need special attention. Black Diamond still needed to be watched and it would take a lot of work to save an undernourished young horse.

I was disappointed about the trip, but I really loved the idea of caring for a foal and a horse that needed rehabilitation. This just fits into my plans for learning to be a vet. I didn't plan on taking over Dad's business, so learning about packing wasn't as important. The trip was more a matter of fun and being with Dad in the high country. I would have to look forward to the next chance to go with him.

Mom gave me a big hug and told me how much she appreciated my maturity. Dad looked me in the eye, nodded, gave me a big wink, promised to take me on the next trip, and went back to work. I knew that he appreciated my willingness to do what was needed. We really were a team.

Mom called Tom saying we would see what we could do for the abused horse. She called Doc Mason and he said he would bring supplements for the horse and show me how to give him any shots he might need. He recommended that we quarantine the new horse until we knew he didn't carry any sickness to our horses. We also had to make sure he was strong enough to take care of himself in a new herd. Horses always do some kicking and biting until the pecking order of the herd is established. Doc said he would come by about 4:00 when the new horse was scheduled to arrive.

Wow, with all we had to do we had this additional excitement to deal with. Mom, Dad, Miguel, Andy, Maria, and I made an efficient crew and we would get it all done.

I went right away to a paddock that we weren't using. I wanted to make sure it was clean for the new horse and I put a clean water tank in it with fresh water. It already had a hay manger with a box that would also hold some grain. If we were going to feed him supplements he would need some grain to mix with them. The fence was solid and the gate was swinging free so the paddock was ready.

I made sure he would have a line of sight to the bigger corral where the horses would be when they came in from pasture. He would also be close to Magpie and when she put her head out over her stall door they could become friends. He would have sufficient company. Of course, I would be attentive, too.

Mom and Maria were making sure the guest house was clean and all the beds had clean sheets. Our guests would arrive late in the afternoon tomorrow for a departure early Monday morning for the high country.

Maria was also doing some extra baking and she was marinating some buffalo steaks that we would barbeque for our guests first dinner at the ranch. It seemed like the number of details to think about in preparation were endless. However, Mom and Maria were used to this and they had it all planned out to the last detail.

I checked Black Diamond and Magpie. I hoped the arrival of a new horse wouldn't be upsetting to them. Magpie seemed like a steady sort and I didn't think she'd be bothered by another horse close by. It was in Diamond's genes to have an even disposition since both Bess and Diablo (Spanish for devil), despite his name, had reproduced their own good dispositions. Therefore, a good disposition should be a sure thing for Diamond. Plus Quarter Horses are known for their even, dependable temperaments.

Magpie was nodding with her head hanging above the sleeping filly. Her maternal instincts were attentive even as she dozed peacefully. When she heard me she raised her head and nickered. I gave her a small amount of grain. I would continue giving her hay and grain several times a day in small amounts to help her maintain her strength during this foaling and nursing period. Magpie didn't even approach the food until Black Diamond roused up with the activity and Magpie could carefully walk around her to the feed bin. What a great surrogate mother!

We used to have a beautiful mare that was very aggressive when she had a foal. Dad didn't keep her because he didn't want anyone to get hurt. We understood that she didn't trust people and she was just caring for her baby, but we felt she just wasn't a horse we wanted around. Dad sold her to a big breeding ranch where they wanted her beauty and didn't care so much about her being overprotective. Magpie, like Bess, had a disposition that fit in better on our ranch.

About four o'clock we could hear a truck pulling up the hill. It was Tom Norton bringing the homeless horse. Tom pulled over by the barn and we all gathered to see what we were adopting.

After greeting everyone in his usual friendly manner Tom said, "This poor guy doesn't seem to have been physically abused, but he sure was hungry when we got him. We just couldn't save his stable mate, but he is younger and probably more resilient. He seems to have a good chance at full recovery. He may have some sturdy Mustang blood in him somewhere in the distant past. His disposition seems quiet and he doesn't show any nasty ways. We decided that maybe someone could save him. That was when you came to mind Colin. You have a reputation of taking good care of your horses."

"Thanks, Tom," Dad replied. "We sure try. There is no reason to take on the responsibility of animals and not treat them right. Plus, for us, our horses and mules are wage earners. We depend on them. We'll do the best we can for this guy. I'm leaving on a trip Monday, but Doc Mason is going to look in and Emily is going to take care of him. I think if anyone can pull him through, that pair can," laughed Dad.

Putting his arm around my shoulder Tom said, "Well Emily, I know you will do well. You seem to have horse in your blood." That compliment swelled my heart with pride and I could see that Mom felt good about it, too.

"Let's get him out and see if you want to change your mind about him," Tom said as he moved to the back of the trailer and opened it. Standing in the front was a skinny horse that nevertheless showed alertness and hope in his pricked up ears and attentive eyes. He was no doubt very confused about his moves and separation from his friend. He looked around at me with a look of bewilderment.

"Tom, is it okay if I get him out?" I asked.

Tom looked at Dad and Dad nodded. "She'll be his caretaker," he said. "They might as well get acquainted."

I moved slowly into the trailer talking gently to my new charge. He was a bay with a black mane and tail. Up close now, I could see that he was in bad shape. His bones protruded, his coat was rough and dull, and his hooves were cracked and broken. My heart went out to this poor creature that looked nothing like our other horses. I had to pause as the full meaning of this horse's condition struck me. I determined immediately that I would help him.

The first impression wasn't all bad. He sniffed me and showed an unmistakable spark of life. He hadn't given up and that meant he had heart. He showed me that he had the "grit" to work with me toward his new lease on life.

He had a nice white patch on his forehead and that was his only white marking. I thought we had two new horses, both with white on their foreheads, usually referred to as stars. Stars are signs of hope.

I walked up to where he was tied and patted and rubbed his neck. I let him smell my hand and he seemed very accepting of me. I wanted to throw my arms around his neck, but I knew that might frighten him, so I restrained myself. I gently untied him.

The trailer was big enough that he could turn and walk out forward. It was probably only his second trailer ride, but he wasn't sweating or worked up. He must be pretty sensible and maybe deep down in had a bold streak like Diamond. That was a good sign. He followed me out of the trailer and stood taking in all his surroundings. He nickered once, probably because he could smell the other horses, though he couldn't see them yet. I wondered why someone had abandoned him. I guess I'll never know.

Mom came up to him and held out her hand for him to sniff. He was friendly, but somewhat distracted by trying to take in everything at once. Mom reached in her apron pocket and pulled out a carrot. He sniffed it and took a bite. As hungry as he must be, he behaved politely. He munched that carrot down and seemed to have accepted Mom as a friend already.

"My, he is skinny, isn't he? I think you have your work cut out for you, Emily. Oh dear, it is so sad to see his pathetic condition, but he has a spark in his eye. I think he'll come out of this just fine," Mom said, with tears in her eyes. "I'm so glad he is here."

Mom was right; I did have some work ahead. But I was encouraged by the fact that he was taking interest in what was happening. I felt an iron determination rise up in me and I promised myself to bring him to his potential. Despite his thinness he looked like he had good straight legs and a quality bone structure. His conformation showed that he was well put together. When I could get him filled out and muscled up I knew he would be a good looking horse.

I led him around to his corral and on the way let him greet Magpie at her stall door. They touched noses, but Magpie warned him to keep his distance by laying her ears back as Diamond came over to see what was going on. For once she wasn't sleeping and missing everything. She was already, in just a few days, becoming an explorer.

With Magpie close the new horse wouldn't be lonely. They would get acquainted from some distance. Maybe in time, when I put him out on pasture, I would be able put him with Magpie and Diamond. I'd see how compatible they were. Then when Magpie went home, Diamond might be able to depend on this new horse to be her friend and protector.

Tom and Dad had followed me back to the barn to make sure I didn't have any problem handling the new guy, but he was behaving just fine. I turned him loose in his area and hung his halter on a peg by the gate. He explored the corral and checked out the water tank. He took a long drink. That was a very good sign. He checked the feed manger, but there wasn't anything there yet. I would start feeding him small amounts several times a day, like I planned with Magpie, but first I wanted him to get a little adjusted and make sure he was relaxed.

Since I was the expert in the family who named the horses, I was pondering what to call this noble and courageous horse. I could tell he was proud by his attentive carriage, along with having a sensible attitude. I wanted to name him something that measured up to what I saw in him. I remembered Dad's love of the ancient Persian historian, Herodotus. Herodotus was known as the Father of History and Dad admired his writings. It seemed like a good way to shorten Herodotus would be to call this horse Hero. I hope I'm a hero to him and can make a good life for him.

"Dad, what would you think of calling him Hero in honor of Herodotus?" I asked.

"That sounds like a fine idea," Dad said enthusiastically. "You are certainly our horse naming expert. Looks like I'd better trim his feet before I go. We need to get them in good enough shape to shoe him."

Hero was about five years old and pretty much the same size as Falling Star, though a little taller. Once he fills out my new saddle would fit him fine.

Tom said, "We don't know about whether he has been ridden or handled much. Often horses that have been abused have problems, but this guy seems to have kept his natural disposition even when hungry. Probably best, though, to take your time with him. Well, I'd better head back. The missus will have dinner ready by the time I get home. Let me know if you need anything this week or have any problems with him while your dad is gone," Tom said to me.

We thanked Tom and he left.

"This week, just look after his feeding and getting to know him. I don't want you to try doing anything with him until we know him better. Okay Emily?" Dad instructed.

"Of course, Dad. I'll be careful. The last thing I want to do is anything that sets him back. He seems to have a nice temperament and I want him to get to trust us. Besides, he just needs rest and food now. He really looks poor. I want to see us get some weight on him and hopefully Doc Mason's supplements and medications will improve his coat and his strength," I said.

"Well, you sound like a vet already. That sounds like a good diagnosis and treatment plan," Dad said. He gave me a big hug and we contentedly watched Hero explore and take in all that was around him.

"I'll get him just a little hay to get him started," I said.

"Good idea," Dad patted my back. "I'd better get back to work."

A couple hours later Doc Mason showed up to check on Hero. I was a little concerned about whether Hero would be okay to walk up to and halter, or whether he would be spooky about me approaching him and restraining him.

When I saw the Doc driving up, I ran back to Hero's corral to try to catch him before he saw others coming. By approaching him quietly with a bucket of grain I was able to get up to him without spooking him. He really wanted to put his nose in the bucket and get that delicious food. I let him eat a little and then very gently slid the halter on. I was delighted with how sensible he seemed.

Doc looked in on Magpie and Diamond first. When he came over to the corral he said they were doing fine. "That is a healthy looking filly," he said. "Magpie is doing her job very well. No one would guess Diamond she was an orphan."

"Magpie is a god send. She sure has saved me a lot of work," I agreed.

"How does this fellow seem?" Doc asked.

"He has just been here a short time, but he is settling in already. He had a nice drink, has explored his new home, and eaten a little hay. I didn't have any trouble catching him just now," I reported.

"Well, let's have a look," Doc said and he came through the gate. Hero became alert to the Doc's approach, snorted, and showed his wary side, but Doc knows horses and he soon had Hero accepting him.

Doc checked him over taking his pulse and temperature, checking his gums, teeth, and eyes for signs of irritation, ran his hands gently over him checking his bones and muscles, and in general checked his coat and looks.

"He certainly is underweight, but overall he looks healthy enough. You need to put him on light feedings several times a day. I'll give him his shots and I'll just worm him today with a paste. I think with your care he will be fine. There doesn't seem to be any permanent damage to him, but we'll watch for signs of digestive or heart issues. Emily, you must realize this will be a slow process." Doc said.

"I know. I'll be patient. I was planning to give him hay several times a day in small amounts for a couple weeks and we have a good grain mixture on hand. Miguel will pick up more when he goes to town this week. What supplement do you recommend?" I asked.

"I brought the one I like. There should be enough to last about a month. For the time being use the smallest recommended dosage. We don't want his intake to be too rich too suddenly," Doc advised.

Doc gave Hero his shots, showing me how to put the shot in his rump muscle. Then he squirted the worm medicine into Hero's mouth. We had accomplished a lot for Hero's first day. Probably more than he had seen in his life till then.

"You'll need to give him one more vitamin shot, say about Tuesday. I'll leave the serum and syringe with you." Doc instructed.

"Ok. I'll wait a few hours for the worm medicine to be absorbed and then I'll give him another light feed of hay." I replied.

"I think this guy just got lucky," Doc said. "He should recover just fine and make a nice horse. It will just take time and lots of work on your part. Let me know if you see any signs of distress from him. Going slow is important so he doesn't founder." Doc explained to me.

It was reassuring to have Doc remind me of all the details I needed to remember and to know that what he recommended was exactly what I had planned.

"Thanks Doc, I'll watch him close," I replied.

Doc went to speak with Dad before leaving and I sat on the fence watching Hero. He seemed content. After wondering around the corral some more he came and stood close to me. This was a horse that really wanted a friend, I thought. I knew that since I would be feeding him he would learn to feel safe with me as long as I didn't do anything to scare him. I needed to be consistent around him to earn his trust. I was excited about the prospects of working with him. It was as though I could see the beautiful bay horse that he would become.

After dinner I went back to check on my charges. I replenished Magpie's hay and gave her a small amount of grain. She ate peacefully. Probably tomorrow I'd take her out of the stall for the first time so they both could get some exercise. Magpie needed the fresh grass and Diamond needed to get some sunshine and room to run.

I got a feeding of hay for Hero. I put it in his feed rack and sat down near it. He was a little wary of my strange action, but he was hungry enough that he moved to where he could snatch some mouthfuls. I just sat still and talked quietly to him some, but some of the time I just sat there. It would help him get accustomed to me.

Before he finished eating he seemed comfortable standing beside me and eating without the wariness. It took a long time for him to eat it all, but I just stayed and kept him company. When he was finished he sniffed me and checked me out pretty thoroughly. I waited for him to move away before I got up. I planned to check him one more time before I went to bed.

"How is he doing?" Dad asked when I went up on the porch where he and Mom were having an after dinner cup of coffee and enjoying their rocking chairs at the end of a busy day.

"He ate well and seems settled," I said. "Doc gave me instructions on how to feed and watch him. Is it okay if Miguel goes in to Jim's Ranch Supply and picks up a few bags of grain?"

"Sure. I'll tell him. Jim will just put it on a bill for us," Dad offered. "You'll be a busy girl while I'm gone. I know you'll do fine. It makes me feel good that you'll be tending our special cases."

"Thanks Dad. I think I'll get a glass of lemonade and join you guys," I said as I felt the fatigue of the day setting in.

Before I went to bed I walked out one more time to check on Hero. I peeked around the barn to see how he was doing before he was aware of my presence. He was standing quietly by his water trough. I thought he was standing where he could hear Magpie in her stall and see her when she put her head out over her half door. He no doubt liked the company.

I spoke to him to let him know I was coming and he nickered softly. That sign of acceptance made me feel an abiding affection for this horse with a big heart. He let me walk right up to him. As he munched a carrot with relish, I thought he must think he had arrived at a fine restaurant. I rubbed his neck and head for a while. Then I just had to head back to bed. I was bushed. It had been another exciting day.

Chapter 6

Sunday morning we were all up before sunrise again. Though we had all been working for a week on preparations for Dad's departure, there were still a lot of last minute details to attend to.

I headed out to the barn to help Miguel with the feeding and to check on Diamond and Hero. Diamond was lying down. She raised her head and blinked as though she couldn't remember where she was. But it didn't take long for her to get her legs unwound and get up. She gets up and down much more gracefully now. She found her breakfast very quickly.

As Magpie contentedly ate her hay and grain, Diamond soon found all that Magpie did to be quite entertaining. She seemed to feel entitled to nose into everything. It was hard to believe she was just a week old. She was continuing to fill out, and her coat was getting sleek.

When Miguel and I started around the barn toward Hero's corral, he could hear us moving close with the hay wagon and he was standing at his feeder quite ready for breakfast. I gave him a little grain and a feeding of hay. I checked his water tank and refreshed the water in it. He was drinking well and all his feed from last night had been cleaned up. I would spend time with him later.

We all had a last big breakfast together before guests would arrive. We were a quiet bunch. It seemed like Dad had given me all the instructions for the week. He and Andy reviewed their plan of action for the day and their route for the week.

"I think the trail should be snow free going up to Ole' Baldy. We should be able to ride as far as Sky High Pass tomorrow. Then we'll take the west trail to Baldy. We should get there by mid-afternoon on Tuesday. We can spend a couple days riding up there or fishing and loafing—whatever the guests want. We should then be able to come down on Friday in one day. That way we will only have to set up camp a couple times," Dad reviewed with all of us.

Mom and I marked our map of the area so we would know where to expect them to be every day. Then everyone dispersed to their various tasks. It always felt a little sad when Dad was leaving. He ran eight to ten adventure trips from late spring through the fall and it always felt funny to have him gone.

I spent much of my time checking on Diamond and Hero and giving Hero and Magpie regular feedings. I didn't have much time to work with Hero, but the coming week would be different. I also helped pack the panniers (bags that hold the gear on the pack saddle frames) with some of the heavier equipment that we would want balanced in the bottom of the pack saddles.

About 10:30 Luke arrived to help Dad with the final preparations. Mom saw Luke coming and sent him back to the barn where Dad, Andy, and I were still working on the pack saddles.

"Good morning all," Luke said cheerily. "Thanks Mr. Campbell for letting me help on this trip. I'll work hard and be the best hand I can." He dropped his small duffel in a pile to be loaded.

"Hey Luke," Dad replied. "I'm very glad to have your help. We had to change our plans at the last minute and you are a life saver for us. I understand you've just returned from a pack trip with your family?"

"Yes sir. We just got back from a trip. I think I'll know how to do everything, but I know it will be different with guests," Luke answered. Dad briefed him on the itinerary as we all worked.

"Emily, why don't you show Luke the horses and mules, sort of introduce him to them. Then, Luke, you can come help us finish with these packs. The guests will arrive in a couple hours and we'll have a cook out for dinner tonight. With six guest horses, three mules, and the three crew horses we'll have a lot of work this week. We have a very seasoned string which helps." Dad instructed me and Luke.

Andy came around the barn. "Welcome aboard. We'll be working you like you were in the Army this week," he said to Luke. "It will be fun though, too. Can you sing campfire songs?"

"My skills tend to be more in the line of livestock care and camp set up," Luke said. I could tell that singing wasn't going to be his favorite thing.

"That's okay," Andy crowed. "I'm a fine baritone myself, so that will be no problem."

As Luke and I walked away from where Andy was working I told Luke, "Oh lord! Andy can't carry a tune in a bucket, but he loves to sing the old cowboy songs. It helps get the guests into it and lowers their inhibitions when they see how enthused Andy is about campfire songs and how badly he sings."

Luke laughed. "He sounds like just the guy we'll need. Did you get good enough grades to be a freshman next year?" Luke asked.

"Sure. Straight A's," I told him. "What did you expect?"

"I guess that is what I expected," he replied. "You know I'm planning to take you to the Homecoming Dance. You are very lucky as a freshman to have a sure date with a sophomore," he informed me seriously.

"What makes you think I'm going to any silly dance you dumb cowboy?" I asked.

"Oh, the peer pressure from your classmates will force you to put on a dress and dance with the handsomest sophomore," he bantered.

"You should be so lucky," I said disdainfully. All the time I was thinking that Luke Winslow was growing into a very handsome, tall young man. The idea of him taking me to a dance sounded interesting. Maybe I should nail him down on that right now so he couldn't change his mind. I guess I was too proud to do that, but I hoped he would be true to his word, even if I was unsure about going to a dance.

When we got to the corral I introduced him to the guest horses by name and rider so he would begin to know who he would be putting on which horse. He picked it up very quickly. Then I pointed out Dad's big gelding Topper, Andy's horse Peanuts, and the horse he would be riding, Ole Ben.

"I don't know why he is called Ole Ben," I told Luke. "He isn't old and he is a very peppy horse. I would have ridden Falling Star—the Buckskin over there. Dad bought him for me, but Dad felt you would want a bigger horse. Ole Ben is very good at quietly moving up and down a string of horses without upsetting any of them. That way you can ride anywhere in the line that Dad needs you. One of the guests is a boy about your age. I think he is seventeen. You guys may enjoy riding together. Of course, you may prefer to ride with the daughter who is fifteen. Maybe after this week you won't want to take me to any ole' dance," I hinted.

"Well, we'll see about that," Luke said. "Is she pretty?"

"I don't know. I haven't seen her yet, but I think she has a big wart on the tip of her nose. You just failed the fickle test!" I reprimanded him. He just laughed.

Then I showed him Diamond and Hero. He was interested in Hero's story and said I was just the one to get that horse into beautiful condition. He thought Hero showed a lot of promise. But he was smitten by Diamond.

"She's the spittin' image of Diablo," he said. "She is going to be a top horse. She'll be a fine mount for you in a few years when you are the queen of the rodeo."

"Ugh! I don't have time for that kind of folderol," I exclaimed, but I was flattered.

Our guests arrived about 2:00. They would stay in our guest house. The Johnsons seemed like a nice family and they were excited about the trip. There was Mr. Johnson, Mrs. Johnson, son Rick who was 17, daughter Sally who was 15, and son Ted who was 13. Mr. Johnson's brother Bill was the sixth person. They all rode back east, but riding all day in the mountains would be a new experience. I felt a little disappointed that I wouldn't have fun with them this week, but I tried to remind myself that my week at home was going to be fun, too.

In the evening we had a cook out of buffalo steaks, beef steaks (for those unaccustomed to buffalo, if they didn't want to try it), baked potatoes, tossed salad, and apple strudel with ice cream.

"Gee, it was worth the trip just for this meal and the beautiful place to eat it," Mrs. Johnson said after dinner. Her family agreed wholeheartedly.

Dad said, "We sit out here about every night and enjoy the stars. The scenery around here feeds the soul."

"I can see how that would be true," Mr. Johnson said. He worked in an office back east. But I could tell he was an outdoorsman. He seemed comfortable in his skin. I could also tell that he wanted his kids to learn the value of this country.

"Eating that buffalo makes me feel like Kit Carson," Ted said. "I feel stronger already."

"You're still just a scrawny kid," Sally teased him. "Buffalo meat can't change that."

Ted ignored her and asked Dad, "Mr. Campbell, can you teach me to track this week?"

Dad laughed. "Yes, I can show you some tricks, but I can't teach you all about tracking in one week. I'll show you tomorrow how to pick out the track of your horse from the others in the group. That way you could track your horse if he got away—which I hope he doesn't."

Picking himself up straight and tall, Ted said, "Don't worry. My horse won't get away. What color will my horse be?"

"He is a black and white named Apache," Dad replied. "You'll like him. He is a top trail horse—very sure footed and bold on a narrow trail."

The party broke up early because everyone was tired and we would be up before sunrise to get the trip headed up the trail. I noticed that Luke had fit in very nicely with the guests. He is a good listener and I could tell he was going to be Ted's new hero. The others seemed to like him, too. I knew he would be a good helper on the trip for Dad.

I wished more than ever that I was going. I had to remind myself again that what I would be doing was important. Both Mom and Dad thanked me again when I was going to bed.

Luke was headed into the guest room when, outside of Mom and Dad's hearing, he said softly, "Sorry about trying to sneak a kiss from you at the end of the school year. I really like and respect you. I sort of messed up and I was ashamed. I won't do anything like that again without your permission."

"Well, you're not likely to get that permission," I made him suffer, though my respect for him had just grown. "Maybe someday you'll be so lucky. Maybe after I finish vet school."

"Geez, I'll be an old man by then!" he chided. "But it'll be worth the wait. I'll do a good job for your dad this week while you take good care of Diamond and Hero. Good night."

All of a sudden he looked like the hero of a western movie to me. Geez, what was going on here?

CHAPTER 7

MOM, DAD, ANDY, Miguel, Luke, and I were up before light to get the final packing accomplished, get the horses in and fed, and get all the packs finalized and ready to load. Maria was cooking a huge breakfast for twelve people and I think she must have been up since 3:00 o'clock.

By 6:00 o'clock the Johnsons came rolling out of their cabin dressed and ready. We had a noisy breakfast with the excitement level running high.

By 8:30 Dad, Andy, Miguel, and Luke had gotten all the packs loaded on the mules. It is a tricky business to load pack saddles so they are balanced and tight. The weight needs to be the same on both sides of the animal. The packs have to be very tight so they won't slide around to the side of the mule or rub sores on his back. It is a difficult skill to learn.

There is nothing worse than a bucking, recalcitrant pack mule which can scatter loads far and wide. But when our mules settled into their work they were the best. Dad had them well trained and conditioned for the trail. He treated his mules very well and they responded by being good workers.

Soon the riders were ready to mount up and head north into the beautiful Sawatch Range. They had their rain slickers tied on the back of their saddles and their lunches in their saddle bags along with some personal gear.

Ted looked at Sally's horse and started the teasing. "Wow, Sally, I hope that nag can carry you all day the way you flop around on a horse."

"Oh yeah," she chimed in. "Just who was it that won the horseman-ship class at the show last fall. Not you, skinny britches." As I watched her, I could see she was smitten by Luke. I felt the sting of something that had to be jealousy, but I shook it off.

"Could you two just grow up," Rick said disgustedly. "I expect both of your horses will be ready to commit suicide before they are done hauling you two around all week. On the contrary side, my tall black steed will mourn my departure at the end of the week."

Their Uncle Bill just shook his head. "I can see it is going to be a long week in some ways. Surely they will give you three enough work in the camp to take all that chatter out of you. I can't even hear the birds!"

They all laughed and said he was an old fogey and beamed with smiles on their faces. Being in the wild with horses and living outside always seemed to bring the best out in our city slicker guests.

When they were all mounted up Dad led the way to the trail. Mr. Johnson and Bill rode right behind Dad. That way all the men could visit. Rick and Ted followed them. Mrs. Johnson and Sally rode along together. They all seemed quite comfortable in their saddles and with their horses.

Luke and Andy rode drag where they could help keep an eye on everything to make sure no problems were developing. Andy, along with keeping an eye on things, was also leading Buster with Thornton and Ears tied in a line following Buster.

They made quite an impressive procession. It was so exciting to see everyone lined out with all our animals doing their jobs as they should. Dad really trains his remuda (that's the Spanish word for herd of horses and mules) well. I felt so proud of him. To me he was the handsomest cowboy ever, even over Luke. I gave Dad a big wave when he turned to look back at us.

As they rounded the bend and went out of sight, Luke turned in his saddle and gave me a wave, blowing a kiss. We laughed and Mom put her arm around me and said, "I think that handsome cowboy is sweet on one of us."

"Oh, Mom," was all I could say. I have to admit his attention made me feel warm all over. Thoughts of him would intrude on my mind in the days ahead. During the quiet evening hours when we had time to think about how they were all doing in the mountains, Luke especially came to mind. We had been friends forever, but something different seemed in the wind.

It was always sort of melancholy around home after Dad left. We always missed him so much. I thought, when I get to go with him, I'll miss Mom just as much. We were really a close family, working and living together as we did.

We had a quiet rest of the day around the ranch. I spent a lot of time with Diamond and Magpie. They seemed to be thriving.

I would sit in the corner of the stall and wait for Diamond to come and investigate me. She would lower her head and perk her ears up and study this strange object in her new world. It wouldn't be long until she would ease over to me and start sniffing me from head to toe. She was identifying what I was. When she sniffed my cheeks her nose felt so soft and warm. She would explore me with her upper lip and sometimes she startled herself. I would try not to move while I spoke softly to her so she would become familiar with my voice. When I did move I did it slowly and she seemed to think that was fine.

Later while Diamond slept I eased out of the stall and went to sit with Hero. He was grazing in the far end of the corral where there was a little nice grass. I made sure he had a good supply of water and then I wondered over and lay down in the grass.

It was a gorgeous day with fluffy white clouds against a deep blue sky. I wondered how far Dad and his charges had progressed and how things were going. It would be really nice up in the valley once they crossed the first ridge in their climb. I could picture it all. I dreamed of riding Star up there on our next trip. I would have to be sure to ride him as often as possible to keep him in good condition and to get my new tack broken in.

Hero eventually came over and nosed around me. He was getting familiar with me, just as Diamond was. It was important to spend this kind of time with both horses so they would learn to trust me and realize that they didn't have anything to fear.

I hoped to eventually start riding Hero. My plan was to get him buddied up with Star so that when I worked with one on the trails I could pony (lead) the second one along. That way I would be conditioning two horses at once and getting them used to the trails and working together. That was going to be so much fun and an efficient way to work them when I was back in school.

After a while I wondered back to Diamond's stall. She was having brunch, so I sat in the straw again. After she ate she came right over to me. I think she was already looking for a playmate. This time I was able to reach out and touch her nose and pet her. When she tired of this diversion she lay down again beside me and the first thing I knew she rolled out flat with her head on my legs. That was so awesome. I dared not move because I was so thrilled and I didn't want to scare her. It was as though I was accepted as one of her small family. It wasn't long until my legs were cramping up, but I endured it.

When Mom rang the lunch bell to call us all in, Diamond raised her head. I slowly got up and backed away and she just watched me. She was really showing signs of a calm and sensible nature. Those were traits we watched for in a trail horse.

"What have you been up to all morning?" Maria asked.

"I've been keeping Diamond and Hero company. It seems like I'm not working, but it is important for me to spend time with them so they become comfortable with me," I told her.

"Well, aren't you quite the horse trainer these days," Maria laughed.

"Don't forget about Star, my dear," Mom said. "You need to keep working him too, you know."

"Yes, Mom, I know. I'm planning to ride him up to the lower canyon this afternoon. I'm anxious to start breaking in my saddle and I want to work with him on the water crossings. He's doing well at going over the logs, picking his way in the rocks, and being alert to wildlife. I want him to be a bit more comfortable with picking his way through the cold water. I can give him a good long gallop up there. I hope that soon I can pony Hero along on some easy rides so that as he puts on some weight he'll start building wind and muscle," I shared my training program for the near future. "I'll also start leading Diamond in a day or so."

"Maria is right. You are quite the horse trainer with a solid plan. Just remember all the safety tips Dad has given you," Mom reminded.

"I will Mom. I think they are ingrained at this point. Last week when I visited Anna Winkle at their place I saw things that seemed careless to me and made me uneasy. She was particularly sloppy about walking among several tied horses without making sure they were always aware of where she was. I'll be careful and go slow." I tried to reassure Mom.

I could hardly wait to try my new saddle on Star. I planned to ride it a couple times to loosen up the leather before I oiled and treated it for waterproofing. Tack needs to be cared for. I'd do the same for the breast plate and bridle. The breast plate would help keep the saddle in the right position on Star when we climbed steep mountain trails.

After lunch I brought Star in and brushed him, combed his mane, cleaned his feet, and generally checked him over as I groomed him. He was always paying attention to me and what I was doing. I placed a nice saddle pad on him and eased my new saddle into place on his back. It looked gorgeous on him and was a good fit. Dad knew what he was doing when he picked this saddle. I put the breastplate on and buckled it in place. It was another nice fit. I didn't need to ride Star with a bit in his mouth because he was well trained to go in a hackamore. With some adjustments to fit his bridle, without the bit, to his head, we were set to go. Mom and Dad picked a nice color for my gear on a Buckskin horse.

I headed out toward the canyon following a fairly level trail at first. Star had a wonderful forward moving walk that was easy to ride and covered a lot of ground. He paid close attention to his footing and his surroundings. I was always tuned in to his body language because there were many things he would see or smell before I was aware of them. I also felt his steps in my seat so that if he would hit something that hurt his foot or caused a misstep I would be aware. Riding is a real partnership between horse and rider. It is important to give your horse a full fifty percent of the management of the ride as he picks his way on a trail.

I found so much solace cantering Star up into the foothills. That was where I could find peace. I understood what Dad and I shared in our souls when I felt the freedom of a horse traveling a trail in the splendor of this gift of nature.

About a half hour up the trail Star's head popped up a little and his eyes and ears pointed off to the left telling me he was aware of something there. Sure enough, a coyote jogged up the rise and into some trees. I enjoyed seeing the wildlife and I was grateful to Star for making me aware of what was there. That coyote was surely why we hadn't seen any rabbits along the trail.

We came to a stream as we began to climb. Lower Bluff Creek runs year round with a cold fresh snow melt from up in the mountains. I let Star take a drink. He liked playing in the shallow water pushing the water with his nose and pawing large waves of water onto his stomach. After he played a little we pushed on across the stream picking our way through the rocks.

Now we began to climb earnestly up the canyon. The pine trees were whispering with a light breeze and the crows squawked their usual racket. I listened to the birds, not only because I enjoyed them, but because, if there was a bear or mountain lion around they would fall quiet. I was always watchful to try to see either one because they were shy and we didn't see them very often. It is hard to spot a mountain lion, but sometimes we would see a bear feeding. That makes a horse real alert, but if you can keep at some distance and not surprise the bear, it is an exciting event, though not a dangerous one.

We continued climbing along the rising canyon floor for about an hour and then joined a steep switchback trail that took us to the top of the ridge. The view from up there was really inspiring. Star worked pretty hard on the climb, so I got off and sat at the rim to let him cool off. He grazed a little, but mostly stood quietly with me looking off into the distance. It was a very peaceful place. I thought of it as my secret hideaway where I could go anytime I needed some alone time to think.

My mind wondered. I thought about Dad, Andy, and Luke and how they were all doing. I thought about school this next year, but I didn't let school interfere with my time for very long. Soon enough I would be back in the classroom and only able to ride to the ridge on the weekends. I thought about Diamond and what she would be like in a couple years. I pictured myself riding her at the annual rodeo parade. She would be so handsome. I thought about Hero and how satisfying it would be to make a life for him knowing that he came close to not having a very long life. Maybe in a couple months he would be ready to make the climb to this ridge, too.

I had to admit to myself that I was thinking more about Luke than I wanted to. Dang him. He was such a tease, but he was also thoughtful of people. That was important to me. I just couldn't like someone who wasn't respectful of others. He was handsome, but he also rode a horse with a lot of grace. That counted with me. He always remembered to ask me about my dream of being a vet. I thought he was worth liking. But I'd have to think about that a lot more. For some reason thinking about him was pleasant, but unsettling.

I must have dreamed away an hour. This wasn't the way a hard working rancher was supposed to spend time, but my mom and dad had always allowed me to have this kind of time to wonder the country, ride a horse, and dream.

"Ok, Star, we better head back," I reluctantly said. "It will be feeding time by the time we get home."

Just then Star's head jerked up from the grass and he whirled to look to our left. A black bear emerged from out of the trees near the head of the trail. He was a big, full grown bear just browsing along about 300 yards away. He wasn't aware of us, but I preferred to keep it that way. We were down wind of him so he hadn't picked up our scent.

I patted Star and tried to reassure him. I moved around to his left side and mounted. We started easing away in the opposite direction of the bear, but when we moved he sensed us there and stood up on his hind legs to see us better. He was big. My heart was pumping like a racing horse.

I knew not to run and just turned Star away and increased the distance between us. Bless Star. He was startled, but he did what I asked of him when he would have liked to take off running. We moved on up the ridge and I watched the bear for as long as I could. He didn't seem alarmed by us and, to my relief, he turned to go back into the trees. Both Star and I breathed a thankful sigh.

The dilemma was that I needed to wait a while to return to where the head of the trail was located. I wanted to give that bear some time to move away before we started down the narrow trail. So I loped star up the ridge where the grade was gradual and grassy. We waited about a half hour and didn't spot the bear again from that high vantage point. When I felt it was safe to return to the trail head, we started down.

Star made good time on the trip down and we soon returned to the barn.

Miguel was beginning to look for me because it was feeding time and he knew I should be there to help.

"You're late, Missy," he said grumpily. "You been off sky larkin' and it's time to feed."

"I know. I'm sorry, but there was a big male bear up near the trailhead off the ridge and I gave him plenty of space before I could head down the trail. Fortunately, he headed back up into the trees. I didn't want to upset him or have to share a trail with him," I explained.

"Okay. That makes good sense. Let's get these horses fed before the dinner bell rings," he said.

I had cooled Star out on the last part of the ride and I pulled the tack off and put him in the corral. Then I joined Miguel to feed. When I went to Magpie's stall, Diamond was trying to peek out over the top of their half stall door. I think she was ready to get out and see the world. I decided to give her and Magpie some outside time tomorrow.

When I heard the dinner bell ring I was sure ready. I avoided mentioning the bear to Mom because she would just worry. Dad had taught me how to handle that kind of situation and it worked out just fine. Star and I both had a new experience under our belts.

Chapter 8

AFTER A FEW days, if our foals were doing well, we took them out with their dams to run free in a grassy field so they could develop their muscles and balance. Just living in a stall all the time was too stagnant.

If Magpie had lived, in time I would have ridden her for short rides and let Diamond follow along. That would have helped Diamond learn to watch her footing in the rocks, to get used to crossing a stream, and to running up and down hills. She would develop strength and confidence with those activities.

Since Magpie wasn't our horse, I didn't ride her. I didn't even know if she was trained to ride. In time, I planned to teach Diamond to lead and I could take her out with Star. But for now, I had to depend on turning Magpie out for short times with Diamond so they could exercise.

Shortly after first light the next morning I pulled on my boots and jeans and went to the barn. Miguel and I fed before breakfast to allow the animals to eat and digest before any of them were put to work or out to pasture.

Miguel was already sitting on the porch drinking his ritual cup of coffee. I dropped down beside him.

"After breakfast and some warmth from the sun hits the corral, I'll turn Magpie and Diamond out for a couple hours. I can hardly wait to see Diamond's reaction," I told him.

"She'll give you a show, I don't doubt," he chuckled. "I'm going to start cutting the hay in the south field this morning, so you'll have to do the turn out and keep an eye on things around the barn."

"Okay. Let me know anything else you want done. I'll run ahead and feed Magpie and Hero. I'll be ready to throw hay then when you finish your coffee." I just couldn't wait any longer to see Diamond. "You can loaf over your coffee like a proper gentleman."

"Ho, listen to you. Just run along and get to work, you young whipper-snapper," Miguel said with a big grin.

It was a beautiful morning with the sun not over the mountains yet. I could feel that the day was going to warm up even though it was still a bit nippy. The birds were certainly happily greeting the day and I felt a wonderful carefree happiness.

As I approached Magpie's stall she nickered low in greeting and stuck her head out over her half-door. I gave her the expected carrot and rubbed her nose gently. I could hear the straw swishing and I peeked over the door. Diamond was up, but looking sleepy with straw hanging from her coat. She looked at me curiously as though I was the wonder. She shook her head and boldly moved up beside Magpie.

I got hay from the hay shed and gave Magpie her portion with a scoop of grain. I moved quietly into the stall and put her feed in her feeding bin. Magpie went right to eating, which pleased me. She seemed to be feeling fine in her new home and with her new charge. I gave her a fresh bucket of water and cleaned her stall with new straw.

Diamond ignored me until she had her fill of breakfast, but then she came right over to watch what I was doing. She wasn't shy and several times I had to nudge her out of the way. When I pushed on her she shook her head defiantly, but she moved aside. I could tell she was going to be a pet with a mind of her own.

When I finished and had rubbed her back for a minute, I left to see how Hero was doing. Having heard me greeting Magpie and working in her stall, Hero had moved curiously to the fence closest to the stall. I got his hay and went into his corral to put it in the hay rack. I mixed his supplement in a little grain and delivered it to a hungry horse.

From the feed and tack room I brought out the shot to give Hero. Miguel arrived just in a time to help. I put a halter on Hero while he didn't miss a bite and Miguel took his lead rope. Miguel turned Hero's head toward the side I was on and took a tight hold in case Hero might kick when he felt the shot. I stayed in close to Hero's side and out of reach of his back foot and put the shot in his rump muscle like the Doc had showed me. Hero jumped a little and looked around, but he didn't make any aggressive move. I thought I took him by surprise. He had a 'what the heck' look. Miguel took the halter off and Hero resumed eating contentedly. He was very focused on his food.

Miguel and I left my charges eating peacefully and loaded up the hay to distribute to the other horses in the corral. With all the mules and nine horses gone, there weren't that many to feed.

A couple hours after the horses were fed, I opened the gate to the corral for the riding horses and they trotted out to pasture. They would come back in the evening for a little hay. We liked to have them close to the house at night.

I was excited to take Magpie and Diamond out to pasture for Diamond's first look at the world. As I took Magpie from her stall Diamond lingered behind rather confused by this new move. She nickered plaintively a couple times. Then she shuffled through the deep straw and looked out the door at her disappearing step- mother.

Magpie nickered reassuringly to her. Diamond blinked at the sunlight and capered out the door. She trotted over behind Magpie, as though hanging on to a security blanket.

I took them to the small grassy pasture and turned Magpie loose. Magpie was delighted and dropped down in the thick grass to roll. Then she went right to cropping the fresh grass with appreciation. Diamond stayed close watching this perplexing behavior and then tried her wings with a few running strides that seemed to surprise her. She stopped and looked around in wonder at what she had accomplished and dashed back to Magpie.

Diamond studied all the sights and decided to try that dashing thing again. She ran off and made a circle around Magpie. This time she threw in a few bucks. I couldn't help but laugh at her. Her long legs were better coordinated than they looked like they would be. She was getting them to work together amazingly well. Had she been born in the wild she would have run with the herd in an emergency, just as nature prepared her to do.

She began building confidence as she moved further from Magpie on each venture into this new, big world. Soon she decided that she had burned enough energy to deserve a morning snack and Magpie patiently let Diamond nurse rather vigorously. When Diamond was satisfied Magpie trotted off around the paddock stretching her legs a little and Diamond decided it must be a race and ran circles around her step-mother.

When Magpie settled down to graze again, using this opportunity to enrich her diet and her milk, Diamond soon lay down in the warm sunshine and took her first outdoor morning nap. All was well and peaceful. I felt I could safely leave them to their bonding and exploring. It was back to work. I sure loved raising horses.

Before lunch I returned Diamond and Magpie to their stall where they could rest peacefully. Periodically all day, I would check on them to make sure Diamond was okay, but more to watch her and laugh at her antics than in anticipation of any problem. Mostly she slept, but sometimes she got up on her spider-like legs long enough to nurse. I loved it when she tired and decided she needed another nap because she just dropped down and went right to sleep. Sometimes she made noises in her sleep. It was as though she was dreaming. She was a fascinating little animal.

Chapter 9

Since we believed Hero was about five years old he may have been trained and handled some. With no knowledge of his experience, I'll have to start at square one with his training. If he had been worked with he would just advance faster or he might need some brushing up on his past experience. He seemed gentle and sensible so I didn't anticipate any big problems. Dad said not to do much with him this week, but I'll just work on leading and simple things that he seems to know and see how he progresses. So far I had only handled him for Doc and to feed him. There was still a lot of unknown.

I got his halter from the tack room and went into his corral. He saw me and probably remembered the carrots I carried and he walked toward me, but he was hesitant when he got close. Maybe it was the sight of the halter. In the last few days his world had been turned upside down, so his confidence was still a little shaky. He probably felt some fear about what would come next.

I talked softly to him and leaned on the fence in no hurry. He watched me closely and tentatively took a few more steps. I just let him think about it. When I held out a carrot, he cautiously stepped up to bite part of it off. As he chewed it he stepped back a little, but he didn't seem afraid. I held out the rest of the carrot and let him take it. This time he didn't move away, but began nosing around to see if I had more.

I stepped to his side and slipped on his halter. The way he took the halter made me feel sure he had been handled some. He didn't show the fear of a wild horse.

I started to walk away to see if he followed. At first he baulked as though he didn't know what was expected. I moved to his side and urged him forward by swinging the lead rope toward his rear and soon he was walking nicely beside me. This was a very pleasing result. At least he seemed to be familiar with the concept of leading. When I had led him from the trailer he had seemed familiar.

I led him around his corral for about fifteen minutes turning both ways, stopping, starting, and even backing for a few steps. He seemed to pick all this up very quickly as though he liked the attention and something to do. I felt he might be a good learner. That happens in horses just as it does in people. Horses like to please if they haven't learned a reason to fear.

Finally, I decided he would be okay outside the paddock to look around and I could familiarize him with his new home. I eased open the gate and took him out into the barn area. I led him all around the barn and corrals and even up toward the house. I let him graze in some thick grass. He could only have a little grass because his digestive tract was not accustomed to such rich food. However, just a little grass with all its nutrients, his natural food, would be good for him.

He looked alertly at everything around and snorted and pranced a little, but again his calm, sensible nature prevailed and he didn't act spooky. Mother saw us and came out with another carrot for him. He sniffed her hand and accepted the carrot as though he remembered his friend. After all, she gave him his first carrot on arrival.

I decided that was enough for one session. I led him back to his now familiar corral and turned him loose. He lingered beside me as though he liked the company so I sat on the ground and leaned on the fence to keep him company for a while. He went back to nibbling his left over hay, but moved near me and sniffed me several times in greeting. I thought he was going to be one wonderful horse to work with and I was pleased with his progress.

CHAPTER 10

MOTHER AND I missed Dad. Home seemed very quiet. I had to admit I'd thought some about Luke, too. I hoped he was doing a good job and enjoying learning the ropes of packing with guests. I looked forward to hearing all their tales when they returned.

The next couple days were pretty mundane. I was busy looking after Magpie and Diamond. I loved watching how Diamond ventured further each day and how her running and bucking skills looked less and less like impending disaster.

I led Hero further and further each day and let him get some grazing time. After Dad got back, we would probably turn him out with Magpie and Diamond. He would gain weight better on a gradual increase in his time on grass. Thank goodness he had healthy teeth and his digestion wasn't ruined by being so starved. His age had certainly been on his side and it looked like he would make a full recovery.

On Wednesday evening everyone seemed tired from the extra work and responsibilities. We all decided to turn in early, glad that everything had been running smoothly.

For some reason I awakened wondering what time it was. That was uncharacteristic of me. I checked my alarm clock and saw that it was two in the morning. What the heck woke me at this hour, I wondered. I laid my head back down, but was shocked to hear a horse whinny in alarm. It was a shriek of fear and my hair stood on end. I jumped out of the bed and began pulling on clothes.

As I ran toward the door Mom came out of her room.

"What is going on, Emily? I thought I heard a horse," she said.

"I don't know, but I'll soon find out," I said as I flung open the door and grabbed the flash light that hung on a peg by the door.

"Wait," Mom yelled, but I was out the door and running toward the corrals. As I passed our small bunk house Miguel came out in his pants and long under ware shirt carrying a shot gun.

He joined me as we hurried toward the pens with the flash light off to avoid anyone seeing us coming. Again we heard a horse shriek.

"That's Hero!" I said.

Miguel and I moved cautiously toward Hero's corral. Then I also heard Magpie whinny and I knew something was awfully wrong.

As we moved closer Miguel stepped in front of me in a protective manner and we stopped to listen. Hero was running around in his corral and I could hear Magpie pawing in her stall.

Then we saw the problem. The black bear I had seen earlier in the day had come down from the ridge and was moving around just outside Hero's gate. We yelled at the bear and he stood up on his hind legs looking about ten feet tall. I was scared out of my wits, but thankfully Miguel had a gun between me and that bear.

Miguel yelled again, "Git outta' here. Go on, git. Nothin' for you here." That bear didn't seem intimidated. He probably smelled our chickens, but he certainly was alarming the horses. On the other side of the barn I could hear the horses snorting and moving around.

When Miguel yelled the second time, the bear let out a snort and snarl that brought heart rates to a new high. He just stood there and seemed to be deciding what to do. Then he turned and lumbered off, back toward the ridge. I felt myself slump with relief.

Miguel went around the corral to make sure the bear was actually moving away and not circling around. I went to Hero's corral and entered to calm him. He was snorting and charging around watching where that bear had gone. I approached him talking calmly in hopes that he wouldn't sense my own fear. He let me walk up to him and pat his neck, all the time I managed to talk calmly to him. I could feel that he had broken a sweat, but he didn't seem any worse for wear.

He soon relaxed next to me as though he was feeling some trust in me. I praised him for raising the alarm, though the words were really meant for me. I was so glad that he had awakened us all before that bear did any damage.

I went to Magpie's stall to calm her, too. Fortunately, she had been in the barn and not as close to the bear as Hero. A new foal would have, no doubt, looked like a fine meal for a bear. And that was not a small bear! Magpie was tense, but she seemed to be settling down. Diamond was on her feet, only wondering at all the excitement in the middle of the night. She hadn't been around long enough to know what routine was, but all this chaos had her on the alert.

Miguel came to the stall. "I'm glad these horses woke us. That bear should not have been comin' this close. We'll have to call wildlife protection in the morning. They'll look into why he was so bold. That just isn't natural." Miguel said.

Mom arrived about this time and was glad to see that everyone was okay.

"Thanks Miguel for rushing to the rescue with your shot gun. I'm glad you didn't have to use it. Why don't you both come in and we'll have a calming hot chocolate before any of us tries to sleep again," she said as she put her arm around me and pulled me close. "You were very brave, too. I guess we'll have a story for Dad that may top any story he brings home."

"Man, I was scared, Mom. I'm so glad Miguel was here and could scare that bear away. Hero did a good job of raising the alarm," I told Mom. "He is already living up to his name."

"He sure is. He sounded plenty concerned," she replied.

I checked Hero, Magpie and Diamond one more time as Miguel did another circuit of the area and checked the other horses. We all walked back toward the house beginning to feel our adrenaline levels settle some, but I wondered if I would sleep again.

Chapter 11

I GUESS I did get back to sleep for a while because I awakened after the sun was well up. Being late was not like me, so I jumped out of bed and dressed quickly. Mom and Miguel were already on the porch drinking their coffee.

"Well, Sleeping Beauty, it's about time. I guess the excitement last night was too much for your highness," Miguel said. I knew his teasing was his way of loving me.

"Of course, a Princess deserves extra rest after being torn from her bed in the night in violent horror. I needed extra rest to avoid stress lines in my face," I haughtily responded, holding my nose high in the air.

Mom chuckled. "I sure can do without another night like last night. Miguel, do you think our marauder will return? I expect his smell lingering near the barn will keep the horses on edge today."

Miguel thought for a minute. "I think there is a chance he will return. He didn't seem intimidated. I think you should call the wildlife ranger. They'll check out where he went. Chickens are a tempting draw, as that foal might be too, though keeping her in at night will help."

"I think I'll stay real close to the horses today to see if they are uneasy. I don't want Magpie's concern to upset her milk and effect Diamond," I commented.

"Yes, you should stay close today. Don't be riding up on the ridge. Just work in the corrals," Miguel directed.

"Keep your gun handy Miguel, if you are away from the buildings," Mom said.

"Well, a shot gun won't do that bear much harm, but the noise should chase him away," Miguel said distractedly.

"I'll call wildlife first thing," Mom assured us. "I'd like you both to be here when the ranger comes. He may have advice or more information on this bear for us." Miguel and I both nodded agreement.

Mom got up. "I'll make breakfast while you two feed."

Miguel and I headed for the barn. Magpie seemed calm enough while I fed her and Diamond was her usual self. She was getting nosy and watched my every move. I could rub her all over now and she liked the attention. I knew that when Magpie and Diamond were going to be out today, I would watch them closely. That bear might think he would like a foal for lunch.

Hero seemed more anxious than Magpie, but then the bear was at his corral and he was the one who set off the warning. I talked to him while he started to eat. I could go up to him and pet him now without him being shy. When I turned to leave to help Miguel with the other horses, he left his food and followed me to the gate. It made me feel good that with his anxiety he seemed to look to me for reassurance. I realized we were becoming partners and that was important to our progress in training. I was getting anxious to ride him, though I wouldn't neglect Star. I decided to give Star a day of rest today since I didn't want to ride far.

After breakfast Mom called the ranger station and I headed out to work with Hero. He had finished eating and was standing by the gate. He seemed to get bored in the corral by himself. I took a lunge line from the tack room and put his halter on with the long line attached.

I wanted to start showing him how to lunge. That means to exercise him on the long line in a circle around me. With lunging I could start teaching him stop, start, reverse direction, and take different gates. For the time being I would only walk him because of his poor condition, but as he gained weight I wanted him to build muscle and that would take lots of exercise.

From the center of the corral I let him out on the line and cued him to go left at a walk. He got the idea pretty quickly. It took a couple tries to show him how to reverse and walk in the other direction, but again he seemed pretty quick to learn. It wasn't long until he was taking all the cues at a walk.

Since this corral, also called a round pen, was circular and not real big, I would work him tomorrow in the same way, but without the halter. That was called working in the "round pen" and provided the horse the opportunity to make choices about obeying cues. I didn't think Hero would be any problem because he wanted to please and wasn't showing any apprehension.

When I was done working him I rubbed his face and petted him and praised him. He responded to my voice and the rubbing. Then I pulled a carrot from my pocket and he got the reward that he anticipated.

Tomorrow I would try turning him in the bigger corral with the other horses for a short time. He would have to learn to get along with them and they would teach him the pecking order. They would teach him who the leaders of the group were and to keep in his place. He would still eat separately for a while to ensure that he got all the feed he should have. At the bottom of the pecking order, where he would be, he might not get a lot to eat when with the others. In time he would learn to hold his own in the group.

Later in the day Ranger Hal Summers came around the barn and found me watching Magpie and Diamond in their small pasture. He stood with me for a few minutes watching Diamond work off some of her energy. She put on a good show.

"Now that is a fine filly," he said admiringly. "I hear you had a bear visit. Ya'll better keep her close by for a while. She'd look yummy to a bear."

"Don't worry. I'm keeping close tabs on her," I said.

I walked him around the area and described what had happened in the night. He took a close look at the tracks and followed them a little distance. When he came back he was shaking his head.

"That's a good sized bear. Have you seen him around before?" he asked.

"I think he was the same bear that I saw on the ridge earlier in the week when I was riding," I explained.

"That's not good. Bear like that shouldn't be comin' down this time a' the year. Them chickens may draw him. I think I'll bring a couple boys out and we'll track him up a ways. Then we'll leave a trap for him and haul him up further into the mountains. Hopefully that will take care of the problem," he said.

"It's great to see bears when we ride high, but having them in the yard in the middle of the night had everybody up last night. We'll be glad if you can arrange another territory for him to roam," I urged.

"Not to worry. We'll do just that," Ranger Summers said as he moved to his car. In his car he made a radio call to his office and put into motion his plan for re-settling the bear.

Mom came out and we thanked him with relief.

CHAPTER 12

THE NEXT MORNING I was working with Hero in his corral. I was now working him free and he was learning the signals very well. I took his halter off and then I'd stand in the center of the round pen. I had a lead-rope in one hand. I positioned him near the edge of the pen and moved to the center. Then I'd hold my arm out to tell him which direction I wanted him to go on the rail. Then I moved a little to his rear and waved the rope to urge him to move in the desired direction. When I wanted him to speed up a little I took steps toward his rear and swing the rope to sort of drive him in the right direction and to speed up. When I wanted him to stop, I stepped to his front and when he stopped he should turn and look toward me.

The idea was to get him to "hook on" to me. In other words, he needed to focus on me and not be distracted by anything else. Then I had him reverse his direction. I had him walk and jog a little. As he gained in strength and energy, I would work him at his other gates. He had nice smooth gaits.

As I finished up I noticed a large black car coming toward the ranch buildings from the distant road. I didn't recognize the car so I praised Hero and left his corral. I walked up to the house and called in to Mom that someone was coming. She came to the door.

"Who could that be?" she wondered. "I sure don't recognize that car, do you? It looks like a limousine."

"No, I have no idea who that could be. Can't say I've seen a limousine before," I replied.

The car pulled up to the house and an older man got out from the back. The driver stayed in the car. A very pretty young woman followed the older man. The man was dressed in very expensive looking western clothes—a suit, boots, and hat. The woman was dressed in western riding pants, boots, and hat. She sported lots of turquoise jewelry. They walked toward Mom and me.

Mom came out the door and greeted them. "Hello. You must be lost. Can we help?" she inquired.

"Hello. I'm James Butler from up near Denver. I raise Quarter horses. This is my daughter Jessica," he replied. Jessica nodded hello, but in a rather snooty manner.

"I believe we are in the right place. Bill Summerhill, who owns Diablo, told me that you have a Diablo foal that was born this season."

"Why yes," Mom replied. "She is just a few days old."

"A filly," Mr. Butler seemed pleased. "We were wondering if we could see the filly. We have been looking at several Diablo foals. We're thinking of buying him."

"I'm sure Emily would be glad to show you the filly. By the way, this is my daughter Emily and she is our horsewoman. I'm Anna Campbell," Mom said.

"I'm pleased to meet you. If you want to follow me I'll show you Black Diamond," I led them toward the barn.

"So she is black?" Mr. Butler said.

"Yes, coal black with a white star and three white feet. She is a nice strong filly," I told him.

Mr. Butler and Jessica followed me. Jessica seemed to be looking over our facilities somewhat disdainfully. I guessed she must come from one of those high end ranches near Denver. Our place was clean and neat, well kept, but definitely a working ranch.

As we approached Magpie's stall she stuck her head out to greet us. I moved her back and opened the door so they could see Diamond. She was lying in the back of the stall, but she got up and stretched when she saw something going on. She nickered softly and curiously came over to me.

"Is the mare touchy?" Mr. Butler asked. I guess he knows horses I thought since some mares can be very aggressive about strangers approaching their foals.

"No," I told him. "I should explain. Our mare, Bess, was bred to Diablo, but she died during foaling. This mare, Magpie, has stepped up as a surrogate and has been doing a great job. She is quite relaxed and I've been handling the foal a lot. They both have nice dispositions," I assured him.

Mr. Butler stepped into the stall and petted Magpie on the head and neck reassuring her. He was looking her over very carefully.

"I can see this mare is not the dam," he commented.

Then he turned his attention to Diamond. He looked her over, and then approached her holding his hand out for her to sniff. She wasn't shy. He petted her on the neck and ran his hand along her back. She liked being scratched and arched her neck up at the good feel.

Mr. Butler walked around her and checked her legs, assessing her confirmation with the eye of an experienced horseman.

"When did you say she was foaled?" he asked.

"Last week on Monday night," I replied.

"She has filled out nice already. This mare must be a good producer. The filly looks straight and strong already. Have you had her out?" he asked.

"Yes, I turn them out each day for a short time. She is quite nimble and active. It gives Magpie a chance to stretch her legs and get some grass. Would you like to see them out?" I asked.

"Yes, please," he replied.

I haltered Magpie and led them out into the yard.

"Could you walk and trot them up and down a couple times?" Mr. Butler asked. I thought that a little strange, but assumed he wanted to see how a Diablo foal moved.

As I walked and trotted up and down Mr. Butler observed them from the front, back, and side. Diamond was frisky and pleased to be out in the sunshine. She capered around her dam, raced away in several different directions only to realize she was alone, and came dashing back to Magpie. Then she pranced and snorted at this exciting event. Magpie was quite calm about this show Diamond was putting on, but she kept a close eye on Diamond.

I led them over to their paddock and turned them loose. Magpie took a few turns around the area at a gallop, obviously feeling very good. Then she settled to some grazing, but Diamond was still full of it. She finally ventured over to where I was standing, approaching me with head and ears up, and then whirled and raced away. She was quite the show off.

"Do you have papers on the dam," Mr. Butler asked. Again this seemed strange to me since he had said he was interested in the kind of foal Diablo produced and that had nothing to do with whether Bess was a registered Quarter horse.

"Yes, I believe Dad has her papers, "I replied.

"Thanks for showing the filly. Could we speak with your dad?" Mr. Butler asked.

Again with the baffling questions! I began to think he hadn't totally represented his interest.

"My dad is an outfitter and he is out this week with a trip. I guess you could speak with my mom, but Dad won't be back until late Friday," I explained.

"Could I speak with your Mother then, please?" he queried.

I made sure the corral gate was latched properly and left Magpie and Diamond in the paddock for a while. We walked to the house and entered. Mom heard us and came into the living room.

"Mom, Mr. Butler wanted to talk to Dad, but I told him that Dad won't be back till late Friday. Mr. Butler asked to speak with you," I explained.

"Won't you come in and have a seat," Mom graciously invited. "Would you like a glass of lemonade?"

"No, thank you. We must be moving along on a tight schedule. Emily has been very graciously showing us your fine foal. I should explain myself more fully. As I mentioned, I'm thinking of buying Diablo for our breeding program at Golden Gate Canyon Quarter Horses. Jessica and I have been traveling to see some of his foals to help us with that decision. I must tell you, I'm very impressed with your filly. She is the best progeny we've seen. In fact, I'm impressed enough to tell you I would like to buy her. I can make the sale very worthwhile for you," Mr. Butler verified my suspicions.

My heart took a terrible turn. Sell Diamond! No! No! Dad wouldn't do that. I noticed Jessica seemed as surprised as I was, but she hadn't spoken a word the while time.

"Oh, that is a surprise. I don't think the filly is for sale, but you would have to talk to my husband. We have bred her for our own string of trail horses and she shows all the promise we had hoped for," Mom said.

What a relief. Mom was standing pat against the idea of selling Diamond. I was sure Dad would do the same.

"Well, let me leave my card. When your husband gets back he can contact me or I'll try to get hold of him. The offer I'm prepared to make is this: I'll give you $15,000 for the filly. I'll buy her now and pick her up in six months after she is weaned. She has convinced me that I really like the Diablo line and I think she will be a top notch example to use in the show ring to promote the stallion. I really would like to buy this filly," Mr. Butler offered.

Geez, no. $15,000! That is a huge amount of money. I know my mom and dad could really use that kind of cash. Oh, but I hoped they would say no. But could they? My heart would break if they sold Diamond.

"I'm sorry you lost your mare. To sweeten the pot, though, I'll even include a return breeding to Diablo for any brood mare if you wanted to breed to him again." Mr. Butler added.

My life is over, I thought.

"We must be on our way. I certainly thank you for your gracious reception of us today and I hope you'll accept my offer. I'll look forward to talking to your husband on his return," Mr. Butler said and he and Jessica got up and walked to the door.

"Thank you, Mr. Butler, but I wouldn't want to hold out much hope to you. I really don't think my husband will want to sell the filly," Mom reiterated, to my relief.

After the Butler's left, Mom and I collapsed on the sofa.

"Can you believe that?" Mom said.

"Oh Mom, you guys wouldn't sell Diamond, would you?" I moaned.

"I don't know. We'll have to talk to your dad. $15,000 is a lot of money. We've never had a horse before that was worth that kind of money. Wow, we better take good care of her," Mom gasped.

"This is a threat worse than a bear" I groaned.

"Now Emily. You know we have to be practical when running a ranch," Mom reasoned.

As I left I slammed the door. As I dragged myself back toward the barn my mood was on the ground. I loved Star and Hero and the other horses, but sell Diamond! I couldn't bear the thought.

I decided that with my low spirits it wasn't a good time to ride. Horses sense your mood. This seemed like a good time to turn Hero in with Magpie and Diamond to see how they got along. It would be good for him to have closer company and Magpie seems pretty tolerant and friendly.

I led Hero to the small pasture and took him through the gate. Magpie's head popped up when I did that. I knew she would be protective of Diamond, but I hoped Hero would keep his distance.

When I let Hero loose he trotted toward Magpie, but to his surprise she laid her ears flat back and charged him. Poor Hero reversed course on a dime and dashed away from her. Magpie didn't pursue, but only sent the message to keep his distance.

Then Diamond entered the introductions with no qualms about upsetting things for Hero. She headed over to see what Hero was and that triggered another charge from Magpie. Poor Hero was confused by all this, but convinced that he should keep some distance from these threatening beasts.

However, it wasn't long until Magpie was grazing and Hero grazed nearby, keeping a constant distance that he judged kept him in a safe zone. Diamond loved all this excitement. She capered about, but avoided Hero. He watched with curiosity that seemed like amusement. I knew they would sort themselves out so I went to clean Magpie's stall, put her feed out, and refresh her water. Then I put hay in Hero's corral and checked on his water.

An hour later I went to see how things were going. Hero and Magpie were grazing together and Diamond was getting a nap. It seemed they have worked things out to determine that Hero was a friend. I sat on the fence top and watched them, realizing how they calmed me. It felt so painful to think of losing Diamond. I just had to trust Dad.

Diamond got up from her nap and felt it was time to break Hero into living with her. She wondered over near him and put her nose to his. Magpie raised her head to watch, but wasn't alarmed. I guess Hero seemed harmless. Then Diamond went around to Hero's side and gave him a kick and galloped away. Hero looked like 'what was that for?' but was unperturbed. It wasn't long till I could see that Magpie had gained a tolerant babysitter. I could now put them out together every day without worrying about them not getting along.

CHAPTER 13

SOON I WAS recovered enough from Mr. Butler's visit to feel I should ride Star. I tacked him up to give him some work, but I wouldn't ride off the ranch today. I would check the pastures. I let my mood effect Star as we slumped along through a large pasture. There was no lift in either of us. He dutifully took a course along the ranch boundary where I often rode to check for any down or damaged fencing.

I rode along hating Mr. Butler and his snooty daughter. How could rich people just ride onto your property and start throwing around their money? He already had a lot of horses and was going to buy Diablo—why does he need Diamond, I wondered. She's just a baby and won't produce any money or acclaim in the show ring for him except to promote Diablo. I was really feeling sorry for myself.

Suddenly Star jerked his head and ears up. I reflexively came alert and looked where he was looking. The gate at the far end of the pasture had a chain and padlock on it. It gave us an outlet to the road if we ever needed it for livestock. The chain was intact, but there were tire tracks by the gate where the ground was torn up and some of the fence was cut. This was alarming and certainly unusual.

I got off and had a look around. The tire tracks looked like they were made by a truck and there were foot prints along the fence. The hair on the back of my neck stood up again. This was as scary as the bear. Why would anyone be tampering with our fence? I wondered why they had not completed the job.

Man, just because Dad was away everything was going crazy. First the bear, then a rich guy wanting Diamond, and now possible rustlers! It made me anxious for Dad's return. I swung up on Star, patted his neck and praised his alertness, and urged him into a gallop toward the ranch house. Suddenly we both were recovered from our doldrums.

I galloped into the ranch and jumped from Star. I knew he wouldn't wander off anywhere. I ran to where Miguel was working.

"Miguel, I found a place in the lower pasture by the gate where it looks like someone was messing with our fence. I came to you so I wouldn't alarm Mom," I blurted out.

"What did you see there?" Miguel asked as he dropped his tools.

"It looked like a truck had been parked at the gate, there were footprints, and some of the fence was cut," I explained.

"That doesn't sound good. Put Star up and I'll get the truck. We better go check," Miguel said as he headed for the truck.

I quickly removed Star's tack, gave him his treat, and put him in the main corral. Then I ran to the truck as Miguel was already going into the pasture. We drove to the end of the pasture where Miguel checked the signs I had seen and agreed that this was strange. He took some wire from the truck and patched up the damage. We sure didn't want any horses getting out on the road.

"I think we should talk to the Sheriff to see if there has been any problem in the area with rustlers," Miguel said as he got back in the truck.

When we got back to the ranch headquarters we went to talk to Mom and have her call Sheriff Martinez. After she explained our concerns to the sheriff, she soon hung up.

"Sheriff Martinez will head out this way to check what you saw. He said there has been some problem with rustlers north of here, but this is the first possible problem in this county that he knows of," Mom told us.

"Boy, Mom, I'll be glad when Dad gets home. We're having too much excitement," I told Mom.

"I know what you mean. But we're handling things. Not to worry. He'll be back late tomorrow," Mom tried to assure me. "Miguel, would you talk to the sheriff when he gets here," Mom requested.

"Sure," Miguel said as he returned to his work.

"He is a steady sort, isn't he Mom? Someone we can rely on," I said to Mom after Miguel left.

"My, aren't you sounding mature," Mom laughed as she gave me a hug. "You and Star did some good detective work this morning. Now run along to your chores."

Chapter 14

ABOUT FOUR O'CLOCK Sheriff Martinez drove up to the house. I was cleaning and conditioning my new tack when I saw him. I ran to the house as the chief witness and investigator into the rustling probe. Okay, maybe that's getting a bit carried away.

Mom came to the door just as I skidded onto the porch. Sheriff Martinez was a noticeably tall man who totally looked the part of a western sheriff. He had broad shoulders, thick dark hair, a trace of beard, long legs, and walked like he'd spent a lot of time on a horse. As he came up to the porch Mom opened the door and invited him in.

"Thank you Mrs. Campbell," he said.

"Can I get you a glass of lemonade?" Mom said as she indicated he should have a seat in the living room.

"That would be nice," he said.

Man of few words, I thought. He took his hat off, sat down, and nervously fidgeted with his hat.

"We have a beautiful new foal and we just adopted an abused horse," I told him trying to fill the quiet time while Mom was in the kitchen.

"Well, I reckon that will keep you busy this summer," he replied.

"I'm the one who found the suspicious tracks down by our pasture gate. We wondered if someone might be trying to get to our horses," I informed him.

"Well, we'll have to look into that, won't we?" he replied.

I was out of things to say and it got quiet. Mom came in with the lemonade and gave us each a glass. Sheriff Martinez sat his down on the end table. He seemed tense and troubled in a manner that didn't fit with our rustler suspicions.

"Mrs. Campbell, I'm afraid I'm here about a different business than what we talked about this morning," Sheriff Martinez struggled to say.

"Oh? What is your business?" Mom inquired.

"I'm afraid I have some bad news, real bad news. A report came in a few hours ago that there was an accident up on the other side of Sky High Pass. It came in that an outfitter had been hurt. When we got there I found that it was Colin. It seems his horse slipped on a damp embankment and fell. He fell on Colin. I'm afraid Colin's injuries were fatal," Sheriff Martinez told us with his voice cracking. "Colin was still alive when we put him in an ambulance, but I got a report from the hospital that he had passed away shortly after arrival there."

My Mom gasped. With disbelief she said, "You mean Colin is dead?"

"I'm afraid so," the Sheriff replied.

I froze. Did he just tell us Dad is dead? That wasn't possible. I felt numb. My mom and I just sat there trying to wrap our minds around what the Sheriff had just said.

"Are you sure?" I asked in disbelief. The sheriff nodded his head.

"The accident was reported to the ranger station by campers. A ranger is bringing your clients and your stock home. You will have to make arrangements with the funeral home regarding Colin," the Sheriff said gently. "I'm so sorry to have to bring you this news."

My mom looked at the Sheriff as though she didn't know what he was talking about, but it was just the shock. I went to her and kneeled down and put my head in her lap. She stroked my hair and tears poured down her cheek.

The Sheriff stood up. "Is Miguel here? I'll let him know what's happened."

"He's at the barn," I said between sobs that began washing over me. Sheriff Martinez put his hand on my shoulder as I sat at Mother's knees.

"I'm so sorry," he said again and then he left for the barn.

"Oh, Mom," was all I could say. Words just didn't seem to form. I couldn't imagine life without my steady, caring father. I could only think about how my mom and I would get through the coming days. We would have to be as strong as he would have expected us to be.

Miguel walked in. "I'm so sorry to hear about Colin," he said as he stood there hat in hand.

"Sit down Miguel," my mom said and we all just sat there in a stupor. The phone rang and Mom rose with effort and answered. She seemed to have little to say and just said "Thanks" and "yes" periodically. When she hung up she said it was the funeral home and she was to go there tomorrow.

We heard a commotion in the yard. I looked out and it was our string of trail animals with our clients and a couple rangers coming in to the barn. My dad was so conspicuously missing. Topper carried an empty saddle.

"Mama the string is back. I'll go see to the animals," I said. Miguel got up to go with me to help.

"I'll see to the guests," Mama said and I saw her pull herself together enough to do what was right by everyone. We already knew that our guests had been through a traumatic experience. I was glad Mama could deal with them. I only felt like talking to our horses right now.

When I went out the guests had dismounted and they came right to me to express their sorrow. They hugged me and comforted me. When Mom came out they walked off with her to their guest quarters.

"I guess you are Emily? I'm Jim Stewart and this is ranger Roberto Ortiz," Ranger Stewart told me.

"Thanks for bringing our string and guests home for us. I'm sure you've had your hands full. If we could just tie them up at the hitching rail, Miguel, Andy, and I can untack them. We'll hose them off and make sure they are relaxed before we feed them," I said.

I heard myself talk as though I was looking down on myself. I sure sounded tougher than I felt, but Dad would have wanted me to take care of the livestock before all else. That's the Cowboy's Creed; take care of your horse first.

"Where is Luke Winslow?" I asked when Ranger Ortiz led Ole Ben forward without a rider.

"He said he would stay with your father, so we led his horse down. He said he would ride to town in the ambulance and call his dad for a ride from the hospital," Ranger Ortiz said.

"Miguel, would you drive the rangers back to their station?" I asked. He seemed glad to have a task and to be busy. I could understand that. I could see that Andy looked like he was still in shock. He seemed exhausted.

"Andy, why don't you go on home? I can take care of the animals," I said. He gave me a hug and mumbled that he needed to have some time. I assured him that he should take whatever time he needed. He seemed to drag himself to his Jeep and it was like there was a dark cloud following him.

I was glad to finally be left alone with the horses and mules.

I went to Dad's horse, Topper. I wanted some quiet time with him. I could see my dad riding out of the yard only a few days ago, sitting high and proud on his favorite trail horse. He was so happy when he was riding a horse into the mountains. I laid my hand on the stirrup leathers and imagined that I could feel Dad's warmth still there. I remembered how he turned and waved as they rode out of sight.

I un-cinched Topper's saddle and removed his breast plate. When I pulled Dad's saddle down it about bowled me over. It must have weighed fifty pounds with the saddle bags still attached. But my dad handled that saddle daily without noticing the weight.

Then I went to Ole Ben, the horse Luke had ridden. As I unsaddled him I thought about how brave Luke was to stay with Dad and ride to town with him. That seemed very grown up to me. He seemed older than his sixteen years.

After I had all the horses untacked and hosed down, I left them tied to cool. I wondered out to Hero's pasture. He nickered to me and walked right up to me. I lay my head on his lowered face and again the dam holding my tears broke and I sobbed. It felt like I was crying my heart right out of my body. I simply couldn't comprehend life without my dad. The sobs just rolled and rolled.

When I felt so depleted that I could hardly stand, Hero hadn't moved a muscle. He was there to be with me as long as it took. He sensed my sorrow. I moved around beside his neck and lay my head on him. I don't know how long I stood there, but Hero only moved to reach around and put his nose on my arm. A bond was born between that horse and me at that moment. It was as though Dad had made sure I would have this strong, intuitive partner at this hour. He really was a hero.

When Miguel returned we fed all the horses and mules, making sure they had a good fresh supply of water. I felt like a zombie as I moved through these tasks, but I was grateful for something to do. The animals instilled a peaceful feeling in me.

After I turned out the trail string, I went to Magpie's stall. I spent time petting Diamond while Magpie quietly munched her feed. Diamond liked having her back rubbed and she even made me laugh when she stretched into the rub and leaned against it. I knew Dad would have chuckled to see her antics. What a gift she was.

Suddenly I realized Mom was standing at the stall door watching me.

"That is a picture your dad would have loved," she said.

"I was just thinking of how he would have laughed at her antics," I said.

I went out of the stall and stood with Mom watching the peaceful animals. Magpie continued eating without a care in the world. Diamond nursed and then laid down for yet another nap. Mom said the guests had packed their car and left, no doubt out of deference to our needs. I was glad they weren't around. Mom and I and Miguel would need time for our thoughts tonight.

"Your dad loved this ranch and these animals so much," Mom continued.

"I know you both have poured your heart and soul into this place, Mom. You both have given me such a good life here." I told her.

Mom spoke quietly and with many pauses, "Tomorrow we must get through the process of planning a funeral and getting through the next week. It will be so hard for both of us, but we must do the things that would make your dad proud of us. We must be strong. That doesn't mean there won't be a lot of tears. We'll lean on each other and on our friends. Soon we will have to think about what we do from here, but we can put that off for a while."

I felt a sense of alarm at her words. Would I be strong enough? What would the future hold for us without Dad? How will I provide the help that Mom would need? How would I not roll up under the covers of my bed, never to come out?

"Not to worry honey. We will get through this together. We will keep Daddy with us," I felt Mom draw up tall as though she was gathering her strength as she boosted my courage.

"Mom," I said, "Luke sent Ole Ben down with the rangers and he rode in the ambulance with Dad. I think that was very grown up of him."

"Yes, it was," she replied. "We'll have some time to talk to him in the next few days and to thank him for his thoughtfulness. He seems like a fine young man . . . and only sixteen."

"Sixteen and a half," I reminded her. That half means a lot to a teenager.

That night we were very quiet and ate little at dinner time. Miguel joined us on the porch as we watched Dad's sunset. He always loved to sit out on the porch and watch the earth bed down at night, just as he had taught me to watch how the earth settled down in the fall for a long winters nap and awakened in the spring. I marveled at the beautiful art work in the sky created by Mother Nature.

The tears just seemed to keep coming with quiet sorrow. I felt a pain I didn't think I could bear.

Then we quietly dispersed for bed at an early hour. Mom soon came into my room. I sat up and we held on to each other. We didn't seem to have any words. We were exhausted. Where would we get the strength to go on?

"Try to rest and get some sleep if you can," Mom said as she got up.

"Good night, Mom," I said.

CHAPTER 15

THE NEXT MORNING I didn't feel like I had slept at all, but I must have dozed off at some point. I lay for a long time watching the dark sky begin to lighten and knew I should get up to start my chores. But my body just wouldn't move. I felt paralyzed. I guessed this was what grief felt like. My world was now a totally different world. With our terrible loss I knew it was time for me to do a lot of growing up whether I was ready or not. I ached inside to hear my father's voice.

When I went into the kitchen Mom was standing and staring out the window as the tea kettle whistled on the stove. She seemed in a trance. I went to her and put my arms around her. We both had tears running down our cheeks.

Today was the first day of our changed lives. But I didn't speak of that to Mom. It was just too sad.

When we saw Miguel coming across the yard for breakfast we saw a man who seemed almost unable to walk. He had worked for Dad for a long time and they were close. They seemed to work so compatibly that they didn't need to talk—they just both knew what needed to be done. Miguel had lost a friend.

Mom startled and moved to rescue the tea kettle and I set the table. Miguel took his hat off and sat at the table. I saw a tear run down his face. My sense was that Miguel would not verbalize his pain, but that he felt it just as we did. I put my head on his shoulder and he hugged me.

"You were his precious," he said quietly.

Mom scrambled some eggs while Miguel babied his first cup of coffee. We were quiet until Mom sat down and she seemed to grow into her new role of captaining the ship and being there to help us keep things together. I was proud of her strength at that moment.

"I'll have to go to the funeral home this morning," Mom said. "Do you want to go with me, Emily?"

"Yes," I said.

"You know it will be tough to discuss the things we'll have to talk about and they'll ask if we want to see Dad," Mom warned.

"I know," was all I could say, though the thoughts of what it would be like scared me. I didn't know if I could do this at the same time that I knew that I must.

"I will take care of all the ranch chores," Miguel reassured us.

"I'll help feed. There is plenty of time before I have to get ready to go," I told Miguel. I really needed to pat Star, and Hero, and Diamond. They grounded me and were my support.

After breakfast and the feeding, I was walking to the house to clean up for the trip to town when I saw Luke cantering up the lane on his pinto. I was pleased and surprised. He had never ridden over here before. Sometimes we would meet half way and ride together into the foot hills. He rode up to the hitching rail by the stable and tied his horse.

When he came over to me I felt my tears start to roll again. "Emily, I'm so sorry for what happened to your dad. It was a terrible accident." Luke put his arms around me and for the first time, in front of another person, I broke down. While I stood there I felt that I couldn't keep living. It was just too hard.

After a while, I said to Luke, "What happened?

"You sure you want to know? It all replays in my head and it isn't easy," he said.

"I think I must know," I mumbled. "I feel so bad that I wasn't there for him."

"Emily, I'm glad you weren't there. I tried to do the things you would have wanted me to do. I felt there was a reason that it was me there instead of you," Luke said as he stood back and looked me in the face. All I could say was, "I'm grateful. Please tell me."

"It happened so quick—one second he was riding up a damp embankment leading out of camp, and the next he and the horse went down. Topper landed downhill on your dad and when he struggled to get up he hit your dad's head with a foot. I think Mr. Campbell also had internal injuries. At the hospital that is what they told me," Luke said as he laid a hand on my shoulder.

Then Luke pulled me into his arms and I couldn't help but break down in sobs again. Soon his holding me felt very natural to us both and I was so grateful for such a kind friend.

"You were so brave Luke to go with Dad on short notice and then to stay with him after he was hurt. I'm so thankful you were there. Dad liked you a lot." I told him.

"I'm glad I was there," Luke said.

Mom came out of the house to see if I was coming to get ready. When she saw Luke she put her arms around both of us.

"Thank you so much for everything, Luke," was all she could say. We all seemed suddenly tongue tied in our grief. We walked to the house and sat on the porch.

"My mom and dad send their thoughts to you. They said anything that you need, just let us know," Luke said.

Then we saw a car coming up the lane. Doc Mason parked and walked up to the porch.

"Anna, I don't have words for what I feel. Everyone is shocked by what has happened," Doc spoke with tightness in his throat. He sat down quietly.

The phone rang. "Emily, would you get that," Mom said.

I took the call and it was one of Mom's friends at work. She was crying and said she wanted Mom to know she was thinking of her. I thanked her and said I would convey her thoughts.

Soon another car arrived. It was Maria. "I've come to look after things here at the house for a few days," she told Mom. "You will be busy with all you need to do and there will be company and people bringing food by. I can help with all that."

Mom went to her and hugged her. "Maria, I can't tell you what this means to me. I've always been able to count on you. Thank you so much. Emily and I need to go to the funeral home. Maybe you will take care of any visitors who might come while we're gone," Mom said as they went into the house.

"Thanks Doc for coming by. Mom and I have to go to the funeral home," I said as I got up.

"I'll just take a look at your charges and then I'll be on my way. Let me know if you need anything," Doc said and he headed for the barn.

"Luke, I have to get ready to go with Mom. Thanks for coming by. We really appreciate all you've done," I said as I turned toward the house. Luke pulled me back and hugged me again. It was almost more than I could handle and I pulled away to go get a shower. I was beginning to get feeling back and it was too painful to bear.

As I walked away, I heard him say, "See you later."

CHAPTER 16

THE NEXT FEW days and weeks were a blur to me. Somehow Mom and I got through the funeral leaning heavily on our friends. We had so much wonderful support from the community with food, visits, and kind offers of help. It really brought home to me how respected Dad had been.

The next few weeks I plodded through the work we had to do to care for the livestock and the ranch. When Mom went back to work, Maria just stayed. She said with her kids grown and gone, she could just stick around. She and Miguel are family to us. Though they both have homes, they often stayed at the ranch.

We managed to keep the place going, but the memories of Dad as I went through the routines we had shared brought more tears. Finally, I felt that all the tears had dried up, but there was a heavy feeling left in my chest where my heart was located. I had to carry that weight with me everywhere. It was like a piece of me was gone and I'd never get it back.

At the funeral, Luke's mom and dad told us that they could spare Luke during the summer for any help we needed. We took advantage of that and he came over a couple times a week. He was a great extra pair of hands when something needed to be done that Miguel and I couldn't handle alone. We needed to get the hay baled that Miguel had cut. That took all of us pitching in.

Hero had been filling out well and I'd been working him with a saddle and bridle. When it got to be time to get on him for the first time

I, of course, didn't know for sure what his reaction would be. He hadn't shown any buck, except for a couple crow hops when he was feeling good. I asked Luke if he would help me the first time I planned to get on. He said he would be glad to do that.

"In fact," he said, "it might be good if I got on him first. I get that job at our place and I'm used to it. And, of course, it is a man's job."

I swatted him on the shoulder. "Right, it is a man's job because landing on his head won't make any difference in his smarts," I countered. I warmed to his teasing. "Besides, your humongous weight might break down a horse recovering from malnutrition." It was nice to laugh again. Sometimes I was afraid to be happy. It might mean I didn't still miss my dad.

"Had he been handled before you got him?" Luke asked.

"We don't really know," I replied. "Why do you ask?"

"Well, he has progressed very fast. I wondered if anyone else had been on him," Luke replied.

"We'll never know, but I think it is testimony to my great skill as a trainer that he has come so far," I said.

"Oh, without a doubt," Luke laughed.

"Get out of here," I said as I drew up in sham indignation.

"Could you be serious for a moment?" he drew back and scowled at me.

"Like I'm the one that starts the teasing," I replied. "But sure. What's on your mind?" I asked.

Luke grew solemn. "My family has decided to throw a big barbeque on the fourth of July. I know this isn't really a time for you and your mom to feel joyous. We respect that. But we also decided that it might be good for both of you to be out among friends and neighbors to spend the day. Everyone will be sensitive to your situation, I'm sure. Would you consider coming?"

I thought about that for a few minutes while Luke patiently gave me time. "I can't imagine going without Dad, but it's very nice for your parents to think of us. They have been Mom and Dad's closest friends for a long time. I suppose it would be good for us to be among friends on the holiday. Can I talk to Mom about it and let you know?"

"Sure," Luke said and he put his arm around my shoulder again. Could he possibly be any kinder or more considerate of me and my mom? I felt like my feelings for Luke as a fun riding companion were growing into feelings in me that went well beyond "liking." I gently pulled away from him at the same time that I imagined him leaning down and kissing me. Oh gad, where did that come from?

Getting myself together I said, "Okay, tomorrow we saddle and ride Hero. When we get him going well, maybe you would ride Star and we could go out together. It really helps a young horse to learn the ropes from an experienced and sensible horse. We would be training and having fun like in the past."

"Sounds like a plan," he said. "I'll see you tomorrow."

When Luke left, I found myself thinking about him. I wandered to the paddock where Magpie was grazing and Diamond was napping, as usual. I eased through the gate and walked up to Magpie. I petted her neck. She acknowledged me and went back to chomping grass.

Diamond raised her head and I sat down beside her and rubbed her neck. Soon she flopped over with her head landing in my lap and proceeded to continue her rest with me as a pillow. I had to chuckle at her. What a peaceful spot for me to do my thinking with the companionship of this extraordinary baby keeping me company in the sunshine. The interlude didn't last long because I knew I needed to go help Mom, but I felt better.

When I told Mom about the invitation for the 4th of July she said at first she probably wasn't ready for any socializing. I told her about how thoughtful Luke had been. She said she would think about it.

CHAPTER 17

THE PHONE RANG as we were sitting down to dinner. Miguel and Maria were eating with us most of the time. I think it provided company for all of us. Mom went to answer the strident ringing.

"Hello. Yes, this is Mrs. Campbell," she said. "Mr. Butler, of course I remember you."

There was a long pause as Mother listened.

"That is very thoughtful of you. Thank you," Mom said.

Another pause.

"Well, I'll have to think about that. I do appreciate your concern," she then paused again. "Thank you. You are most thoughtful. I really hadn't yet tackled those issues, but you are right, I will soon have to."

We listened through another long excruciating pause. I knew what this had to be about. We never got a chance to talk to Dad about Mr. Butler's interest in Diamond. I wished I had heard Mom say," No, we aren't interested," but I guessed there would be issues other than what I wanted. I lost my appetite.

Mom said goodbye and hung up. She came to the table and sat down meeting my troubled look.

"I'm sure you've guessed what that was about, Emily. Lord help us. How much more can we take! Let's set it aside for now and have a pleasant dinner. We'll think about this tomorrow, as Scarlet O'Hara was famous for saying," Mom said.

I couldn't speak. I knew Mom would know my thoughts.

After dinner when Maria and Miguel had left, Mom and I sat quietly on the porch. Neither of us wanted to speak of what we had to talk about.

"Emily, I don't know how we're going to support the ranch and the horses. Luke and Miguel are great help, but without the guiding business we just won't have enough income. My job has been about half of what we take in, but that won't get it. We can sell some hay, but that is a small supplement," Mom said thoughtfully.

"You know I'll do anything I can to help," I told Mom.

"Of course, honey, I always know that. We're going to have to apply some real creative thinking if we want to keep the ranch," Mom pondered.

I just couldn't wrap my mind around what she was saying. "Where would we live if not on the ranch," I blurted in amazement. The ranch was the only home I knew. I didn't want to live anywhere else.

"Emily, we have to consider every option. How will we support a ranch? I don't know yet what we will have to do, but I know it may be drastic," Mom reasoned.

Then the worst dawned on me. "Are you thinking of selling Diamond? We can't do that. Dad wouldn't sell her," I yelled at mother.

I jumped up and ran off the porch toward the barn. I ran like a crazy person until I calmed down. I hadn't put Magpie and Diamond in their stall from the pasture yet, so I got a halter and went to put them in for the night. I just had to be near the horses to calm me.

I couldn't believe that we would have to sell Diamond. She was so beautiful. I knew she was Dad's dream result for our small breeding program. She would be a top horse. Then I had to admit to myself that was why she could bring $15,000 as a weanling. Was this Dad's legacy to us? Would his dream horse help us keep the ranch? Everything in me rebelled against this unfair tragedy!

When Magpie had a drink and Diamond lay down in the fresh straw with her usual lack of dignity, I sat down in the straw with Diamond and had a good cry. The pain felt awful. Why was life suddenly like this? Magpie came over and stood with her head above Diamond and me.

She seemed to sense my anguish. I cried so hard that I eventually laid my head down by Diamond and dozed off.

I was awakened when Mom called to me softly from the stall door.

"Emily, come in and go to bed. We'll talk more tomorrow." Mom said.

I got up and went out of the stall turning to say good night to Magpie and Diamond. Mom brushed straw off me and put her arm around my shoulder and led me to the house.

"I'm sorry Mom. I just hurt so bad," I whispered.

Mom held me tighter and said, "It's okay honey. I know how you feel. We are going to have some rough times, but we have to stick together. That is what Dad would expect."

"I know," I said.

CHAPTER 18

A WEEK LATER Mom called me into the den that Dad had used as a ranch office. She looked very serious and I knew this couldn't be good.

"I've talked to our banker, Doug Olson, and I've been thinking about how we are going to manage financially. I also talked with Orrville Swenson and John Winslow. They were good friends of Dad's and they have been very nice to help me sort out our finances. We've looked at the costs of running the ranch and my income. We fall pretty short, as I thought we would. We've talked about selling some land or selling the whole ranch and you and me moving to town. There are many things to think about. Foremost in my thoughts will be your college. We do have some savings set aside for college that will help, if we don't have to tap into them," Mom said.

I felt like this was heavy duty stuff for me at age fifteen, but was determined to be the best help for Mom that I could, despite the anger I felt toward our situation. Moving to town sounded like the end of the world and I sensed that would be our outcome.

"What about the horses?" I asked with a shaky voice.

Mom continued, "John said he could help us sell the pack horses and mules. I can't imagine how we can keep them if we aren't guiding. One of Dad's outfitter friends may take them, knowing that we have a good string. And, of course, I told them about the potential sale of Diamond. Mr. Butler's interest in her is very timely," Mom finished.

"What about Star and Hero?" I asked with a horrible feeling of foreboding.

"I don't know. If we sell everything and move to town, maybe you could keep one riding horse. I think John might buy Star. He knows that Star is a very good quality horse and Luke likes him. They think with his bloodline he probably has cow sense," Mom said.

"Star," I moaned. "I love him so much. He is the finest riding horse around."

"I know honey. At least if John bought him you could still go and ride with Luke and take Star up in the hills like old times," Mom commiserated.

I thought my world had fallen into a black hole when Dad died. Now I was beginning to see what the implications would be for Mom and me. The losses just kept piling up. My body felt like it was made of lead.

"Without Dad our lives as we knew them are over, I'm afraid," Mom said. "Do you think we can handle all this?"

"What choice do we have? Couldn't I keep running the packing trips with guests? I know how to do everything. Cooking, caring for the horses, leading the trails, everything," I almost begged.

"Oh, honey, there is no way one fifteen year old girl could run that business. It is a lot of heavy work. I remember how tired your dad would be when he got back after a week and he always had at least two men helping him. You are brave to think of it though," Mom shot down my ingenious idea.

"Maybe when I'm older and through vet school I'll run trips like Dad did. I think I'm cut out to be an outfitter in the mountains. I would do that in memory of Dad," I planned, as another impractical idea was planted in my mind.

"We'll spend a little time making our decision, but I'm afraid there really won't be much choice for us when all is said and done. Mr. Butler said he would call me back in a couple days. He had read about Dad in the paper. He said he wanted to assure me that he is still interested in Diamond. I hope he sticks to his original price. I'm so sorry, Emily. She may save us in the short term while we get readjusted to this new life," Mom told me.

How I had wished Mr. Butler dead and now I had to think of his buying Diamond as a saving grace. He did seem nice and would be a good owner for Diamond, but I must insist on having visitor's rights if he took her away. I'd had so many visions of what she would look like as a grown horse. I knew I must not lose track of her. I railed at my fate for a few selfish minutes, but I knew in my heart that I would have to deal with losing Diamond and Star. It helped that it seemed like I was going to be able to keep Hero.

Then Mom said, "I've been thinking about going to the Winslow get together on the 4th. I guess it would be good for us. The Winslows are good friends and I expect some of their other guests will be friends we've known for a long time. I know it isn't good for you to be closeted away from people all summer. It won't be easy for either of us, but why don't you tell Luke we'll go over for a while."

"Thanks, Mom. I understand that it will be hard to go without Dad. I almost can't think about it. But I think the Winslow barbeque will be good for you, too. You should have friends to talk to and lean on," I told her.

Mom chuckled, "I was thinking the same thing about you." She hugged me to her and we both had a cry. "Small steps," she said.

In the end I thanked my lucky stars that Mr. Winslow agreed to buy Star. We said we would sell him to the Winslows for one dollar. That was the only deal we would make. We knew he would find a good home with them. When they picked him up to go to his new home it was the first of many heart breaking departures.

CHAPTER 19

THE FOURTH OF July arrived right on time with both Mother and me wondering if we really wanted to go to a party. It just didn't feel right. We were still both subject to tears being triggered at the slightest reminder of Dad. We didn't feel very rational.

I worried about being a sad sack and bringing the party down or being hurt by others having a good time without considering our sadness. When I told Mom how I felt she agreed that we had to try to have some fun and not ruin things for other people. We decided hiding away wouldn't do any good.

"I think we should be ready to help each other to keep things light, in tune with the spirit of the day," Mom suggested. "Here's what we'll do. If either of us feels like we are losing control we'll go to the other and say, 'Help me get something from the car,' and then we'll find privacy together. I really think we will do fine and will enjoy the company of our friends. I'm sure that is what Dad would want us to do."

"I think that is a good approach in a risky situation," I agreed, though not heartily. "I expect we will be distracted once we get there."

So we got ready and headed to the Winslow ranch shortly before noon. We agreed that, once we got started, it just felt good to dress up a little and go out among other people. We've been isolated in our grief.

When we drove in Luke greeted us at the car. "Gee, I'm glad you guys could come. It means a lot to us that you chose to be here with us today," Luke said.

"We are glad to come over and see our friends," Mom said.

Betsy Winslow met us as we walked toward the patio where people were gathering. She and Mom made eye contact and I could see the non-verbal communication that passed between them. Both were pleased to be together and I saw that Mrs. Winslow understood our dilemma. The love and understanding between those two friends was enviable.

Mr. Winslow came and hugged Mom. Then he turned to me and winked. "Maybe we'll have to sneak out later this afternoon and get you a ride on Star. We are so impressed with him. I wonder if a good gallop on him wouldn't do a lot for your spirits."

"Oh yes," I said. "I hadn't thought of that, but it would make a grand time for me on the 4th of July. You know me too well."

"Come on up to the tables and have something to drink. We have the meat cooking and we'll be ready to eat soon. I think you know the Swensons, Tom Oberholtzer, and Doc Mason. I'll introduce you to the Donaldsons, who have a ranch about ten miles west, and the Bryce brothers, who ranch the old Carson place," Mr. Winslow said. He was good at putting us at ease.

Soon everyone was gathered with drinks and reacquainting or getting to know each other.

Luke introduced me to Robert and Brenda Donaldson. Robert was seventeen and Brenda was fifteen like me. We decided to throw some horseshoes before we were called to eat. It turned out to be fun.

A couple hours after we ate Luke asked Brenda and Robert if they wanted to go for a ride. They were enthused about that and I felt the whole party was taking a turn for the better.

Luke and I led them to the stables. Suddenly there was Star standing and looking at me when I went around the corner.

He knew me and walked to me when I called his name. As the tears welled up I thought, oh no, Mom isn't here to help contain me, but I swallowed the tears and threw my arms around his neck. I rubbed and petted his head and neck and checked him all over.

"Star, I've missed you so much," I whispered to him. Our bond was renewed as though we had never missed a day.

"Emily, this saddle fits him well," Luke said as he laid a nice saddle on Star's back. He handed me a bridle, patted me knowingly on the shoulder, and left me to prepare Star like old times. Luke made himself busy setting up Robert and Brenda with nice mounts and saddling his own horse.

It was very thoughtful of Luke to realize how I treasured those extra quiet minutes with Star while he kept everyone else busy. By the time he had Robert and Brenda mounted, I was sitting on Star much more composed and ready to go.

We left the ranch riding abreast and headed toward the foothills. Being ranch kids we were all riders so we soon picked up a ground covering canter.

My soul soared as Star stepped into his smooth stride. I relaxed as I hadn't relaxed since our last ride. I felt whole again, at least for the time being. Luke smiled at me as he cantered stirrup to stirrup with me. He knew what this meant to me.

After a good long lope, we picked up a trail that climbed up a ridge. On top of the ridge we turned up ridge following the top of the ridge line to where it leveled out on a plateau. It was a gorgeous day and the view was something to behold.

Our horses had begun to sweat so we put them in a leisurely walk as we climbed to the end of the gentle rise of the plateau. At the top we all dismounted and sat on some convenient rocks near the edge where we could look down on the ranch far below.

"That was invigorating," Robert said. "Are you a rancher, too, Emily?" he asked.

"I grew up on a ranch near here. Have you always lived on a ranch?" I asked, avoiding discussion of the uncertainty of my future situation.

"No, but we moved there five years ago. Dad always wanted to raise cattle and he had made enough in construction that he could buy a small place. Our mom isn't too happy living the lonely life in the boonies, but she puts up with it," Brenda chimed in.

"Are you going hunting this fall? I really enjoy shooting," Robert asked, turning to Luke.

"Probably not. My dad and I aren't much into hunting. We do love to take packing trips into the mountains in the fall and we usually fish," Luke said.

"Are you excited about starting high school this fall?" I asked Brenda.

"I sort of dread it, but at the same time I'm looking forward to it. I hope high school will be more exciting than middle school," Brenda said. "Will your mom and dad let you start dating now that you'll be in high school?"

"If the answer is yes, I'd like to put in first dibs," Robert said.

Geez, I didn't like the way this conversation was going. Robert, at seventeen, was interested in different things then Brenda or me.

"I guess you didn't know that Emily's dad was killed earlier in the summer. He was an outfitter and his horse fell on him. I was with him when it happened," Luke stepped in to control the conversation.

"I'm sorry. I guess we heard about that accident, but I didn't realize it was your father," Brenda said.

"That's rough," Robert added.

"Well, maybe we better head back," Luke said, breaking the tension. "They'll be sending out a search party."

As we went to our horses Robert went over to Star and held my stirrup while I mounted. "Any time you need a fix riding a ranch, you'd be welcome to come to our place and ride," he said looking up at me.

"Thanks," was all I said. I noticed Luke observing Robert's chivalry with a bit of a scowl.

Brenda rode over by me and winked as the guys started ahead of us. "I think Robert has taken a shine to you," she said. I smiled and moved Star forward to catch up.

When we had turned the horses out, we headed back to the house and Robert, rather than Luke, walked at my side. I found that unsettling, but didn't really know how to handle it, so I just walked briskly to the patio.

The party was breaking up. I found a moment to thank Mr. Winslow for suggesting the ride. "You couldn't have given me a better fourth of July," I told him.

"I think we are kindred spirits when it comes to our horses," Mr. Winslow said giving me a pat on the shoulder. "You are welcome to come and ride Star any time."

"Thanks to you and Mrs. Winslow for being such steadfast friends to my mom. It means the world to her." I told him.

Mrs. Winslow walked up to me as I said that and she hugged me and whispered in my ear, "Friends forever."

Mom and I were very quiet on the ride home. I think we were emotionally drained. We did agree that it had been good to spend the day with friends.

"Mom, riding Star made me feel like I might come back to life," I told Mom somewhat guiltily.

"You will in time, honey. You are young, strong, and resilient," she assured me. "I'm glad you felt that way."

"I think Robert was flirting with me on the ride," I confessed shyly. "I don't think Luke liked it."

"No, I suppose he wouldn't. You've been special friends for a long time and he probably feels a bit jealous of another boy giving you attention. However, lots of boys are going to flirt with you, so he might as well get used to it," Mom chuckled.

"But Mom, I wouldn't want to hurt Luke in any way." I told her.

"And that is as it should be honey," she said.

CHAPTER 20

AND SO THAT summer of nightmare went. In the end we had to sell the ranch and make plans to move to town. An outfitter friend of Dad's bought Thornton, Ears, and Buster. He said he knew that Dad had the best trained pack mules around. I was proud of that.

Mr. Winslow helped us advertise the trail horses and an outfitter from Wyoming bought them. As his stock trucks took them out our driveway I couldn't watch. I ran to Hero's corral and sat in the dirt sobbing. My heart felt broken again. Dad and Miguel had taken such good care of those horses, never overworking them. There was no guarantee what their lives would be like with the stranger. With Star safe at the Winslow ranch, this was the first time I knew the pain of giving up animals that I loved to an unknown future. It was wrenching.

The outfitter who bought the trail string hired Andy to come work for him. Mom gave Andy a strong recommendation and we were glad he wasn't going to be without work. It was a sad good-bye, but it had been hard for Andy to be around the ranch. It was as though he somehow blamed himself for Dad's accident. We felt this was a good move for him; a fresh start.

Word got around in the ranching community that our ranch was for sale. We advertised it, too. It wasn't long until potential buyers, from close and far away, were coming to look at it. Our set up was a perfect place for horses or a small herd of cattle. Eventually well-to-do brothers from

Denver made us a fair offer and we agreed to sell. I'm afraid I was little help to Mom during that process. I just had to hide away somewhere when she had to show our home to strangers. I just couldn't cope with everything.

The grieving process for Mom was devastating. Not only missing Dad, but losing her home and having to create a sensible future for me, was a terrible course for her to navigate. I really tried to help all I could, but there was so little I could really do. Her friends gathered around her and that helped a great deal. I think she and Luke's mom, Betsy, became even closer. And more than once I saw her sitting and crying while Maria just quietly stayed by her side.

Living in the country, as we had, I didn't have close girlfriends. I had a couple chums at school, but I lived too far away for us to spend time together outside of school. I guess Dad and the horses had always been my best friends. And, of course, Luke remained a steadfast friend that summer. He couldn't come by as often as we had planned because he was working for his dad on their ranch, but he came by a couple times a week to help Miguel and we did manage to have some lovely evening rides up in the foothills.

When we rode together, Luke rode Star toward our place and I rode Hero to meet him. For a while we just walked the horses together until Hero learned about my cues from on his back and until he got used to the balance with someone on him. However, it wasn't long until Hero could jog, trot, and canter along with Star. They were very companionable and Hero learned from Star. It was very nostalgic.

Luke felt bad that I had to move to town, but he assured me that he would soon have his driver's license and he'd come see me whenever he could, if I wanted him to. I was really glad for that, but I acted cool. I said I would probably be very busy, but it would be nice to have him come by sometimes. He said his dad would let him drive to school during football season and he could give me a ride home after school sometimes. I said that would be nice.

I don't know why I said that when I was wishing I would see him every day. I think I had such a feeling of loss at the time that I felt that somehow everything important would be lost. Since he would be a sophomore and I'd be a lowly freshman, I really worried that he would decide I wasn't old enough for his attentions. Maybe he would even get a girlfriend at school. I knew I should behave differently, maybe more appreciative of him, but I just wasn't dealing with any real feelings. It seemed like a risk to care about anyone.

The bank would close the sale on the ranch before school started, so Mom and I went to town several times to look for a place to rent. We wanted to be close to school and her work if possible and to have a place close by where I could keep Hero. Mom had decided that I would be able to keep Hero.

Hero had filled out nicely. I would continue through the winter working on his strength and conditioning so I would need a place to ride him. I felt having him with me would go a long way to preserving my sanity. He was becoming a really good looking horse now that he was healthy.

Mom told me that with the money we got from Mr. Butler, her job, and the appreciation we would get out of the ranch, we would be safe and pretty comfortable if we lived modestly. She said that she would open a savings account for my college with the profit from the ranch. Dad had built the ranch up to a very good facility and she would be able to save a pretty good amount of money. I think she was determined to set aside money for my schooling since that had been an important goal for Dad.

After some very discouraging house searching, we decided we were going about our search the wrong way. We got a map of the city and plotted Mom's hospital and my school, and then searched for a stable. Amazingly, we found a nice stable close by that housed a lot of pleasure horses and some nice Quarter show horses.

We met with the manager, Beth, and she showed us several ways we could rent space. We chose a nice outer area of stalls that had small runs so a horse could stay in his stall or go outside into his private pen. There would be many horses around for company and we also opted to have Hero turned out every day in a large pasture with other pasture horses.

Having located all that we needed, we turned to finding a small house to rent that would be central. That took long enough that we were getting worried, but one day Mom came home from work with the news that a friend had mentioned a small, but clean and neat house for rent in a nice quiet neighborhood near the school. Mom called the number and made arrangements for us to go see the house on Saturday.

When I saw the small house and the tiny yard, I felt the open spaces and freedom of the ranch pulling me back. This was going to be harder than I had imagined. But then I had never thought about living in a town.

The house was a cute place with a breakfast nook off the kitchen that was sunny and bright. It had two bedrooms and we would share a bathroom. There was plenty of room for two people and I could walk to school and the stable. We told the people we would think about it and call them.

In the car Mom said, "Well, what do you think?"

"Wow, I think we are really going to miss the ranch. Just seeing the sunrise and sunset will be impossible," I moaned.

"Yes, you are right about that. It will be hard. But I think it is a bit of an exaggeration to say we won't see the sunrise or sunset. We've had it so good, but now we'll have to make adjustments. The house is safe, clean, and handy. You can walk to school and we'll get you a bike so you can get to the stable after school," Mom reasoned.

"I have to learn to ride a bike!" I blurted.

"It's easy, I can show you how to do that. It will be important for you to get around," Mom assured me.

"It sounds like you think we should take this place," I said.

"Well, we haven't found any other option that seemed to work," Mom said.

"I guess you're right. I just feel like I'm in a vortex. And you can forget the bike idea. I'll walk." I complained, indulging myself in a self-pity pout.

Mom laughed. "I know what you mean about the vortex. Maybe by Christmas we will be resettled and make our adjustments so things will seem like a new normal. I can't help but think your dad is watching us and understanding why we have to make these difficult choices."

"You are right about that." I paused to think and we were quiet for a few minutes. "I guess we better take this place, but I'm not crazy about a new normal." I said.

And so Mom and I made our decisions and changed our lives in ways we could never have imagined. I wondered 21 – Diamond's Fate if that was just the way life goes.

CHAPTER 21

TO TOP OFF our losses, Mr. Butler spoke with my mom a couple days later. He asked Mom if she had decided to sell Diamond. Mom told him she was very reluctant to sell, and that if Dad hadn't died, we never would have, but now we would sell out of necessity.

I have to say Mr. Butler was kind and generous to us. He could have reneged on his offer, knowing that we really needed the money. Instead, he said he would buy Diamond at his original offer. He said Bess produced a nice foal and Diamond would be worth a lot to him for promoting Diablo. Putting a $15,000 check in the bank would provide a lot of relief for Mom.

Mr. Butler told Mom, "Tell your daughter I will take very good care of the filly and she will have a good home. I know what it is like to love a horse and she is facing a great sacrifice for a young girl."

"Thank you," Mom said. "We truly appreciate the thoughtful way you have treated us. We feel vulnerable right now and your respect means a lot to Emily and me."

"We could pick up the filly and her nurse mare on Thursday, if that works for you?" he asked. "I usually send a man with a van, but in this case I will come with my handler to help watch over the horses' welfare on the trip. I've arranged with Magpie's owner to keep Magpie with Diamond until the filly is weaned. I'll pay him for the time that Magpie has been with you, too."

"Thank you, once again you are very generous," Mother said and they hung up. Mom just looked at me and said, "Thursday."

My heart sank. I turned and slowly walked out of the house. I went to Magpie and Diamond's pasture to be with them. As soon as Diamond saw me she came to see what activity I would bring to her peaceful day. She was always ready for some attention and action. Maybe at her new home she would be turned out with other foals. I imagined how she would happily run and play with them.

Magpie kept peacefully grazing after she ate a carrot. I talked to her and told her what a faithful, wonderful step-mother she has been and that we appreciated her. Diamond nipped me on the back in jealousy at all the attention I was giving Magpie. I rubbed her all over and talked to her and played with her for a long time. She had learned to lead and would be ready to go with Magpie to her new life. I was proud she was so smart and growing so well. How I would miss Black Diamond.

I finally dragged myself back to the work I needed to do at the stable to leave everything ship shape for the new owners.

Thursday would be a sad day.

Black Thursday arrived much too quickly. Promptly at 10:00 a horse van showed up. Mr. Butler and his handler jumped down from the cab after backing up close to the barn. Miguel and I left the barn to greet them.

"Hello, Miss Campbell," Mr. Butler said and he nodded to Miguel. "I'm glad that you have decided to sell your filly though I know it was a hard decision for you. I want to assure you again that she will be well cared for and you will be welcome to visit her any time."

"Thank you Mr. Butler. We would never have sold her if circumstances had been different," I told him. "I'll take you up on that offer to visit anytime."

Mom came out of the house. She gave Mr. Butler the registration application papers for Diamond. "We haven't registered the filly yet, but I've included all the information that you'll need," she told Mr. Butler.

"Thank you Mrs. Campbell. This is a cashier's check for the filly," he said as he handed Mom the check that would help feed us for a while.

"I'm grateful," Mom told him. "I'm sure you realize how timely your visits have been for us."

"I'm sorry I never got to meet Mr. Campbell. I'm sure, from what I've seen of his family, he was a fine man. I was just telling your daughter that she is welcome to visit Diamond any time. I've attached my card to the check so you'll always know how to contact me," Mr. Butler said. "Mrs. Campbell, I also have planned to tell you that, if your daughter is interested in a summer job while she is in high school, I would offer her a summer position working at our stables. She could be involved in the filly's development that way. She seemed rather sincere about wanting to be a horse vet and we could see to it that she could get some practical experience."

"Wow," I said. "That is an awesome offer that I accept. And you should call me Emily."

"Whoa young lady," Mom laughed. "We will certainly think about that and it is an amazing offer. Thank you again, Mr. Butler. It seems we are eternally in your debt."

"Not at all. Well, we should get on with it, Emily. It might be best if you and your helper would bring Magpie out. Does the filly lead?"

Proudly I responded, "Yes, I have taught her. And my helper is Miguel. He has been on the ranch since my father built it and is like family."

Mr. Butler shook Miguel's hand. "We appreciate your help, Miguel."

Miguel and I went and haltered Magpie and Diamond. He led Magpie out and gave her some time to look at the van. Diamond pranced excitedly at all this activity and I kept her close to Magpie. When Miguel led Magpie to the ramp she loaded quietly. Diamond jumped up the ramp to follow her step- mother and I barely kept my feet. The van was roomy. We tied Magpie and left Diamond free with her halter on. Miguel helped close up the back of the van while I said goodbye to Diamond.

I swallowed hard to avoid any more tears. I rubbed Diamond's back for a few minutes the way she liked it.

"Diamond, I'll be coming to work with you next summer. We must both count on it," I told her. I didn't know for sure if that would work out, but for now it comforted me to believe it. For the last time, at least until next summer, I laid my head gently on her neck. She was too wiggly for that to last long and I had to laugh at her curiosity about what was going on.

Then I left the van. Mr. Butler was anxious to get on the road to return and get the horses settled into their new stalls. Mom had brought lemonade for everyone and then Mr. Butler and his helper climbed up into the van and drove away.

Mom and I didn't even try to talk. How much more sadness could we take. I put my saddle on Hero and took a ride with him around our nearly horseless ranch. He was quiet and seemed to sense my despondency. I prayed that Dad would feel that we made the right decision with his 'pride and joy' filly.

CHAPTER 22

WHEN THINGS FINALLY got sorted out—the ranch sold, the livestock moved, the house in town rented, and our things ready to move—the heartache of leaving the ranch was upon us.

Neither my mom nor I could sleep the night before. We finally got dressed and walked together, on a beautiful moonlight night, to places where we had so many wonderful memories stored.

I recalled with Mom the night Diamond was born with my fear, Mrs. Swenson's lifesaving help, and the sadness of losing Bess. And I remembered how pleased I was to see that I'd been able to save Diamond, with lots of help, of course.

My mom's memories started many years ago when she and Dad had moved to the ranch. "We were so excited to set up a home where he could live his dream of working in the mountains as an outfitter. I was pleased that I got a good job so I could help with the financial responsibilities. And we knew this would be a grand place to raise a child, not yet, of course, knowing who that would be," she chuckled.

I enjoyed hearing her memories of when she and Dad were young. She sometimes talked about how hard it was to get the business started and how money was short. But the memories were never sad or unhappy. I understood that they took on the challenges together and enjoyed their success. They weren't afraid of hard work and had pride in making their own way.

"Then when you came along our lives were complete. You were such a joy to us. Your dad spoiled you, but not in a bad way. He just couldn't say 'no' to you. I worried when he started taking you out with him around the animals. I thought he might be working and forget to watch you. He told me, 'Don't worry. She is right underfoot all the time. I can't lose sight of her.' and he would laugh. Those were good times," Mom reminisced.

"I remember when he used to put me up on the horse he was working with and let me ride along. How I loved that. When he got off to fix a fence or clear water flow in the stream, my job was to stay on the horse and keep it following him. Man, I thought I was a real horsewoman. Of course, the horse just followed Dad," I told Mom.

"How rich we are," she said. With that we grew quiet, each in our own thoughts.

We looked in on Magpie and Diamond's empty stall, visited the corrals where we had known so many horses and mules, and stopped by Hero's corral. As the only horse left he was lonely. He nickered to us. We spent some time keeping him company.

"You will soon have a new home, Hero, with lots of company," I assured him.

"Hero doesn't look much like the horse that arrived here a couple months ago. You've done a great job with him. I'm glad we decided to try to save him and I hope he provides you with good company in town," Mom said.

"Star and Diamond will always be a part of me, but I'm glad you could let me take Hero with us. I'll be able to visit Star and, hopefully next summer, I'll see a lot of Diamond," I said in an effort to keep that plan in front of Mom.

"What will I do without you all summer," she said.

"You'll be so busy with your friends and your job that you won't know I'm gone," I teased her back. She gave me another big hug.

We walked up on a hill that looked over the ranch buildings in the moonlight and stood there quietly taking in the beauty of the place. "You and Dad sure built a great home," I told Mom.

"Well, honey, it is time to build a new chapter in our lives. It will be very different, but together we will make it happy. It won't be that many years until you'll be going away to school. We have many chapters ahead," Mom encouraged.

We finally walked down the hill, as a rim of light in the east began to dissolve the darkness, to face moving day. We are no longer ranchers.

Chapter 23

MOVING DAY WAS a nightmare. It took the movers a couple hours to load the few things we were taking with us. All that I was taking of the ranch was my new saddle, bridle, and breastplate. Since Hero had filled out so well, my tack fortunately fit him well. He was about the same size as Star, though a little taller and not as bulky.

When the van was loaded we gave the address in town to the movers. We would follow them in Mom's car. That gave us a few minutes to walk around the house to make sure we had everything we were to take. Then we packed all the smells, sights, memories, and love that the house held, into our hearts and minds. We hugged and held each other on the porch recalling all the beautiful, peaceful evenings we had spent there at the end of long wearisome days. The tears flowed.

We didn't have any words left. I fed Hero for the last time on the ranch. Mr. Winslow and Luke would pick him up with their trailer tomorrow and bring him to his new stable. I made sure he had plenty of water for the night and assured him I would see him tomorrow. It would be lonely for him with all the horses gone, but only for one night. I was glad the rangers had moved our bear into another territory.

Then Mom and I drove after the van. When we arrived at our new house, Maria and Miguel were both there to help us unpack and arrange things. It didn't take long for the movers to get everything into the house and then they were gone.

Miguel had his tools and he went around making sure that anything that needed to be fixed or adjusted was set right. When he was done, my bedroom door would swing freely and all the locks on the doors and windows were working smoothly.

Maria brought vegetables from her garden and some of her home-made apple pie. She helped Mom get things into cupboards and closets. Beforehand we had figured out how we wanted things arranged. I had pictures of Bess, Star, and Diamond that I arranged in a prominent place. And, of course, I had a good picture of Mom and Dad from our last Christmas on the ranch and their wedding picture.

Miguel and Maria had a quiet dinner with us. And then it was time for us to face things on our own. Fortunately, they both lived nearby.

"I'll come by every week to check on things for you," Miguel said as he left. He hugged me long and hard and I saw tears in his eyes. "I will never forget how you toddled after your Father," he said. "Even when I watch you graduate from vet school." We all laughed through our tears.

"I'll be dropping in too," Maria said. "How about we have a pact that we will all have Thanksgiving dinner together?"

In unison we said, "Agreed".

"We will look forward to it. You are invited to our new house," Mom said.

Miguel and Maria had both decided to retire and I hoped we would be seeing them often. It was comforting to know that they each lived close by.

And then they were gone. I could no longer count the things that were gone. The house felt very lonely.

"I think we have done enough for today," Mom said wearily. "Let's just crash for today and get some rest, before starting tomorrow." I could feel her let down. Even Mom's strength flagged sometimes.

"Remember, I'll meet Mr. Winslow and Luke at the stable to get Hero settled in tomorrow. I'm to meet them at 10:00," I reminded Mom.

"Okay, I think that will keep you busy tomorrow, honey. Thanks for being so brave. We will both have some tough days ahead, but I think having Hero will be helpful to you. I can't imagine you being here with no horse," she said.

"Yeah, that would be a disaster. I'd get in trouble in no time flat," I teased her. "I'm excited to think of having a summer job next summer at Mr. Butler's stable."

"We'll see how things work out," Mom said.

"I have some reading to do before I can go to sleep. I think I'll do it in bed," I said.

"Good idea. I'll say good night in a few minutes," Mom said quietly.

When I finished my English reading assignment I was ready to turn out the light when Mom came into my room. She sat on the edge of my bed.

"I feel depleted when it comes to talk, but I just have to thank you again for being the amazing young woman that you are. You give me strength Emily," she said as she looked deep into my eyes. "Dad left me with the gift of you and a reason to go on." It was a moment with my Mother that I'll never forget.

"I could say the same to you, Mom. I love you. Thanks for devoting yourself to making a home for me. We are survivors," I opened my heart to her.

She hugged me for a long time and kissed my cheek as she got up to go to her room. This house felt like an empty place tonight, for both of us.

I turned off the light. I was so tired, but first I went back to the ranch and galloped up into the hills with Star. Then I said goodnight to Diamond. I knew that I could go back to the ranch in my mind anytime and the beauty and peace would be with me.

I added an addendum to my plan to be a vet. Someday I would go back and buy the ranch, even if I wasn't an outfitter. I sure had some goals to focus on now.

CHAPTER 24

WHEN I WOKE up next morning it took a few seconds to realize where I was located. Talk about disoriented! It hit me pretty quickly that I wasn't at the ranch and that I didn't need to get up at first light to feed. I guessed it would be good when school started that I wake up early. I was sure it would be a hard habit to break.

The sadness of these realizations hit me like a baseball bat. I didn't feel like getting up so I just rolled over toward the wall and cried a few tears. I laid their thinking about the immediate future and the long road ahead, getting through school and buying the ranch back. It would take years to accomplish all that. I chastised myself for dreaming so big now that reality was soaking in. One day at a time.

After a few minutes I heard Mom go into the kitchen and I knew I had to get up and start functioning if I was ever to get down that long road. Digging deep and finding the courage just to rise out of bed was a new experience for me. Thoughts of what Dad's expectations of me would be motivated me.

I dressed and went looking for Mom. I followed the smell of coffee to the kitchen and sat down at the table.

"Morning Angel," Mom said with a bright enthusiasm that I marveled at.

"Urgh," I groaned.

"It's a new day in the rest of our lives," Mom said as she came over and hugged me. "Time to face the music of the future."

"You're just full of bright, clever sayings this morning," I groaned.

"And you sound like a slow starter," she laughed.

"I'm afraid reality is hitting home," I said with a hanging head.

"I know," Mom agreed with the enthusiasm sucked out of her voice. "It hit me too. But we have to keep each other focused on making our bodies perform ahead of where our hearts are lagging."

"That's a good way to put it," I said. "Thank God for Hero and the need for me to look after him today. It will give me a purpose that will bring happiness to me. I have to wonder how Diamond is adjusting when I think of settling Hero into a new place. I wish I could have been there for her, too."

"I know. So many things have been so hard for us this summer. We simply must be strong. We should keep goals in front of us that are attainable short term," Mom consoled.

"Well, last night I added a difficult and very long term goal to my determination to go to vet school," I confessed.

"What is that?" Mom asked.

"You'll think I'm nuts," I avoided confessing an ambition that seemed so unrealistic.

"Come on. We've never kept secrets," Mom pressed.

"Okay. Here goes. After vet school and getting a practice going, I'm going to buy back the ranch," I reluctantly told her.

"Well, that is ambitious, but also very commendable," Mom sighed. "I guess that could be a great goal for us to share in our dreams of the future. That would certainly honor your dad and all that he put into building the ranch. As a reality check, you might consider that you will have to move somewhere else to set up practice or that you might have a husband by then. You might have to temper that dream with the needs of a family."

"I suppose. But I'm not giving up on this dream yet. I might just choose to be a spinster," I said determinedly.

Mom laughed. "Where would Luke or some other young man fit into that plan!"

"Oh, Mom. Luke will be a sophomore and probably wants a sophomore girlfriend. He won't pay any attention to a mere freshman. And I'm going to be too busy studying for a good ten to twelve years. He'll have four kids by then," I said while hoping none of that was true.

"Well, one thing we've learned is that we don't know how the future will unfold, but having goals needs to motivate me to get ready for work today and you to go and care for Hero. What do you want for breakfast?" she said.

About 9:00 I walked to the new stable. I wanted to see the manager and have Hero's stall ready when he arrived. When I got there I was directed to where Beth was overseeing the stable hands with morning chores.

"Good morning," she said brightly. "Welcome. This is a big day for you and your horse. Will he arrive soon?"

"Yes, in about an hour. I wanted to get his stall ready," I said, suddenly feeling a little unsure of myself. This was no longer my stable or one where I knew the routines. I didn't want to make mistakes in this new situation.

Beth showed me to my stall assignment and where to find the bedding. Soon I had the stall cleanly bedded, fresh water available, and had made sure that Hero's run outside the stall was clean. I wanted to do all these things for him daily that I could to help keep the costs down. It might be different after school started.

Beth soon came around to see how I was doing. Two girls about my age followed her. Both were dressed, much as I was, in jeans, cowboy boots, and shirt.

"I can see you know what you are doing around a stable," Beth said. "I thought you might like to meet Sandi Sawyer and Jennifer Brenton. Sandi is a freshman like you and Jennifer is a sophomore." Sandi and Jennifer acknowledged me and I greeted them. Beth said she would leave us to get acquainted and left.

"It will be fun to have another rider for the trails," Sandi said. "I assume you ride a western horse."

"Yes," I said. "I brought an abandoned and abused horse with me. We got him a couple months ago and I've been working to bring him back from malnutrition. He is doing well now and I hope to make a nice riding horse out of him. I call him Hero. He's named for a famous historian that my dad admired."

"My horse is a paint Quarter Horse," Sandi said. "Jennifer rides a Quarter Horse too, but hers is a show horse. She rides him in pleasure and trail classes."

"Yes, he is a top horse," Jennifer added. I had a feeling right away that she was very proud of him. "Where are you from?"

"My mom and I just moved into town yesterday. We lived on a ranch about ten miles from here," I replied.

"If you lived on a ranch didn't you have a better horse to bring than an abandoned nag?" Jennifer asked.

"Don't call her horse a nag. That is insulting. For all you know he is a fine horse," Sandi scolded her.

"I don't know the pedigree for Hero, but he looks to be a Quarter Horse." I said. "I want to be a vet and saving his life and making a friend of him has been a wonderful experience for me."

Jennifer turned and walked away. "I have to saddle up," she said.

"Don't mind her. She is pretty rude sometimes. Her dad owns the local John Deere dealership and the family thinks highly of themselves," Sandi laughed. I thought that I was going to like Sandi.

I saw the Winslow horse trailer turning into the drive. "Here comes Hero," I said as I went to direct Mr. Winslow back to my stall. Sandi tagged along and I was happy to have already made a new friend.

"Hi, Mr. Winslow. Thanks for bringing Hero," I said as Mr. Winslow got out of the truck. "Isn't Luke with you?" I inquired.

"No, I'm afraid I had to leave him at the ranch. We had two cows with new calves that he needed to bring in. But your horse just walked right into the trailer for me so it was no problem for me to bring him.

How's your mom doing?" Mr. Winslow asked rather gently, looking me in the eye.

"She is doing fine. It was a rude awakening this morning, but we're going to make things in our new life work. This is my new friend Sandi," I said.

Mr. Winslow tipped his hat to Sandi. Then he opened the back of his stock trailer and I walked in to Hero. He certainly knew me and he nosed me gently looking for a treat.

"Welcome to your new home," I said softly in his ear as I rubbed his head and neck. I led him to his stall and turned him into it.

"Wow, he is no nag," Sandi said. "It looks like you did a great thing saving this horse. He looks like he has some good quality."

I was proud of the way Hero looked and behaved. He was always sensible, which showed good breeding. His coat was shiny now and he had filled out a lot. He was even beginning to muscle up. He sniffed everything in his stall and put his head out over his half door at the front of his stall to see what we were doing.

"He has a nice disposition and you've done wonders with him," Mr. Winslow said.

"Thanks. I'm proud of him. How is Star doing?" I said with a terrible lump in my throat.

"He seems settled in and has made a friend in the herd that he hangs out with," Mr. Winslow said. "He is a good horse. You should come out on the weekends to ride him. He has good cow sense and Luke is using him this morning. He's become Luke's favorite."

"I would love to come out and ride with Luke. We always had a lot of fun riding together. Tell him I send my best," I replied. I felt a twitch of disappointment for not seeing Luke.

Mr. Winslow closed up his trailer, wished Mom and me good luck and said to stay in touch. Then he drove away. I felt like a piece of me was heading back out to the country with him.

Sandi turned to me and said, "He was very nice. Is this Luke your boyfriend?"

"No, just a friend," I said. "The Winslows were our neighbors when we lived on the ranch."

"Why did he ask about your mom? Is something the matter?" she asked curiously.

"No, everything is okay. He is just being a nice friend," I evaded. I wanted to be seen as a new friend and not someone to pity.

"If Hero seems settled down enough, do you want to take a ride? We could show you where we ride and start getting our horses used to each other," Sandi suggested.

"I'll have to take a rain check. My saddle is at the house and I walked here. I'll have Mom run me over here after work and we'll put my tack in the tack room. I'll take a rain check for tomorrow, if I can," I explained.

"Sure, that will be fine. I'll just get Tonto and bring him over here and we can introduce Hero and him," Sandi said.

"That's a great idea. Let's do that," I said. Sandi seemed very sincere about being friends. I was glad for that.

When Sandi brought Tonto up to Hero's outside run Hero came right out of his stall to meet this new horse. They did the usual squealing and snorting and pawing the ground to get acquainted and then decided to be friends. I thought Hero was settling in nicely. He seemed very adaptable.

I spent the afternoon with Hero keeping him company and grooming him to perfection. He was eating and drinking normally. I didn't think Hero would ever choose to miss a meal. Before I left in the afternoon I gave him a little more hay, freshened his water, and closed his stall door out to the run so that he would rest safely inside through the night. Once he was adjusted I could leave the run door open so he could go in and out as he pleased.

When Mom got home I told her about my visit with Mr. Winslow, how Hero was settling in, and about my new friend that I would ride with tomorrow. She was very pleased that I was making an effort to adjust to our new circumstances. She said we would take my tack over to the stable after dinner so I could ride tomorrow.

"I think Hero will be a saving grace for you. It will be good for you to be able to go after school and care for him and to ride with a friend. It will keep your hand in the things you've always loved doing. We'll make an effort to get you out to see Star as often as we can on the weekends," Mom said.

"Good plan. How was your day?" I asked her.

"Well my job is the same. I don't have to spend as much time commuting, which will be nice. I'll have more time with you in the evenings. And in about ten days you'll be starting back to school. I think we will be very busy," Mom assured me.

After we delivered my tack to the stable Mom said, "I have a little surprise for us this evening. We used to love to all curl up in the evening and watch a movie together. I thought it would be fun to do that tonight. I rented an old favorite, *To Kill a Mockingbird*. We haven't watched it in a long time."

"Awesome idea," I said. "That was such a favorite of Dad's. I gotta' tell you I almost named Hero, Atticus."

Mom laughed. "That would have been a mouth full for a horse," she said.

We made some popcorn and snuggled on the sofa to enjoy a quiet evening of mother-daughter bonding. I ended up with my head in Mom's lap and dozed off before the end of the movie.

CHAPTER 25

A COUPLE WEEKS before school started Mom informed me that we needed to do some clothes shopping. Ugh! I hated shopping for school clothes.

Anyway, after feeding Hero on Saturday we headed for town and did all the appropriate shopping. Mom said that since we had some money in the bank now, I could get some Vans high tops. I like them. We got some jeans, tee shirts, and a jacket. All in all it was fun and we had some laughs.

After we did our shopping Mom needed to get a haircut. I decided to go to the book store and spend some time while I waited for her. We were going to meet then and have a fun dinner out together.

Just before I was going to turn in to the book store a man came around the corner and bumped into me.

"'Scuse me," he grunted.

"And me," I said.

"Say ain't you that girl from the Campbell Ranch?" he asked rather rudely. He was of medium height, looked rather scruffy, wore a worn cowboy hat, and smelled bad.

"Yes, I'm Emily Campbell. Do I know you?" I asked as I drew back away from him.

"Well, I just thought I knowed who you were. Was you the one that reported rustlers to the Sheriff Martinez?" he asked.

"Well, we did have someone tamper with our fence. I don't know who did it," I said sensing that this inquiry felt threatening and not knowing why I felt that way.

"You should learn to keep your mouth shut," he said.

Just then I saw Brenda Donaldson coming up the street. I stepped away from this guy and called to her.

"Hey Brenda, wait up," I called. When I did that he hurried away in the other direction.

"Hi, Emily. It's great to see you. Are you doing your school shopping?" Brenda asked.

"Yes, Mom drags me out annually to do this. She's getting a haircut now," I said. "Are you ready for school?"

"Shopping wise, yes, but emotionally, no," Brenda laughed. "I prefer the freedom of summer."

"Me too," I said.

"I'm late to meet Mom. Gotta run. Call me some time," she said as she turned to go on.

"Okay, I'll do that. Good to see you," I said and I turned into the book shop. The strange encounter with that man and his comment about me keeping my mouth shut was very puzzling. I knew I didn't know him and wondered how he would know me. How did he know that I talked to Sheriff Martinez? It was weird, but it soon went out of my mind as I searched for a good mystery.

My thoughts were more on starting high school. It felt like a big step. I had attended a small middle school in a very large school district. For high school all the distant schools would come into central building. Living in the country I had always gone home to the ranch to work with Dad after school and had never really developed many close friends. At least now I knew Luke, Sandi, and Jennifer.

As a freshman I thought my studies would be a lot harder and that I had to focus on all my college prerequisites. I was taking science, math, literature, history, and Latin with computers as an elective. Fortunately, they had let me put off the physical education/health semester courses until later so I could take the Latin course.

I guess it was somewhat unusual for students to take Latin these days, but we had a lady in town that had taught it for years and was willing to take on the small class of kids who expected to need it for science or medical careers. It seemed like the Latin was important for my future.

When I went to my homeroom the first day, I found that Sandi was in the same group with me. I was really enjoying her friendship. We had been spending most of our time at the stable and messing with our horses so we'd become good friends.

To my surprise Luke showed up as I was going into homeroom.

"I hoped to see you before class," he said. "How are you and your mom getting along?"

"I'm glad to see you. I guess we are doing as well as can be expected. I had to spend last weekend with Mom doing some shopping in Gunnison, so I didn't get to visit Star. How is he doing?" I inquired.

"He is doing fine. He is very good working with the cattle. You have him beautifully trained," he replied. "The bigger question is have you missed me as much as the horse?" he pouted kiddingly.

"Yeah, I hate to admit it, but I have missed you. Thoughts of your brilliance and beauty just won't leave my mind. It makes me worried that I won't be able to concentrate on my studies." More seriously I confessed, "I enjoy the sweet memories of our gallops in the hills."

"Ah, you wax poetic?" he continued teasing me.

The bell rang and I started into my room.

"Wait," Luke said. "I'm thinking ahead here, but I want to beat the other guys to the draw. The Homecoming Dance is in a month and I've been hoping you would go with me. Will you?"

"Hmm. The Homecoming Dance. Is that formal? Do we know how to dance?" I asked doubtfully.

"You'll be surprised to find that I'm a good dancer," he puffed up "After all, I danced with all the girls last year while you were still in kiddie middle school."

"Oh brother. No wonder many of the sophomore girls have a stunned look. I guess I'll have to think about it and talk to Mom. If I go, I would want to go with you, unless someone cuter and smarter asks me, of course," I said.

"Oh good, since there is no one cuter or smarter than me. It isn't formal, just dressy. Not to worry. You'll look lovely in whatever you wear," responded Luke.

"Gotta' run. I'll get back to you on that. Thanks. " I said as dashed away.

As I took a seat by Sandi she whispered, "Who is the hunk?"

I just winked and said, "That's Luke."

At lunch time Jennifer came by to say hello. "I hear that you know that hunk Luke Winslow. All the girls were after him last year. I'm hoping he'll ask me to the Homecoming Dance."

Sandi piped up joyously, "He already asked Emily."

"Why would he do that!" Jennifer blurted. "You're only a freshman. Oh well, he may change his mind between now and a month from now."

"Luke and I were neighbors before I moved to town and we've been friends all our lives. We are close," I said.

"Maybe he likes younger women," Sandi prodded.

"It sounds like a pity date to me," Jennifer said and she turned and flounced away.

"Sorry, but I have a problem with her," Sandi said. "You hadn't mentioned that your dad died. My dad said he thought he had read about it in the paper some time ago. Is that why Mr. Winslow asked about your mom the other day at the stable?" Sandi asked.

"Yes," I said. "Dad was killed in a horse fall early in the summer." I hadn't faced talking about it to other people. "I don't talk about it much, but I guess as you get to know me, you'll hear me say things. I don't mind questions about where I came from," I explained.

"I'm sorry. I'm glad we are friends," Sandi said, showing her natural compassion.

"Me to," I said somewhat bashfully. "Not to change the subject, but I guess we should try to get along with Jennifer. Especially with the stable bringing us together all the time," I changed the subject.

"As you wish," Sandi glowered. "Will I see you at the stables after school today?"

"Yes, I have to go take care of Hero. Maybe we'll have time for a short ride. I seem to be accumulating a good amount of homework as the day goes on. But I can't abandon Hero."

"Well, you're taking all the hard subjects. I guess vet school will demand that. Thank goodness I want to study languages. I don't think that will be as hard," Sandi said. Too soon we were off to our afternoon classes.

That evening at dinner I broached the subject of the dance with Mom.

"Mom, can you teach me to dance," I asked.

"Good grief, where did that come from? What kind of dance?" she asked.

"Well, I don't know. The kind of dance that high schoolers do at Homecoming, I guess," I stammered.

"Well, I haven't danced in years, except for a few square dances. Why are you suddenly interested in dance," she questioned.

"Well, I saw Luke today. He asked me to go with him to the Homecoming Dance next month," I confessed with some embarrassment.

"How will you get there?" Mom asked with a stern demeanor that she rarely displayed. She had never seemed very protective before.

"Luke has his license now. I guess we would go in his dad's truck or the family car," I speculated, thinking transportation an unlikely concern.

"I don't know about that. I'm not prepared for you to be running around with a boy who just learned to drive and being out late," Mom admonished.

"Mom! I'm in high school now. That is part of going to school. Besides, we know Luke is a good driver and he has been very kind to me. He has driven on the ranch forever. I trust him," I pleaded, surprising myself with my desire to go.

"Well, you will have a curfew. Or he could come here and park his truck and I could run you over to the school," Mom said, looking for a solution.

"Geez, that will be embarrassing," I announced.

"I'm sorry, Emily, but this is a whole new ball game. On the ranch you were home after school and I never had to worry about you. Now, without the help of Colin, I have to deal with you wanting to go out to a dance and be driven around by a sixteen year old boy. I guess I'm going to have to do some adapting, but I also have to think about what the limits will be. Being a single parent is new. I have an increased responsibility," Mom explained rather vehemently, more than I needed to know.

"Mom, you can trust Luke and me. We are like sister and brother. I like him a lot, and know he is sensible. Think about how grown up he was when he was with Dad in the mountains. Luke doesn't act like a lot of teenagers," I tried reasoning with Mom. I guess I'm going to have to ease her into being the parent of a grown up teenager—well almost grown up.

"I'll think about it," Mom agreed.

"I really want to go, Mom. I want the full high school experience," I announced. "But how about the dancing part?"

"Tomorrow night we'll have a dancing lesson and practice. I'll ask some of the ladies at work what kind of dancing we should work on," she laughed. "This might be a whole new adventure for both of us. But that doesn't mean I've made up my mind," Mom back stepped sternly.

I went to start my homework. I realized it might be hard to raise a parent. Ugh!

I had a warm feeling about looking forward to time with Luke and it sort of pleased me to think that the sophomore girls didn't like that he wanted to take me. I knew the phrase, 'pride comes before the fall,' but I couldn't help it.

Chapter 26

FOR THE NEXT month I studied and cared for Hero in the evenings. Mostly I thought a lot about the upcoming dance. Mom agreed that I could go with Luke, but we hadn't yet revisited the transportation issue. I worried that I wasn't a good dancer. I worried that I didn't have the right clothes. I worried that Luke and I would ruin our friendship by going out together. I worried that I wouldn't know what to talk about. I worried.

Sandi worried that she wouldn't have a date. Then Antonio Ortiz asked her to the dance, so she was all excited, too. Antonio was a handsome lineman on the football team. Luke plays running back. I thought Luke might have suggested doubling with Antonio to encourage Antonio to ask a girl to go to the dance.

"Do your parents mind you going to the dance with a sophomore boy?" I asked her when we had a chance to talk about it. I wondered how other parents reacted.

"No, I don't think they care. My parents are pretty busy with four kids and they don't pay a lot of attention to what I do. They seem happy that I have a date and I'm double dating with you," she laughed.

"Boy, my mom isn't like that. She says it's because she has all the responsibility as a new single parent," I explained. "I think we are going to have some battles to get her to let me grow up a little. I'm not in middle school anymore. My mom thinks she has a lot of responsibility as a single parent, but I think I have a lot of duty training her to be a single parent and learning to let go." It was good to have Sandi as a friend who let me vent my frustration.

But in the end Mom decided it would be okay for Luke to drive. She was okay with that since it was only a few blocks. How much trouble could we get into? The driving issue finally worked out without embarrassment, to my relief.

In the meantime Sandi and I went to the two home football games to watch Luke and Antonio play. Luke caught several good passes and scored a touchdown in each of the two games. I was proud of him. We lost one game 10-7 and won the other one 14-0. I wasn't that excited about football and Sandi thought it was totally a waste of time, but we wanted to support Luke and Antonio.

I did get to visit a short time at one of the games with John and Betsy Winslow. "How are you and your mom adjusting to city life?" Mrs. Winslow asked.

"We're getting there," I replied. "It hasn't been easy, but we both are so busy the time goes by and we don't have a lot of time to think about the past."

"That is a good approach," Mr. Winslow said. "The grieving process will be with you both for a long time, but by focusing on going forward you are handling it the right way. You must come out and ride. Star is becoming one of our top cow horses."

"Wow, that is great. I'm glad he is doing well under the tutelage of you and Luke. He is a good horse," I said.

They each gave me a big hug and I rejoined Sandi as she returned from the food stand. She was carrying two hot dogs and two cokes.

I said "Watch out stomach, here it comes."

"I'll have to go back for the ice cream. I couldn't carry it all," Sandi laughed.

Finally, Homecoming weekend arrived. That afternoon of the dance Hero got a short shrift of attention. I just fed him, hugged him, and ran home. I showered and futzed with my hair. I usually wear braids, but because I thought it would be more sophisticated for a dance, I wanted to wear it loose. Ugh! What do I know?

Mom came home promptly to try to calm me down and to help me get ready. This was definitely a new mother-daughter experience for us. We laughed a lot as we worked our way through all the issues.

Mom had taken me to Gunnison to shop for a dress to match my auburn hair and splash of freckles. It was a lovely blue with a high collar and long sleeves, a sash at the waist, and a knee length skirt. I wore flats that matched the color of the dress. Mom brushed out my hair for me and pulled the front part up into a band in the back. She used the curling iron on the ends so it didn't look too bad. Luckily it was a beautiful early fall evening so my hair wouldn't get brutalized by the weather.

To tell the truth, I was nervous. I wasn't sure about this dating thing. I was glad it was only Luke I was going with. We were such long-time friends that it really hardly seemed like a date. Though there were some differences between dancing and riding horses together, like putting our arms around each other. Oh brother! Am I ready for this?

Luke came at seven thirty to pick me up. Fortunately, he was driving the family Lexus SUV. He brought me flowers and looked very fine in his suit.

"Thanks for letting Emily go with me Mrs. Campbell," he said to Mom. "I shall dance the waltz with her as though I'm Rhett Butler."

"Mom, I think I'm in for an interesting evening," I said. Mom and I laughed and she gave Luke a hug.

"I'm surprised you know who Rhett Butler was and that he could waltz like an angel. You just drive carefully," she reminded poor Luke.

"Yes ma'am," Luke said quietly as he nodded to Mom and made eye contact with his gorgeous blues. He is a good communicator.

When we arrived at the school the gym was decorated in a Parisian theme. The parents were providing nice refreshments and the DJ played a variety of music.

At first I was a little uncomfortable. I realized I suddenly felt a little shy. What was the deal with me? This was Luke, after all. Luke asked about how I felt about high school by now. He seemed at ease and, surprisingly he soon had me feeling at ease.

"It's hard for me to get homework done when I have practice every night and Dad often still needs some help when I get home. I'm afraid "all work and no play" is making Luke a dull boy," he laughed.

"I doubt that," I said rather boldly. "I'm proud of you keeping such a tough schedule. And you know what? You are the handsomest guy here. You weren't lying about that," I told him. Maybe I was getting the hang of this.

"Now you've embarrassed me. Would you like something to drink?" Luke asked.

"Sure. How about a Coke?" I replied. He went off to get the drinks.

I noticed that Antonio and Sandi were already dancing. It didn't seem like Sandi was having all the anxiety about dating that I was suffering. But I felt like I was relaxing as I spent time with Luke. It was beginning to feel like it was just Luke and me again.

Luke brought the drinks and some of his team mates came to tables around us. Soon we had a bunch of kids around us talking and laughing, with and without dates, and I began to get to know many of the football players. They seemed to congregate very naturally. I'm no longer just a country girl with my horses, I thought.

Luke asked me to dance. "Sure I said," swallowing hard. The dance actually turned out to be lovely. Luke was very gentlemanly and Mom's lessons served me well. I realized I liked dancing.

We rejoined our group and I excused myself to visit the ladies' room. When I returned I found Jennifer standing very close to Luke, looking into his eyes, and flirting with him. Well, darn, I thought. A girl can't even go to the ladies. As I walked up she turned to me.

"I was just trying to find out if Luke is on a pity date. You know, caring for his forlorn country bumpkin neighbor. He really ought to hang out with his own kind," Jennifer blatantly insulted me.

I was taken aback at her rudeness. How could she talk so brazenly? I'm afraid the shock tied my tongue, but the kind of manners my parents taught me just didn't produce an answer to her.

Luke saved the day. "Why Jennifer, you know your flirtations have never impressed me. Emily is my world. I'll never date another woman as long as I live," he jested.

"Your loss Luke Winslow," she said as she put her arm around another one of the players who I didn't know.

Luke pulled me back to the dance floor. "Sorry about that," he said. "She is a terrible flirt and is jealous of any other girl who has a boyfriend. Some of the guys like her flirting, but she bores me. My daddy warned me that a handsome dog like me would attract all kinds," Luke said very seriously.

I punched him and said, "Your daddy is biased. You aren't THAT handsome. Besides, I don't have a boyfriend," I said. Luke gave me a funny look, but he didn't say anything. And we started to dance.

After the dance Luke drove me home. He walked me to the door and gave me a hug. "Come out and ride Star when you can," he said. As he drove away I had a funny, sinking feeling, but wasn't sure why.

Mom greeted me and I told her every detail about the dance. I told her that Luke seemed funny when he brought me to the door. I didn't know why he seemed formal and in a hurry.

"He may have been a bit unsure about how to say good night to you in this new kind of relationship. After all, when he tried to kiss you before, you said he was pukey. Dating makes a relationship a little different. You're not just the neighborhood tom-boy to him now. Give him time to sort out how he feels," Mom gave me wise advice.

I'll have to think about all that.

CHAPTER 27

THE NEXT DAY I met Sandi at the stable to take a ride. All she could talk about was how Antonio kissed her good night—three times. Ugh! I didn't need to hear the details.

Jennifer was there. Before we left on our ride, I had Hero tied while I was grooming him and, when she walked by, she "accidentally" poked him in the stomach with the handle of the pitch fork she was carrying. He jumped and grunted and laid his ears back. I had never seen him show anger before, but I could understand why he did now.

"Hey, bitch, your horse is in the way," she said.

"No, he's not," I said. "You know the location of the hitching rail and should be able to walk by without stabbing a horse. You did that on purpose."

"Yeah, and I'll do more like it," she said.

"Why do you have a burr under your saddle for me? I never did anything to you and Hero sure never has," I said.

"Oh, aren't you the sweet talkin' lady. Maybe I'll just take your boyfriend away. Believe me, I know how to get him from you," she threatened me.

"Whatever . . . . He told me how uninterested he is in you, so good luck with that. And besides, watch your mouth," my temper surprised me.

Never having had a sibling I didn't think I really knew how to fight with someone, but I guess her treatment of Hero aroused in me a response that even I didn't see coming.

Beth came around the corner in time to hear us. "Whoa, what is going on here? We don't behave like that around the stable. Anger has no place around the horses. What is this all about?"

"This new girl's horse laid his ears back at me. He's not a safe horse to have around here. Probably because he was abused," Jennifer accused in a raised voice.

"Now wait a minute," I said, but Beth cut me off.

"I will not have this kind of behavior," she said. "Emily, you are new here and we have not had problems with stable mates not getting along with each other. You are on probation here and must conduct yourself in a civil manner."

"But she . . .," again I was cut off.

"Jennifer you go and tend to your horse," she directed. When Jennifer had left Beth went on, "Emily, I have observed you with your horse and you seem like a fine horsewoman, but I'm surprised at your behavior. I just can't have disturbances at the stable. Please keep that in mind."

I could hardly hold back the tears. It felt like the scales of all I've been dealing with since Dad died had just tipped to unbearable. Poor Hero nosed me gently as though he understood that I hadn't poked him, but his sympathy just broke me. I went into the stall and sobbed.

When I got myself together I decided I wasn't going to let meanness defeat me. I saddled Hero and we joined Sandi for a long leisurely ride up the trail along the river. The peaceful quiet of nature helped me. The birds singing, the breeze through the trees, the running water, the blue sky, and Hero's relaxed long strides helped me ground myself. Fortunately Sandi seemed thoughtful and rode along quietly.

Life in town was not going to be the life Dad had made for us on the ranch. I would have encounters with people like Jennifer who directed anger at me without my feeling that it was justified. Staying out of Jennifer's way wouldn't be easy. Spending time with Sandi might require listening to her tales of love, but at least she didn't have a mean bone in her body.

When we got back to the stable I felt I was myself again. I cooled Hero and fed him and thanked him for being there for me. He was good therapy and my partner. I saved him, now he was saving me.

Sandi came by my stall. "What happened between you and Jennifer? She is spreading the word around the barn that you picked a fight with her. Surely you have better sense than that," she commented.

"Before we left she poked Hero with the pitch fork handle accusing me of having him tied in her way. I'm afraid I let her trigger something new in me," I replied. "I couldn't stand seeing her take her anger out on him."

"Well, you better watch yourself. She is mean and I think she hates you because of Luke," Sandi said."

"That's absurd. Luke picks his own friends and he told me he doesn't like her. She was flirting with him at the dance," I told Sandi.

"Oh boy. You've aroused the green dragon of jealously in her. I wouldn't want to be you," Sandi warned.

The next day at school I was called to the principal's office. I couldn't imagine why, but my first thought was that I hoped there was no problem with Mom.

"Emily Campbell, I'm surprised at you. You came into the high school with an exceptional record. But I heard you have been fighting. Though it wasn't on school grounds, I want to make sure that kind of behavior isn't brought to school," Mr. Hill said.

I couldn't for a second, imagine how he had heard about what happened at the stable. Then I realized Jennifer must have carried the tale.

"Mr. Hill, I wasn't in a physical fight. I had an argument at the stable with Jennifer Brenton. She took out her dislike for me on my horse," I tried to explain.

"I know there are always two sides to a story. I know you have had a great deal to adjust to. Many times major changes in our lives cause irrational behaviors. You've had a lot of pressure on you. Are your classes going alright?" he asked sympathetically.

"Yes, the classes are fine. I'm quite determined to have a good academic record so I can get into college. I suppose maybe I am a little touchy. Hurting my horse just isn't acceptable," I tried to defend my actions.

"Well, I hope you will come to me or the student counselor if you are feeling trouble brewing. I know Jennifer Brenton can be a trouble maker. But I warn you, getting a bad reputation among the teachers won't help your cause," he scolded me. "You can go to class now," he said dismissing me.

Geez, I felt a bit victimized. I really didn't want to get off on the wrong foot in school. How would I cope with Jennifer's threat? I guess I better think of a way to win her over, but I had no idea how. What next?

CHAPTER 28

AT LUNCH I was eating alone in the section where freshmen congregate. I saw Luke eating with some of his teammates, but I was feeling wounded and didn't want to talk to anyone.

Miss Baker, my freshman science teacher, came and sat across from me. "I noticed that on your goals questionnaire you mentioned that you plan to study vet medicine and that science is very important to you for that reason. I'm organizing a special project that will involve several students who will be science majors. Would you be interested in participating?" she asked.

"That sounds interesting," I said. "I'm not sure I have extra time with all my studies. I also have to care for my horse every day after school," I explained.

"I think we could work on the time issue. You could come to the science room during your study period to work on it. It is the kind of extracurricular activity that will help on your college application in a couple years," she said, urging me to join the project.

"What is the project?" I asked.

"I want us to build a poster and display for the science fair showing areas of the Rocky Mountain States where animal species are in danger of extinction," she explained.

"Wow that does sound interesting. I would like to be a part. Thank you for asking me," I said, making the commitment.

"Great. We'll meet after school on Wednesday for just a few minutes to set up our plan and schedule. There will still be time to take care of your horse," she laughed. I decided I liked her.

After Miss Baker left, Luke came sauntering through the freshman lunch crowd toward me. Uh oh, a sophomore coming into the freshman area got attention. Most of the girls were taking note. He sat down next to me.

"I hear you are the first freshman to be called to the principal's office. I didn't realize you would be the leading criminal in the class," he chided me.

"Ugh! How did I get in trouble so quickly? I've never had a record before, other than exemplary. I suppose you are thinking of ending our friendship despite many years of neighborliness between our families. Come to think of it, you are why I'm in trouble," I said.

"Oh, no. This can't be my fault. What did I do?" he said in all innocence.

"It is your stunning Spartan beauty and football hero-ness that has caused this anguish for me," I charged.

"What?" he said with a hearty laugh. My illusion to warriors of Sparta with their athletic prowess and warrior physique amused, and I guessed, flattered him.

"Well, it seems I've gained the animosity of a very angry and jealous girl who thinks your attentions should be lavished on her. In her anger she punched Hero with a pitch fork handle, accused me of being in her way, and initiated an argument that got me in trouble with Beth at the stable. Then she reported my strong reaction to the abuse of Hero to our esteemed principal who warned me about the reputation I will get with the teachers who abhor fighting. And now I'm feeling abused," I whined.

"You're definitely in a downward spiral. The trouble maker must be Jennifer. Man, she is nothing but trouble. Maybe if we let it be known that we are going steady it will cool her jets. It would just be a ruse, of course, to get her off your back," he tried to persuade.

"But we aren't going steady. I've decided to give up men. They seem to only bring distress to my irreproachable life," I said grinning widely at him.

"What kind of treatment is that for a man who just endangered his standing among members of the sophomore class by walking into the cesspool of the dilettantes?" he asked from a puffed up posture.

"Do you even know what 'dilettantes' means," I laughed. How lucky I am to have such a devoted friend, I thought.

"Of course, its use is very sophisticated. It means amateurs," he said with pride. "We happened to have that word in our vocabulary list last week and I've just been waiting for an opportunity to use it. So Ha!"

"Thanks for being my friend and cheering me up. You are steadfast in the face of my criminal ineptitude," I said sincerely.

"You sure skimmed over that going steady thing. Oh well, you missed your chance. How about coming out to ride this weekend? If it is okay with your mom I could pick you up and bring you back. We could ride into the mountains and you could have dinner with us," he offered.

"I would love that. I want to see Star and canter with the wind through my hair. I'll ask Mom and let you know. You are my hero coming to the rescue of my sanity," I said.

"Okay, but how will the wind blow through your hair when it is always in braids? I liked it down at the dance," he said as the bell rang and we got up.

"That's too much trouble. What a typical man," I growled humorously as we parted.

CHAPTER 29

ON WEDNESDAY I met with Miss Baker and four other students. Miss Baker explained that we would be just five students working on this project. I didn't know the others, but she soon introduced us.

Shauna wanted to be a physician's assistant, Peter planned to study physics, Morton was interested in biology, and Levy would be a doctor, like his dad. I was the only one not wearing glasses which made me wonder if I wasn't in the company of some pretty studious nerds. I'm not sure where that stereotype came from and the fleeting thought shamed me. Maybe I felt like I might be in over my head, not really being much of a scientist.

Miss Baker explained that our indicated interests, that would require science study, led her to the idea for this extracurricular project. "As I've explained to each you, I want us to build a poster and display for the science fair showing areas of the Rocky Mountains where animal species are in danger of extinction," she explained. "Morton, with your special interest in biology this topic will be right up your alley. For the rest of you, I hope the study will be interesting and help you in terms of how to organize a scientific inquiry."

"I think this sounds fascinating," Peter said.

"Me too," chimed in Shauna.

"Great," Miss Baker said with a smile. She is very likable. "For the freshman project I've selected to study just the Rocky Mountain States to keep the scope of the study doable in the time we have. Emily, would you work with Morton on Colorado and New Mexico. Peter and Levy work on Wyoming and Utah. Shauna would you work on Montana. These handouts will get you started with guidance on study sources," Miss Baker directed.

We took a few minutes to get to know each other and to set up times to meet with our partner. Shauna seemed fine with working alone, but we all agreed to help with anything she might need.

"Emily has after school responsibilities so I promised to keep this meeting short. Let's meet next Wednesday to see how each of you is getting along. You can meet in the science room during school hours when you need to," Miss Baker said as she dismissed us.

I walked out with Morton. "I'm glad to partner with a biology major," I told him.

"I've always lived in the Rockies and loved studying plants and animals with my mom, so I'll enjoy this," he said shyly.

"Is your mom a biologist?" I inquired.

"No, but she reads and hikes a lot so she is pretty knowledgeable about the area," he replied.

"Shall we get together in the library tomorrow during study period to start looking at the suggested sources?" I asked.

"That sounds good," he said.

"Great, I'll see you tomorrow," I said as I headed for home.

I thought, I hope this works well and maybe our efforts would help reinstate me in the good graces of Mr. Hill.

CHAPTER 30

ON SATURDAY I didn't have as much trouble getting out of bed early as I had been having. Just after first light I quietly dressed and left the house. I walked to the stable and fed and watered Hero and cleaned his stall. I left his door open so he could wonder in and out of his stall into his run.

"Sorry, Hero, but today you are on your own. I'm going to see Star at Luke's ranch. I'll be back to feed you tonight and we'll ride tomorrow," I said as I petted him and rubbed his ears.

Then I dashed home to get breakfast and be ready when Luke came to pick me up. Luckily for me, Mom had decided it was safe for me to ride with Luke only. He was used to handling trucks on the ranch and was very responsible. I think she might have talked to Betsy Winslow about it, but I'm not sure and she doesn't want me to know if she did. Luke probably got a lecture about driving safely. Mom and I had many discussions on this issue and I think she was trying very hard to let me be a normal teenager.

Mom was in the kitchen when I got there. "You better eat a good breakfast if you are going to be out riding all day. Do you want eggs and potatoes?" she asked. I could tell Mom still had a lot of hesitancy about letting me go on this ride, but she seemed determined to do what she thought was right for me.

"That sounds great. I'll make the toast. Mrs. Winslow is going to have a lunch made for us to take in our saddle bags. If Mr. Winslow and some of his men are riding up into the hills to bring down some of the cattle, we'll ride up with them and help for a while. I think that will be a blast."

"Well, be sure to take your chaps and slicker. September will be pretty up there, but the weather can be unpredictable. Some of the leaves are probably changing," Mom tried to get into the spirit of the thing.

At eight o'clock Luke pulled into the driveway. I was ready and I ran out with all my gear. Mom waved to us as we pulled away.

"So how are you," Luke asked.

"I'm grand," I said. "You are my hero to rescue me from town and take me riding. I'm anxious to see Star."

"Dad and some of the men will be going up to a high pasture to bring down about twenty cows and calves. We can tag along, if you want to," Luke said as he drove onto the main road out of town.

"I would love that," I answered with boundless enthusiasm. I was so happy and excited.

"Can I ask you something serious while we drive?" Luke asked.

"I guess so. That is sort of open ended," I replied wondering what was coming. Luke usually wasn't all that serious.

"Well, you said the other day that you don't have a boyfriend and when I mentioned, though I was teasing, going steady, you totally avoided the subject. Are you not interested in having a boyfriend?" he asked hesitantly.

"Gosh, Luke, I thought you were just teasing. In the first place you are a sophomore and I never thought you would be interested in a freshman. You are quite a bit older than me. And secondly, I'm so focused on going to vet school that I haven't thought about boys," I explained.

"Well, you are right, I was sort of kidding. But I really like you and I think I'd like to be your boyfriend. If we went steady I wouldn't have to worry about you dating anyone else," Luke smiled at me. "I felt bad the other day when you said you didn't have a boyfriend. I guess I was assuming. And I don't think of high school dating as long term. I'm not asking you to marry me," he laughed.

"Luke, you are way ahead of me on this dating thing. I was shocked when you asked me to the dance. It was fun, but not something that was in my thoughts," I tried to explain as I tried to figure out the answers on the fly. "I really think I should wait until later in high school before I think about such things."

"So I guess you don't care if I date other girls?" Luke probed.

I had to think about that for a while. I'm afraid I've been so focused on horses and our problems after Dad died that dating was the furthest thing from my mind. I guess now that I'm in high school that subject had to come up.

"I'm sorry, Luke. You've been a wonderful friend to me and I like you lots, but being with boys just hasn't been on my radar. I hope you aren't offended. Though I must admit, the idea of you dating someone else doesn't sound that great. Can't we be friends and have fun together without making anything official?" I asked.

"I guess so," Luke said, disappointment on his face. "I want you to know I like you a lot. I didn't mean to rush you. I suppose being a year older and having buddies who are going steady has me thinking of things that you haven't thought about yet. I really didn't mean to rush anything."

"Luke, this summer has been really hard. Sometimes I've wondered how I would survive. For me this escape to the ranch to ride with you and Star makes you my superhero. Can't we relax, just be ourselves, and have fun today. I'm just not capable now of thinking about anything beyond the moment," I told him. "This takes a lot of trust. I haven't confided in any one else about my feelings."

"I'm glad you trust me. That says a lot. Thanks. We shall now focus the rest of the day on joy, freedom, horses, stinky cows, cold lunch, Star, and laughter," he assured me.

I sat back thinking about the things he had said. I guess I just hadn't clarified my feelings about him for myself. I knew that if he went steady with another girl I'd kill her, but I just didn't know how to tell him that. My time with him had always been fun and happy and I guess I was depending on him for that relief. He's been my brother. I put my hand on his arm.

"Forgive me?" I asked.

"There is nothing to forgive," he said. "What did you think about the game last night? Was I as stellar as you expected?"

"Sorry I didn't get to go to the away game, but I heard you guys won pretty handily. It sounds like a real improvement over last week, though you did shine even in the losing game," I said appreciating the change of subject.

Soon we arrived at the ranch. Mr. and Mrs. Winslow greeted me with warmth. Mrs. Winslow gave me a hug and launched into instructions regarding the lunch we were carrying. Mr. Winslow winked and said he was going to put me to work today. I felt a bond with him because he was Dad's friend and he understood how hard it was for me to be away from the ranch.

Soon we had the horses saddled and were ready to ride. Star seemed fit and ready to go. When the group broke into a canter to shorten the time to the cattle pasture, he threw in some bucks and wanted to race. The cool morning and his mistress on his back seemed to make him as happy as it made me.

Working cattle was more fun than a barrel of monkeys. The upper pasture was a beautiful, lush grassland with several streams of melted snow rushing through. On the far end it was wooded.

The cattle had grown somewhat wild over the summer with their freedom. Some cows were compliant when we worked to get them in a group, but some were very defiant. The calves seemed to reflect the attitude of their mothers. When we had twelve in a holding group we still had eight wild ones to find in the trees where they were hiding.

"Jim and Dan hold these buggers here. Luke, Emily, Bob, and I will try to sort the trees," Mr. Winslow directed. I was pleased I didn't have to just hang out and hold the gentler cows. It would be more exciting to bring the unruly ones out of the trees, I thought.

We split up and I headed Star into the trees. I soon found it rough going where there was thick underbrush and that, of course, was where the wary bandits were hiding.

We eased through the shadows searching. Star seemed to pick up on the idea of what we wanted to do. I could tell Mr. Winslow and Luke had been working him some with cattle. Horses with cow sense are invaluable on a ranch. They aren't afraid of the cows and understand how to turn them where the rider indicates they need to go.

I soon found a cow and calf hiding in some rocks and trees. We eased around to the far side of them making sure not to panic them into running. I slowed Star to a very slow walk and moved closer and closer to them. Finally the cow came out and started in the right direction with her calf following. I was feeling pretty good about that. When she wanted to bolt and turn back right or left, I would turn Star that way to cut her off. Soon Star was heading her instinctively.

When we broke out of the trees, instead of running to join the herd, that wily cow started left and then cut right and dashed madly back into the trees with her calf on her heels. Star cut and went after her coming very close to making me lose my seat. Star might have been born to this work, but it caught me by surprise. I was so glad that I hadn't suffered the humiliation of falling off in front of everyone.

We pursued our Demon cow and brought her out again, but this time I was on to her and I pressed her hard until she joined the herd. Just as she joined up another cow dashed out of the herd and headed for the trees. Star was ready and made an amazing move to cut her off.

Luke rode up to me. "Star really has the hang of this work, but you are looking a little marginal," he laughed. "I thought you were going to unload a couple times."

"Well, I'm new to this cow punching and wasn't quite ready. That damned cow looked like I had her tamed when she changed our minds about where we were going," I defended myself.

"The second time Star made a cut you did much better. You'll make a cow girl yet," he encouraged.

"Herding cows isn't easy unless they are compliant," I laughed with him. "How are you doing?"

"I've brought in three pairs, but they weren't as wild as that one you had. She is 'Ole One Horn' and she has the reputation of being non-compliant in all cases. She'll charge a horse," Luke told me.

"Well, good to know. I'm glad she didn't charge us," I said as I turned back to the woods. It was exciting and challenging to work these cattle. I'd worked with trail horses and admired their savvy for their task, but these cow horses knew a very different job. Star obviously liked the work. I was glad he was well placed with a cow man like Mr. Winslow, and Luke, of course.

We soon had the cows gathered and headed down toward the pasture near the ranch buildings. As we started the cows down, Mr. Winslow rode over by me.

"You have a natural cow horse there. We're pleased with him. The boys and I can handle the cows now if you and Luke want to ride up country to have your lunch. You've done good work," he praised as he ducked his head to me tapping the brim of his hat. I felt like a real lady having a handsome cowboy tip his hat to me.

I rode over and told Luke we could take our ride if he wanted to.

"Do I want to? I've been looking at the back end of cows all my young life. There is a great spot for a picnic up on Emerson Creek. Let's ride up there," he suggested.

"Sounds good. Let's go," and I turned up country waving to the men heading down with the cows. "That was fun. I liked working cows," I added.

"Oh, that is so great to hear. You'll make a wonderful wife for some lucky cow man like me," he grinned at me.

"You're impossible," I said as I pushed Star into a canter.

An hour later we arrived at a lovely spot along the stream and under a tree. Mrs. Winslow had fixed us a nice picnic. As we ate we were sort of quiet. The spot was so relaxed and in tune with nature that it didn't seem necessary to talk.

I enjoyed the sound of the burbling stream. The crows and ravens kept up their usual cacophony. A couple mountain jays, known as camp robbers, kept us company. One even came and ate some bread from Luke's hand.

My soul felt like it needed time like this to heal. Luke took a folding rod from his saddle bag and went to the stream and threw his line in.

I lay back on the grass. The sun filtered through the tree leaves above making me feel warm and sleepy. It was a good time for thinking.

When Luke came back, fishless, we decided it was time to head back. I needed to get home in time to feed Hero.

"Thanks for this day," I said to Luke. "It has been just what I needed. A day like this makes me feel like I will survive."

"I'm glad. I could spend the rest of my life with days like this," Luke said. "Too bad we have to go to school and then learn to work. Yuk!"

"Well, we did some work with your dad and it was fun," I told him as we tightened our saddle girths. We made sure we hadn't left anything behind, mounted up, and headed down the ridge toward home.

CHAPTER 31

As we were riding down a steep ridge through some beautiful tall pines we entered a rocky area. I always loved this part of the trail. The rocks were as big as a small garage and the trail wound among them. I was leading and was just entering the part of the trail that made for a great geology lesson. Luke was somewhat behind me dawdling along as he hummed a cowboy tune. He carried a tune just fine.

Suddenly I heard a loud, sharp crack followed by a resounding bang that echoed. Star jumped, but not enough to unseat me. I immediately heard a terrible sounding *ka-thump* behind me. I whirled around to see Luke's horse lying on the mountainside without any movement. And Luke was lying downhill from the horse.

I couldn't imagine what had happened, but having lived around ranches all my life I knew the sound of a rifle. It seemed like the sound had come from up-hill.

I jumped off of Star and ran back to Luke. As his horse went down he had rolled off and was stunned, but didn't seem hurt. He sort of groaned and looked dazedly at his horse. I pulled him into my arms and cradled him momentarily.

"Luke, are you alright?" I asked in a calm manner that belied my fear.

"I think so," he said. "What the hell happened?" Luke's head seemed to be clearing.

"Luke, let me help you behind the rocks. Someone shot at you. Can you come with me?" I said.

At that moment another shot rang out and dirt sprayed up near us. That motivated us to move fast. Luke managed to stagger with my help over behind the rocks. I was afraid that someone up there had us pinned down and would keep shooting. It was obvious that Luke's horse was dead.

"Luke, your horse is shot. We need to get out of here. Someone is trying to kill us. They may be stalking us down the hill," I urged.

"Damn, Emily, we're in trouble. Maybe we should lay low until we know what they are doing," Luke questioned my plan.

I crept over to the edge of the rock and peeked around warily. About one hundred yards above us on the ridge, I saw a man scurry into the trees. I saw he was carrying a rifle, seemed about medium size, was dressed in jeans and a cowboy hat, but that was all I saw in that fleeting moment.

"I saw a man duck into the woods above us. Let's get on Star and keep going down as quickly as we can. We'll use these big rocks for cover until we drop into those trees below," I all but commanded.

"You think Star will carry both of us?" Luke said as he tried to stand. He wobbled some, but managed to keep his feet.

"Oh yes. Come on. You get on him and I'll ride behind you. Hurry." I said as I moved back down the trail into the rocks and caught my faithful Star. We mounted double and I prayed that the man was alone and was not going to keep coming after us.

I knew there was a jeep trail at the top of the ridge and hoped he was heading up there to escape us as we hurried to escape him.

The ride down the mountain seemed to take forever. We couldn't urge Star too fast as long as we were in rough terrain. He had a pretty good load. But when we finally reached the lower meadows we urged him into an easy trot. I knew by now that we weren't going to be shot at again, but I was still scared stiff.

When we rode into the ranch yard, Luke's dad was walking toward the house. When he saw us riding double he knew there was a problem.

"Luke, what happened to your horse?" he called out as he jogged toward us.

"Dad, someone shot him from under me. We were starting down from Emerson Creek where we had lunch and someone shot him dead. I fell and was stunned, but Emily got me behind the big rocks just below the creek," Luke explained, having regained his composure.

"They took a second shot at Luke before we made it to the rocks," I added.

Mr. Winslow called for one of the hands to take care of Star and led us toward the house. As we entered the house he called out, "Betsy come here." When she came running at the urgency of his voice he said, "Call Sheriff Martinez right away. Get him out here. Someone shot at the kids and killed Luke's horse,"

"Oh, my God. Are you kids all right?" she queried.

"Yes, we're okay but scared out of our wits," I told her. Luke and I had both collapsed onto the sofa.

When Sheriff Martinez arrived we had to give him all the details of what happened and I described the man I'd seen the best that I could. Sheriff Martinez looked puzzled.

"Any idea why anyone would shoot at you Luke? Have you been having any trouble with anyone?" he asked Luke.

"Geez, no," Luke said.

"He's about the most popular kid at the school," I said.

"You say he carried a rifle?" Sheriff Martinez asked me.

"Yes, I'm pretty sure. It was all fleeting, but I saw him somewhat in silhouette against the sky and it sure was the shape of a rifle. I think it had a scope. The shots sounded like rifle shots, too." I added.

"And this was near that out cropping of large rocks just below Emerson Creek," the Sheriff reiterated.

"Yes," Luke said.

"I'll take a couple deputies up there at first light tomorrow and look around. Were you below the jeep road on the ridge?" the Sheriff asked.

"Yes, we were under a big tree by the creek. You'll see the dead horse just below where we picnicked and near the rocks," I clarified.

"Do either of you kids feel you should see a Doctor?" he asked.

"Luke took a bad fall," I said.

"I'm okay," Luke said. "I've fallen from enough broncs that I can land okay. Actually I sort of rolled off the horse as he went down. Instinct I guess. Emily got me to cover while I was still woozy. She got us out of there."

"Can you kids eat," Mrs. Winslow asked. "I have a dinner ready. You're welcome to join us Sheriff."

"Thanks, but I need to get back to town and make some calls. I'll put out an APB on this guy and organize a trip up into the mountains for tomorrow. If either of you kids thinks of anything else that might be helpful, please call me right away. And I recommend that both of you stay near home for a few days until we have a chance to find this guy."

We thanked the Sheriff and he left. I called my mom and told her we were just starting to eat a little late, but that I'd come home as soon as we were finished. I asked her to call Beth and ask her to feed Hero some hay. I didn't want to alarm her so I didn't say why we were late.

After a quiet dinner Luke took me home. All through dinner I kept wondering why the sheriff seemed to think Luke and I might still be in danger. Was this not some weird, random incident? Who would want to harm Luke? Or me, for that matter?

As soon as I got home I told Mom everything because I wouldn't want her to find out from someone calling her, like the newspaper. She was alarmed and worried.

"This is beyond my comprehension. Do you think someone has a still or is making meth up there and just wanted to scare off intruders?" she speculated.

"I never thought of that. I guess that would reinforce my idea that this was random—someone just trying to scare us off. But to shoot the horse? Why not just take some random shots to scare us. Their shots were deadly," I said.

"You're right. Just scaring you doesn't seem to fit," Mom said. "I'll call the Sheriff after you go to bed and discuss this more with him. Get cleaned up and get some rest."

I did as I was told and fell asleep imaging all kinds of scenarios. I was determined to not be intimidated by what happened. I have faith in Sheriff Martinez finding out what is going on.

CHAPTER 32

THE NEXT MORNING I was surprised to realize that I had slept so well, given what had happened. Obviously it wasn't the same for Mom. She was in the kitchen drinking coffee and looking haggard.

"Are you okay," I asked her as I started to make a hot chocolate.

"I didn't sleep, as you might imagine. Knowing that you were shot at twice yesterday is more than a bit unsettling. You're going to have to quit roaming around in isolated places, at least until the sheriff catches this person," she said looking very worried.

"I know. That was a very bad situation yesterday. But if someone was just chasing us off, it was a one time fluke. I feel so bad that Luke's horse was killed. He was very lucky not to be badly hurt in the fall. I wish Dad had been as lucky," I told her.

"Boy, I thought about that, too. This summer and fall have been just heartbreaking for us and now this. When does it quit?" Mom moaned.

I put my arm around her and placed my head on her forehead. "We have to keep each other strong," I mumbled. I sensed her total discouragement.

"Until we hear good news from the sheriff I don't want you going anywhere, but to school and over to care for Hero. And ride him locally with a friend," Mom cautioned me.

"Okay, but I hope I'll be able to go see Star, even if I only ride close in," I said.

"We'll see," a very tired Mom said, looking at me plaintively.

About noon Sheriff Martinez called and said he would like to stop by. He arrived shortly thereafter.

"Come in Sheriff," Mom greeted him.

"I know you must want to be kept closely informed on the progress of our investigation," Sheriff Martinez said as he took a seat and Mom set a glass of lemonade beside him.

"Several deputies are up at the crime scene today and they are sending a forensic specialist from Denver to look at the scene. They'll look at what kind of gun brought the horse down, any foot prints and tire tracks, anything on the ground that might be a clue. We are going to talk to one household that is located near where the jeep turned on to the jeep trail to see if they noticed anything," he said.

Mom just nodded. She seemed in a trance of fear. I felt so bad that she had to go through this. First Dad dies in the mountains riding a horse and now I'm shot at up there, though I don't think I was the target.

"I've talked to some other sheriffs around the state about this and there may be a clue in all that they've said to me. Remember your scare about rustlers at your ranch?" he asked.

"Of course," Mom said snapping to attention. "I had about forgotten that, given all that happened shortly after."

"It seems that organized rustlers from Wyoming have been moving into the state. Speculation among several sheriffs has been that maybe the shots weren't intended to kill the horse, but only to scare you out of that area. It may be that they have seen Emily and recognized her from watching your ranch. It may be that scaring Emily away was the main intent," the sheriff said hesitantly.

"You mean to say, Emily was the target?" Mom asked incredulously.

"This is only speculation at this time, but I'm telling you this because I think Emily shouldn't wander in the mountains until we get this sorted out," he replied.

"We had already determined that!" my mom said. It felt like I was about to become a prisoner and I didn't like the sound of that. Roaming the hills and mountains on horseback was what kept me sane. I sure hoped they would catch this guy or guys soon.

"I'll keep you informed on how things are going. All the sheriffs in the area are aware and watching their areas to see what we can find. They may have a camp near where you were yesterday. We're sending out a helicopter from the state police over the next few days to search the area," Sheriff Martinez concluded.

"Thanks for everything," Mom said. "I appreciate your efforts and keeping us updated. I'm scared out of my wits by all this, I'll admit. Mountains and horses right now mean disaster to me. I'm going to be keeping Emily close."

"I'll be on my way," the sheriff said as he got up and left.

Mom looked at me for long moments after he left. "Maybe we should go somewhere until this is settled," she said.

"Mom, I can't miss school and not care for Hero. You sure can't afford to miss work. We'll be okay. They aren't going to come in town to bother us. I'll be careful and alert. Don't worry. We can't run away," I gently encouraged her. "We'll be strong together."

"This being strong thing is wearing thin," Mom moaned, easing the mood. We had a laugh together.

CHAPTER 33

THE NEXT FEW days were pretty normal. Mom calmed down. Everyone at school had heard in the news about Luke and me being shot at and they were mostly very concerned. Only Jennifer had something nasty to say. She said, "Maybe that will teach Luke to stay away from trouble makers. I expect Mr. Hill will really be watching you now."

"I guess you are the one carrying tales to Mr. Hill," I said and went on about my business.

On Tuesday evening I got an unexpected call from Brenda Donaldson.

"Hi Emily. This is Brenda Donaldson. We met at the Winslow ranch on the fourth of July," she said.

"Of course, I remember you, Brenda. How are you?" I greeted her.

"Well, I think the question is, how are you. We heard about you and Luke having a run in with some rustlers. We've been concerned," she told me.

"We don't know for sure it was rustlers, though that is what the sheriff wondered about. We had some indication on our ranch before we sold it that potential rustlers had cut a fence," I explained.

"We just wanted you to know that we are concerned. I hope the sheriff gets whoever did this. I talked to Luke and he was feeling bad about losing a horse, though fortunately he wasn't riding his favorite that day. I think Robert wants to talk to you too. Here he is," Brenda said as she transferred me to Robert.

"Hi Emily. I'm glad you are okay. How weird it must have been to be shot at," Robert said.

"Yeah, it was scary," I said. "Fortunately, if the shooter intended to hurt Luke or me he was a bad shot. It was disturbing that he shot an innocent horse."

"He must really be a bad dude," he said. There was a pause as neither of us knew what to say. Then he added, "Say, I was wondering if you would want to go to a movie with me next Saturday night in Crested Butte. I could pick you up around 5:00 for a 7:00 movie. Game of Thrones is showing."

"That is very nice of you Robert, but my mom wouldn't let me be out that late. I don't really date yet," I told him. I didn't really want to go out with Robert and was surprised at his asking me.

"Well, why don't you ask your mom before you turn me down. If you don't want to go to the movie, we could go out and get something to eat in Alton or Gunnison," Robert pushed.

"I'll talk to my mom, but I'm only fifteen, you know. Mom and the sheriff have grounded me until they find whoever shot at Luke and me," I said. I was glad for my grounding and for the sure excuse it gave me. Though I've indicated to Luke that I'm not ready to go steady, I would feel disloyal to him if I went out with a seventeen year old guy.

"Talk to your mom and I'll call you back tomorrow evening. I guarantee we would have fun," Robert said before hanging up.

"Who was that," Mom asked when I returned to the living room.

"You won't believe this. That was Robert Donaldson. He wants me to go with him to a movie Saturday night in Crested Butte. I tried to turn him down, but he was sort of insistent. I even told him I'm grounded until they find the shooter," I replied. "I don't want to go out with him. He's seventeen for heaven's sake."

"Not to worry. You aren't allowed to drive to Crested Butte for a night movie. You know how I am about you riding with young drivers.

You should be aware that this is just the start of you having admirers. You have to learn to say 'no' politely and stick to it. This dating thing is just starting for you," Mom said with conviction. Her heavy sigh voiced her wish that it wasn't time for dating yet.

"He sort of surprised me. Believe me Mom, I don't want to go with him," I assured Mom again.

Chapter 34

ON WEDNESDAY I stayed after school to work with Morton in the library. We found that four species are endangered or threatened with extinction in our area alone. The Canada lynx, the Greenback cutthroat trout, the Mexican Spotted Owl, and the North American Wolverine are fast disappearing. As I read about these species I noted the reasons for their endangerment. I found that trapping, timber harvests, recreational activity, loss of streams and lakes, starvation and fire have been the culprits. It seemed sad to me.

After an hour and a half of work, Morton and I felt we had a good start on our research. I wanted to go see Hero for a while and clean up his stall, and, of course, feed him. I suggested we call it a day and Morton said he was happy with what we had accomplished.

As I left the school it looked like it was going to rain. Fortunately, it is only a few blocks from the school to the house. As I went around the first corner I was walking rather distractedly, thinking about Hero. I was surprised to see Robert on the curb leaning on the side of his car.

As I approached he said, "How about a ride. It's going to rain."

"Hi Robert. I'm surprised to see you," I said ignoring his offer. Something made me feel uneasy about him being there as though he was waiting for me.

"Surely you would prefer a ride in my fine Mustang to walking in the rain. I'll throw in a stop at the ice cream shop," he pressed.

"No. I don't mind walking. It is nice to get out after school. Thanks anyway," I said as I started to walk past him.

In a few short steps he approached me and took hold of my arm. "Come on, don't be stubborn," he said, as he pulled me toward the car.

"No means no, Robert," I said as I tried to pull away from him. I was stunned by his force.

When I couldn't break loose from his grip he pulled me up to the car and opened the door as though he was going to force me in. I kicked him in the shin. When I did that his demeanor turned dark. He looked enraged. Suddenly he slapped me in the face. I stumbled backward.

At that moment I was so focused on him that I didn't register the screeching of tires. Suddenly Robert was hit and tackled to the ground. Somehow Luke had just arrived in the nick of time.

Robert and Luke were rolling on the ground and hitting each other. When they rolled apart they both jumped up. Then I saw Robert land a blow on Luke's forehead, but Luke landed two upper cuts on Robert's chin. Robert slumped onto the ground. Luke lifted Robert by his shirt and walked him to his car.

"Don't let me ever see you bothering around her again," Luke warned. "Only the worst cowards hit a girl."

"I'll get you for this," Robert yelled at Luke in a rage. Luke just laughed and turned his back on Robert. Robert drove away with screeching tires. "The sound of a coward driving away," Luke said as he came to me holding out a handkerchief.

Only then did I realize my nose was bleeding.

"Luke, how did you manage to arrive just in time like that? Where did you come from?" I said in gratitude.

"It looked like it was going to rain and I knew you had your nerd meeting, so after football practice I decided to drive your route to see if you would need a ride. When I came around the corner and saw him hit you I guess I went crazy. I don't really believe fighting is the way to handle things, but when he initiated violence against you. . . ." Luke's voice trailed off. He seemed surprised at his own actions. "Let's get you home and get some ice on your nose. You don't want to look like a boxer."

"Luke, I think he was going to force me into his car. I'm so glad you showed up when you did. I'm glad you took him out," I attempted to thank him. "It all happened so fast I hardly had time to be afraid of him."

"I don't think he'll bother you again. He sure drove a long way to find you," Luke said thoughtfully. "That seems strange."

"He called and asked me out. I told him 'no,' but he didn't seem to want to accept 'no,'" I confessed.

"Maybe it will penetrate his thick skull now," Luke said looking in the direction in which Robert had driven away. Then Luke turned to me. "I'm glad you told him 'no.' That guy doesn't seem quite right. Come on. I'll drive you home."

I got into Luke's truck still holding his handkerchief to my nose. "Sorry about your handkerchief," I told him. "I'll wash it and return it to you later."

"No problem," Luke said as he thoughtfully pulled away from the curb. "Have you heard any more from the sheriff?" he asked.

"No, we haven't," I said realizing that his thoughts had turned away from Robert.

"I don't like people shooting at you and hitting you," Luke said. "I think I'm getting pretty pissed."

"You don't think the two things are in any way related, do you?" I said following Luke's thought process.

"Not likely, but I don't know. I think we should report this to the sheriff. It is probably coincidence, but he can determine that," Luke pondered.

When we got to my house we let Mom know what had happened. Mom produced ice packs for my nose and Luke's forehead. We discussed talking to the sheriff and Mom said she would call him tomorrow. Luke volunteered to take me over to care for Hero since it was getting late. He called home to let them know he would be late. After we did the chores, Luke dropped me at home.

Mom came to the door, "Thanks again Luke for helping Emily. You seem to have a knack for turning up and being our hero. Really . . . thank you."

"I'm sure glad it looked like rain tonight. I hate to think about that jerk bothering Emily," Luke said. Then he left for home and I had to face homework.

Chapter 35

On Friday I was glad the football game was away. I had no Nerd Team, a title we seem to have taken rather formally, or after school tasks and I could go spend the evening with Hero. It had seemed like I hardly had time to work with him and I missed my hands on horse time. When I rode him he had done well to pick up on leg aids, reining, and his gaits. There was much more refinement to work on, but that would all come with time.

I dashed home from school and changed and went right to the stable. While I gave him a thorough brushing, Hero seemed glad for the attention. Several times he turned and nudged me. I spent a lot of time picking up his feet so he'd know how to behave when I got him shod. While I worked with him I spoke softly to him and spent time just rubbing his ears and head.

When I saddled him I always remembered how Dad spent time choosing such beautiful tack for me and how pleased he was to give me my dream gift. He was with me for a few moments while I worked. I wanted to think he would be pleased with Hero's progress.

I was about ready to mount up when Sandi came by my stall on her horse, Tonto. "Can we ride together?" she asked.

"That sounds great. I'm so glad it is Friday evening and I can spend some time riding," I said with enthusiasm. "Let's head out the trail toward the lake. That is as far as I'm allowed to go."

Camilla Kattell

"Awesome," she agreed. We took a nice leisurely walk through the trees on a lovely two track trail where we could ride beside each other.

"Word got around the school about your run in with that guy from out of town," Sandi said. "I heard that Luke rescued you. We never had so much excitement at school until you moved here," she teased.

"I never had so much excitement before I moved here either. I really just want uneventful days. Boy, on the ranch we didn't know how good we had it with endless quiet days," I told her. "I wonder how it got around at school."

"In this town everything gets around. It can't be avoided," Sandi said. "You're lucky to have a friend like Luke. He seems to be 'Johnny on the Spot.' I broke up with Antonio. He was too fast for me!"

"I'm glad I have a friend in you Sandi. I enjoy riding with you," I said, not wanting to talk boys.

When the horses were warmed up we jogged and trotted them for a while. I wanted to work on Hero's response to gait changes. Then we picked up a nice ground covering lope and soon we arrived at the lake. It isn't a big lake, but it adds ambiance to the area where several houses have been built to take advantage of the view.

Soon the trail led across a road and into the trees. We began climbing up a gradual slope into some lovely hills. We are lucky to have such a nice place to ride right on the edge of town and close to the stable. From the hill we could look down on the town and the stable.

Sandi and I had fun. We enjoyed relaxing at the end of the school week and we laughed a lot. It was nice to have a girlfriend like I'd never had before. When the sun started getting low we turned for home. The horses were relaxed and we could walk along on a loose rein. Hero and Tonto naturally picked up their gate as we headed home. They were ready for dinner, as was I.

When we got back to the stable I went to the outer stall area where I rent and Sandi headed for the big, high dollar barn. I let Hero cool out while I cleaned his stall and his outdoor run. I put in fresh water and a good feed of hay. Hero got a nice big carrot and many thanks from me. He went right to enjoying dinner.

I started to walk to Sandi's barn to say good night. As I approached her barn I heard a horse whinny in an alarming manner. I jerked my head up wondering what the problem was. It was getting dark, but there were some safety lights around the barn area. Suddenly I saw smoke rising from one end of the main barn. I ran toward it with great dread. Barn fires are a nightmare.

A horse continued screaming. I saw Sandi run out of the end of her barn.

"The main barn's on fire," she screamed.

"Run to the office and call the fire department," I yelled at her.

I ran into the barn and the first stall had a panicked horse rearing and screaming as I had never heard a horse. I saw some hay in the corner on fire. I grabbed a bucket and threw a bucket of water on it, but to no avail.

I knew I had to get that horse out of the stall. I ripped off my jacket and wet it in the bucket. The horse was rearing and terrified. I opened the stall door and tried to calm the horse enough to get hold of him. Fortunately, he had a halter on. I clipped a lead onto the halter and eased my wet jacket over the horse's head to cover his eyes. I was able to lead him out of the stall, despite his consuming fear. I turned him away from the burning hay and took him through the barn to a corral where I could turn him loose safely.

When I ran back other horses in the barn, smelling the smoke, were becoming panicked, too. The fire was beginning to spread some so I grabbed two buckets and started pouring bucket after bucket of water on the hay. The fire department arrived and they were able to quickly get the fire under control.

Beth arrived and saw what had happened. "Emily, you are a blackened mess," she said.

"I had to get a horse out of the first stall. I was afraid the fire would spread into his straw and he was panicky," I told her.

Sandi came running up. She and Beth led me to a bench where I sort of collapsed as the adrenaline subsided.

"Emily, you saved Jennifer's horse!" Sandi told me. "She will be so grateful to you."

"I'm sure glad you knew what to do, young lady," the fire chief told me. "That fire could have spread fast," he said. "It could have been disastrous."

"I'm so glad you were here late after everyone else had left," Beth said. "That fire could have taken the whole barn. I'm glad you had the presence of mind to have Sandi call the fire department. She called me too. You are off probation," Beth said laughing with relief. "I believe both of you girls have a free month's rent coming to you. We need good heads around here like yours."

"I'd give you a big hug, but you are all smoky," Sandi laughed. "My parents will love me for getting a month's free rent."

We thanked the firemen as they put their equipment in order and left. Then Sandi and I went to check on Jennifer's horse while Beth went to call Jennifer and let her know what happened.

It wasn't long until Jennifer arrived with her dad to check on her horse, Rocket. When Beth told them what had happened Jennifer and her dad were grateful.

"You saved a valuable horse tonight," her dad said. "Thanks."

"I'm just glad we were here," I said, including Sandi. "I didn't know it was your horse in that stall. Any horse in there was valuable to me," I told Mr. Brenton.

"You are right about that," Jennifer said. "But it was the horse I love. He's very valuable and is worth many trophies. I guess you were out riding late."

"Yes, we were having a long Friday, end of the school week, refresher," Sandi told her.

"Well, maybe sometime I'll ride with you," Jennifer said.

"That would be nice," I told her.

As everyone felt things were settled for the night with Jennifer's horse in a new stall, we dispersed.

"My dad will come and give us a ride," Sandi said. I was glad of that since I wasn't feeling much like walking home in the dark since my encounter with Robert. Mom would be getting worried and I had some explaining to do so it was good to get a ride. I was very tired.

CHAPTER 36

THE NEXT MORNING I slept in for a while. All the excitement in my life this week was beginning to take a toll. When I woke up I could hear Mom in the kitchen. I was glad it was her day off, too. What's to not like about Saturday.

Fortunately, Beth feeds Hero in the mornings now during the school year. It is hard enough to go see him each evening when I have to feed. I was glad I didn't have to jump out of bed today.

Mom tapped on my door.

"Come in. I'm awake," I called to her.

"I'm glad you could sleep in for a while. It was a tiring week. That was quite a story you brought home last night that explained your smoky clothes. I have to tell you, though I'm glad you saved another horse, I worry about you running to danger rather than away from it," she said as she sat on the side of my bed.

"I know. I just couldn't let a horse suffer any longer than it took for me to help it. It was rather amazing that I could lead a terrified horse away from the smoke. The fire hadn't really started spreading fast, but the smoke was upsetting the horses. I'm glad they set off an alarm. I probably wouldn't have gone in if the barn walls had already caught fire," I said thoughtfully, as I remembered the events of the last evening.

Mom handed a small box to me. "Open this and see what you think. I have a matching one," she said mysteriously.

"Wow, a cell phone. For me? I've wished I had one. I didn't think you would change your mind on the rule you and Dad had imposed against cell phones," I said with delight.

"Your dad and I never anticipated some of the dangerous things that have been going on since we got to town. It was always so safe and quiet on the ranch. We're in a very different time and place now," Mom said with regret. "I want you to keep this with you all the time. The guy at the store set them up for us. There is auto dial for 911. Don't hesitate to use it. Better safe than sorry."

"Thanks, Mom. I'll feel much better walking home after dark from school or the stable. The days are getting shorter," I said, feeling like I had a little better safety net in my life now.

"I expect Jennifer is feeling very grateful to you. Do you think she'll change her attitude toward you and be friendlier?" Mom asked.

"Boy, I don't know. It will be interesting to find out," I answered. Just then the phone rang and Mom went to answer it. I got up to dress.

"Emily, its Jennifer calling," Mom called to me.

"Timely. Maybe we'll get the answer to your question," I said to Mom as I took the receiver.

"Hello," I greeted.

"Good morning, Emily. I hope I didn't wake you," Jennifer said to me.

"No, not at all. I slept later than usual, but I'm awake now," I said.

"I want to thank you again for what you did last night for Rocket," she said, sounding very sincere. "I went to the barn early today to check on him and he seemed back to normal this morning. I hate to think of what could have greeted me this morning if you hadn't been there."

"I'm sure glad I was there. He is a fine horse and if he had acted crazy I couldn't have gotten him out. Despite his fear he responded to me well enough to get us both out of there in a hurry," I replied.

"Do you know Becky Osgood? She keeps a show horse in the second barn. My dad offered to hitch up our four horse trailer tomorrow to take her and me up into the state park to ride trails. Would you want to take Hero and go too? I'll ask Sandi, too," Jennifer said, surprising me with her offer.

"Let me ask Mom," I said. Holding my hand over the receiver I asked Mom if she cared if I would ride tomorrow for several hours in the nearby state park.

"I don't mind as long as you get your homework done. The sheriff didn't want you to go out of town, but the park is only a couple miles out and you'll be with a group. I think it would be okay," Mom said.

"Jennifer, I can go. It sounds like fun. Thanks," I told Jennifer.

"We'll see you at the barn at 9:00 to load the horses. I'll go out and feed about 8:00, so I'll probably see you then," Jennifer said.

After I hung up the phone I said to Mom, "Well, I think we have the answer to your question about Jennifer. I wonder, though, how long she'll act friendly."

A little later Sandi called. She was very excited about our coming trip. "Can you believe Jennifer asking us to go with her?" she asked.

"I was surprised," I acknowledged. "I think this says something about how much she loves Rocket. Any girl that really loves her horse is okay by me."

"Me too. We have a bond as horse lovers. I think you've made a huge impression on Jennifer," Sandi agreed. "I'll see you in the morning."

I wondered how Hero would react to going on the trail and loading in the trailer with a group of horses. The only times I knew of him being in a horse trailer were the day he was rescued, the day he was delivered to us, and the day Mr. Winslow brought him to town. I hoped he wouldn't misbehave and ruin my effort to go with the others. However, I knew I couldn't let my anxiety about the trailering transfer to him.

I spent most of the day doing my homework and helping Mom with our weekend chores. Late in the afternoon I went to the stable to feed Hero and clean his stall. Beth was there when I arrived.

"Good afternoon," she said happily. "It is a wonderful day for me knowing what it could have been like if you hadn't acted quickly last night. I'm so grateful to you. I sure misjudged you and I regret that. I hope you'll forgive me. A friend of mine, who shall remain nameless, works at the school and she told me about some of the crazy things that have been happening to you. She said you've earned the respect of many of the teachers for the way you have handled things and kept your focus on being a good student."

"Thanks for telling me that. I'm becoming very comfortable coming here to see Hero, but it will even be better if I know I'm not on your probation list," I laughed. I felt happy and that was a very nice sensation

I told Beth about Jennifer's invitation and told her that I hoped to avoid any other conflicts around the stable. I said I understood how inappropriate that was.

"I'm sorry if I came down on you that day harder than I did on Jennifer. Knowing Jennifer as I do, I suspect I was wrong. I'm very glad you are stabling here," Beth told me.

As I walked back to Hero's stall I thought about Dad, Diamond, and Star. My losses still hurt, but I was gaining traction on my new life. It seemed like I'd won two new friends in Beth and Jennifer.

CHAPTER 37

SUNDAY OR NOT I had to get up early the next morning so I could feed Hero in time for him to digest for a while before loading in the trailer. I ran the several blocks to the stable to feed and water him by seven o'clock.

Then I ran home and Mom had a good breakfast fixed for me. I had packed my saddle bags the night before, so after I ate hurriedly, I grabbed them and headed out for the barn again.

"Got your phone?" Mom called to me.

"I sure do. It is charged and ready. See you this afternoon," I called to her.

While Hero finished nibbling at the last of his hay, I brushed him. During the week he had gotten his first pair of shoes. Andrew, the black-smith, was very experienced with first time horses. He reported that he and his helper had taken their time with Hero and Hero was nice to work with. I cleaned his feet and checked that the shoes were still well set.

Sandi came by my stall about seven thirty. "I still can't believe Jennifer offering to take us on a trip today? Plus we get free stable fees for a month. I'm glad we were here to save her horse and report the fire," Sandi gushed.

"We were lucky. I'm glad you got the fire trucks here as quickly as you did. That probably prevented the whole barn from catching on fire. Are you ready to go?" I asked.

"Ready and eager," she said.

Promptly at eight o'clock Jennifer showed up with her dad and Becky Osgood. We met at Jennifer's stall and she introduced me to Becky. I had noticed Becky's name on the sophomore honor roll. She is tall, with long blond hair and the lithe body of a dressage rider.

"I'm impressed with how you saved Jennifer's horse from what could have been a disastrous barn fire. My horse is in the next barn over, but the fire could have spread there if it had time to really get going," she said to me.

"Sandi and I are really glad we were here late," I said. "Tell me about your horse."

"I've had Silver Sky, known as Sky, for about five years. He's a gray Quarter Horse and, of course, the love of my life. I often go with Jennifer to the horse shows. We have a lot of fun doing that, but I prefer the trail rides like today," she said.

We all loaded our tack into the front of the trailer. Mr. Brenton was pleasant as he rushed around helping all of us load. He was different from what I had expected based on Sandi's description. I could see that Jennifer was the apple of his eye.

"You girls ready to load your steeds?" he asked when all the tack was in the trailer.

We responded with an enthused and simultaneous "Yes *sir*."

I explained that Hero hadn't been loaded much. I didn't know how he might react to this new adventure.

"Well, if he won't load up we'll have to leave you here. We can't spend a lot of time training him," Jennifer said. I thought that maybe saving Rocket hadn't really changed Jennifer's attitude toward Hero and me. I decided to be patient.

Jennifer and Becky's horses go to shows a lot so they are trailer veterans and they walked right into the trailer with Hero watching. Since he knows Sandi's Tonto, we loaded Tonto next and Hero would be next to him.

When I led Hero up to the ramp of the large trailer full of horses, he took a long pause. It was obvious he didn't really find this idea too attractive. I let him look for a few minutes and asked him to take a few steps forward. We let him think about going in for a few minutes and then I just walked in and he followed me. What a good boy he was.

"I guess that didn't take too long," Jennifer said.

We closed the trailer and headed for the state park about twenty minutes away. We had in mind a loop trail, so Mr. Brenton said he would just wait for us while he read a book and the newspaper. That seemed above and beyond the call of duty to me, but I was grateful.

After arriving we were soon tacked up and ready to ride. We let Hero approach Rocket and Sky to get acquainted. We wanted to establish that we didn't have any kickers. With four geldings everyone behaved well. None of these fellows was hostile to any of the others, so we could just relax and ride.

The trail was wide enough for us to ride two abreast, which is companionable. The park had several nice streams and lots of trees. The terrain was rolling. I still missed the mountains near the ranch, but this was very pretty. We even got to see a bald eagle, which was a real treat.

At about the half way point we stopped by a stream and let the horses drink. Then we dismounted, tied our horses, and ate our packed lunches.

Becky sat near me. "I heard you are in the Nerd Club," she said.

"Yes," I laughed. "We aren't an official club. We're just working on a special project for the science fair. It won't be a competitor, but will be on display," I explained. "We seem to have acquired the label, Nerd Club, without any one getting ruffled. I saw your name on the honor roll."

"Yes. I want to go into the Air Force and later the FBI. Good grades will be necessary for me to get where I want to go. I hope I can take Sky to school with me when the time comes, but my parent's think that will distract from my studies," she told me.

"I guess when we have specific ambitions we have to plan on getting the grades. Sometimes I just wish I was going to horsemanship school," I laughed. "That sounds low pressure."

"What are you going to do?" she asked.

"I want to be an equine vet," I replied.

"I guess that is why you're taking Latin. I managed to get around that. Morton is a neighbor of mine and we're friends. He has told me all about you," she teased.

"Morton is a nice guy," was all that I said.

"Is there any progress in finding out who shot at you?" she asked.

With that subject change, Jennifer and Sandi moved closer to join our conversation.

"We haven't heard from the sheriff in several days. I hope they find whoever it was soon. I'm sort of on a short leash because of the shooting. I was only able to come today because we are a large group and Mr. Brenton is our chaperone," I explained.

"I think we should head back," Jennifer said. "Dad will get tired of waiting and maybe Emily's shooters are watching us," she said, I hoped in jest. We all took a good look around and concurred with her unease. We mounted up and headed back around the loop that would lead to the parking lot.

About half way down the trail Jennifer and Becky were in the lead when a man suddenly stepped out of the bushes into our path. We halted about thirty yards from him and Jennifer said, "Hello."

"What's four pretty girls like you doing way out here without a man?" he asked while leering at us.

Just then Hero flicked his ears and sidled slightly at something behind him. I turned and looked and another man had moved into the trail close behind us. The hair on the back of my neck stood up and I recognized this as an 'iffy' situation.

I moved Hero up between Jennifer and Becky to confront the man more close up. As I moved away from Sandi, who showed no alarm, I said softly to her, "Move up tight together."

"I'm not sure what business it is of yours what we are doing here, but you need to step aside. Come on girls," I said and I started Hero forward fast. The man jumped out of the way in time for Hero to miss him. Luckily the others took my lead and were close behind me. We trotted briskly on down the trail.

"I don't know why you are so unfriendly," the man called after us. "Next time you'll wish you was nicer to us."

When we were well away from the two men and where they wouldn't catch up to the horses, we stopped and looked back. My heart was racing.

"Why were you so unfriendly?" Sandi asked. "They weren't doing anything."

"I don't know," Becky said. "Why were they blocking our path? They didn't approach us in a normal manner. They seemed threatening to me."

As I calmed down a little I realized why I had acted as I had. "Something about the man behind us reminded me of the quick view I had of the man who shot at us. Becky is right, they weren't acting normal. Men just don't say things like that to girls unless they mean to be threatening."

"I don't know what they had in mind, but I'm glad you rushed them and got us out of there. People don't usually act aggressive or unpleasant to four people on large horses," Jennifer said. "It seems like this is not a time to be careless."

"I think we should hurry on back to the trailer," I said, leading off with Hero at a brisk, ground covering trot.

When we arrived back at the parking lot, kind Mr. Brenton was there patiently waiting for us. "Dad," Jennifer said. "I'm really glad you are here. We ran into some strange men on the trail a ways back and it was a little scary."

"What! Tell me what happened," he came immediately alert.

"They came out of the bushes, one behind us and one in front. One asked us what four pretty girls were doing out there without a man," Jennifer said.

"Emily got all 'these guys are dangerous' and led us in a rush out of there," Sandi said. "I think they were harmless."

Mr. Brenton turned to me where I stood feeling withdrawn. "Aren't you the girl that was shot at a couple weeks ago?" Mr. Brenton said with recognition.

"Yes," I said quietly. "We should load up and get out of here."

Mr. Brenton came over to me and laid a hand on my shoulder. "You're alright now. Yes, let's load up and head home. I'm sorry you were startled. No wonder you were wary."

We loaded the horses and left the park. When we got back to the stable we unloaded the horses and I escaped to my stall. I fed and watered Hero and gave him big hugs and several carrots. I was pleased with the way he acted all day.

I was especially glad he had alerted me to the man behind us. I wondered if there had been any others. I left Hero with a good feeding, a clean stall, and a new found respect for his sensible nature. It was amazing how responsive he had been to my cues when I needed quick action.

As I was leaving Jennifer stopped me on the lane out of the stable.

"I think it is just too dangerous to be around you," she said. "You seem to attract trouble. Let's not socialize anymore. I have to be more careful about who my friends are."

"I'm sorry you feel that way, but I've noticed how snotty you are toward Hero and me. I'm fine with not being friends," I told her.

I ran all the way home holding my phone in my hand. For some reason I still felt scared. It was as though the adrenaline was still working. I was on heightened alert for every shadow, passing car, and dark corner.

When I dashed into the house Mom came out of her room. "Boy, am I glad you are home," I said.

"Well, honey, aren't I always home," she laughed. "How was the ride?"

I felt cold and hot at the same time. My heart was racing fast again. Without answering her I ran to my room and slammed the door shut. I threw myself across my bed and sobbed as I hadn't sobbed since Dad died. I was so scared.

After a while I heard Mom ease my door open and quietly walk over to sit beside me on my bed.

"Honey, what has happened? Was Jennifer unpleasant? Was the ride not fun?" she asked gently.

For some reason the whole story just poured out of me. Finally, I was able to talk about what happened in a way that I couldn't in the parking lot with Mr. Brenton. I cried and talked at the same time.

"Two men came out of the bushes on our ride back to the parking lot. I felt they were threatening in what was said and their demeanor. Usually when several horses come down a trail, hikers move well off the trail. These men moved to block the trail. Something clicked in me and I sort of panicked. I used Hero to charge past the guy in front, urging the girls to follow and we got away. I thought maybe the guy behind me looked like the guy I saw briefly the day we were shot at. I'm not sure of that, but I wasn't taking any chances. When we told Mr. Brenton about it, he sort of hustled us out of there," I related the story all at once.

Mom tried to give me a hug, but for some reason I resented it and avoided her. "I never should have let you go," she said.

"We had a great time before we saw them. I don't think the others were as alarmed as I was. I don't know if I'm over reacting or whether I just have a heightened sense of danger right now. I know one thing—I'm not going to be a prisoner," I shouted. "And besides all that Jennifer was rude and doesn't want anything to do with me. I tarnish her life," I said as the anger poured out.

"Honey, I don't know why you are reacting like this, but it is better to be aware than sorry. I'm going to call Sheriff Martinez right now," Mom said as she got up.

Within an hour the sheriff arrived. Mom brought me into the living room and sat close by me. She asked me to tell the sheriff just what I'd told her.

When I finished the sheriff was thoughtful for a few minutes. Then he said, "This might be a clue that we really need. I haven't reported anything to you because I didn't want to alarm you anymore. Sheriffs in all the surrounding counties have been finding more indication of the Wyoming rustlers moving into the area. Our helicopter search did not find any kind of camp near the shooting, but they may have moved out right away knowing a search would be coming. In several scattered areas a few horses or cows have disappeared without any trace."

"Then you are thinking rustlers were firing at Luke and Emily to scare them off. Sounds like it was dumb to tip the area off to their presence," Mom said.

"Except that they couldn't chance the kids happening into their camp if they were close," the sheriff countered.

By now I was becoming more interested in this mystery and I was able to shake off the fear I had been feeling. I can't let these people get to me. I told Mom and the sheriff, "I think these guys today really rattled me, but I have to keep things in perspective and not let them get to me."

"Well, it is certainly understandable that you reacted with fear, given your recent experience. Were the other girls alarmed?" the sheriff asked.

"Two of them were concerned and felt there was something wrong about the situation. The other girl seemed unalarmed," I told him.

"Don't question your own judgement. Most times when someone has been through a threatening experience they become more watchful and aware of situations around themselves," Mom said.

"That's true," Sheriff Martinez agreed. "I think the key is that the guy behind you triggered a sense of recognition of the earlier shooter. Your description is very important. I'll put out another APB and reinforce the earlier description. We are mapping the locations of the shooter, all the missing livestock, and now we'll include where you were today. It will help a lot for us to start narrowing down where we might find these guys. I want your description of the other guy from today and I'll talk to the other girls and get their recollections too."

"I felt safe letting Emily go today because she was with several other people. I won't let this happen again," Mom said.

As the sheriff left he said, "We may need your help more, Emily."

"I'm available," I said to him. And then something hit me. "Sheriff, I just remembered something. When Mom and I were in Gunnison shopping I ran into a guy when I was going to the book store. He was of medium height, looked rather scruffy, wore a worn cowboy hat, and smelled bad. I think he was the same guy who was behind us today."

"You never mentioned that," Mom said.

"At the time, it didn't mean much to me, but I'm sure it was the same guy behind us today," I said, feeling enthused that I finally knew what the shooter probably looked like. "I remember now that the guy in Gunnison and the guy today had a noticeable scar across his left cheek.

I'm not sure he was the shooter, but he certainly had the same build and his clothes looked about the same."

"That is a more complete description than we've had before. I'll put that information out," Sheriff Martinez said. "If you see him anywhere again, be sure to stay away from him and let me know right away."

After the sheriff left I told Mom, "I want to get these guys caught so I can feel free and safe again." I was really feeling angry.

"I know dear, but in the meantime, we must be careful. They may see you as a threat. I wonder why they aren't bothering Luke," she pondered.

"The sheriff originally said he thought they knew me from having watched the ranch and seeing me find the damaged fence. The shooter must think I can identify him and he wants to scare me," I reminded her.

Mom gave a heavy, deep sigh. I knew things were weighing heavy on her. "Well, it's back to work and school tomorrow. You better make sure you have all your homework finished," Mom said as she started to leave the room.

This time I got up and hugged her.

CHAPTER 38

THE FIRST FEW days of the school week went rather well. Sandi did warn me not to trust Jennifer too far. She said Jennifer could run hot and cold. I told her what happened after the ride and that I had already felt her hot and cold. Becky had been friendly when I saw her and she was easy to talk to. We seemed equally focused on our dreams, though I was still the lowly freshman.

I've seen Luke several times. He had heard about what happened on our trail ride Sunday. It baffled me how word got around, but it sure did. When I told him my version of the story he became agitated.

"You've got to be more careful. Good Lord, you can't even walk home from school safely. I can't drive you home each day because I'm at practice, but I'll drive by your house on my way home to make sure you are okay. The sheriff has to get on top of this thing," he said adamantly.

"It looks like the sheriffs in the whole state are on it. They'll get it figured out. Don't worry. I'm very careful," I tried to reassure him, maybe more than I felt reassured myself. I was getting a little tired of people telling me I should be careful like I choose to have these scary encounters. "Look, I'll be fine coming home from school. Mom gave me a cell phone and I keep it with me. I can take care of myself."

"Have you heard anything more from Robert?" he asked, wary of my anger.

"No, thank goodness. I don't think I will either," I told him.

Later I ran into Principal Hill. He told me he had heard that I was doing better in adjusting to high school and my teachers were pleased with my work. He mentioned the barn fire and praised my bravery.

"My bravery that night, as you put it, won the esteem, at least short term, of the girl who was giving me a bad time and blackening my reputation," I told him laughing. "She's a bit more civil to me now."

"Good for you," he said as he passed on down the hall.

I felt things were getting better for me, if the rustler problem could just be solved.

Then that evening the news broke that a rancher about a hundred miles from us had found some rustlers in a pasture loading some of his cattle. The rustlers shot and killed him. A terrible shock swept our community. Murder in our area was rare. We believed that was the kind of thing that happened in big cities. Mom heard about this before she came home from work.

"Emily, before I left work I arranged with my boss to be able to take you to school in the morning and to pick you up after school. These modern day thieves are just too dangerous for us to take lightly. I'll drive you to the stable to take care of Hero, but you won't be riding away from the stable area. Whatever you are doing I don't want you alone," she told me. The prison walls were closing in on me.

"Really, Mom. I can walk to and from school. Luke thinks he should come by after school and check on me, too. You guys will smother me," I protested.

"I suppose we can't make a prisoner of you, but you must be alert. It's okay if Luke checks on you after school and you must always have your phone with you," Mom worried.

A couple days later Sheriff Martinez came by the house in the evening. Mom invited him in and offered him a drink, as she usually does. He sat rigid and serious with his nervous hands playing with his hat.

"We heard about the murder. I've all but totally grounded Emily. I'm considering sending her to my sister's in California until these men are caught," Mom told the sheriff.

My head snapped up. Sending me away! We hadn't discussed that again. Wasn't I to be in on the decision? School is going so well right now and I don't want to fall behind.

"Mom! We haven't discussed that. I don't want to miss school," I blurted.

"You can transfer to a school in California," she insisted.

"Maybe that won't be necessary," Sheriff Martinez said hesitantly. "Sheriff Garcia, up in Garfield County, had an interesting run in a couple days ago with a young man named Robert Donaldson. Do you know him, Emily?"

"Yes, of course. We met the Donaldsons at the Winslows' Fourth of July barbeque. Since then Robert has asked me out and one day a couple weeks ago I had a run in with him after school," I explained.

"I meant to call you, Sheriff, but the next day it got away from me. I'm sorry. I should have reported what happened," Mom regretted.

"Did you go out with him?" the sheriff asked.

"No, I didn't have any interest in him. Taking care of my horse, studying, and school activities keep me busy," I explained.

"So what happened a couple weeks ago," he asked.

"I was walking home from school and about half way home I turned the corner and he was there by his car waiting for me. He asked me if I wanted a ride and when I declined he tried to force me into his car. Luke Winslow was driving my route after football practice because he knew I had a meeting after school and it was looking like rain. Luke is a good friend. He saw Robert hit me and he tackled Robert, they fought, and Luke drove Robert off. I haven't seen or heard from him again," I said.

The sheriff turned to Mom," Do you know the Donaldsons well?"

"No, we only met them at a Fourth of July party," she said, showing her growing concern.

"I wish you had reported that incident to me. This Robert seems like a young man on a bad path. Sheriff Adams picked him up and questioned him about a report that Donaldson had been bragging about some rough guys he knew who were camping out in the canyons.

Northern Garfield County is very rugged and empty. It'd be a good place for rustlers to hide out. Tough guy Donaldson didn't want to answer any of the sheriff's questions, but his father forced him to cooperate. During the interview he said that one of these guys knows who Emily is and where she lives," the sheriff paused thoughtfully. "Of course that rang a bell with me because of your report from your ride at the state park over the weekend."

"I can't imagine why they would have any interest in Emily," my mom said.

"We thought maybe they had watched her some at your ranch. Then there was the guy who took a shot at her and Luke to run them off, and then the latest threat at the state park. They may be afraid of her identifying one of them, assuming all these sightings were the same fella. Who knows what Donaldson might have said to them about Emily while trying to impress them," the sheriff seemed to be thinking out loud.

"I never really got that good of a look at the shooter, but he sure had a resemblance to the guy I saw this last weekend," I added. "And remember how, when Mom and I were in Gunnison just before school, I bumped into a guy in the street on my way to the book store. He was rude. He asked me if I was the girl from the Campbell Ranch. When I said I was, he asked if I was the one who had reported rustlers and he said I should learn to keep my mouth shut. If it is the same guy seeing him up close that day may be what triggered recognition of the guy this weekend. He was of medium height, like the shooter, wore a worn cowboy hat, and smelled bad. I wasn't close enough to see if he had a scar."

"That might fit with them thinking you could identify one of them. I think we are making headway. Sheriff Adams and I have been trying to plan a way to get this Robert to lead us to these guys. He may know more than he is letting on," Sheriff Martinez said.

We all sat thoughtfully for a couple minutes. "Well, Sheriff, as a mother who is worried sick, I hope you guys get these men in jail soon," Mom pleaded.

"I think we will," he said as he stood up to leave. "Please be sure to let me know if you see or hear from Robert Donaldson."

After mom saw the sheriff out, she sat down with me again. "Honey, I really would feel better if you spent some time at Aunt Sue's until the dust settles. I can't sleep nights for worrying about you," she said.

"Mom, I'll be okay. School is going well after all the adjustments and I don't want to leave you or Hero. If the sheriffs are starting to pick up information about these guys, arrests can't be far behind. I'll be careful," I promised.

"I suppose you've had enough disruption in your life lately," she said, accepting defeat on the idea of sending me away. I knew she wanted me safe; I sure didn't want to get shipped to Aunt Sue.

Chapter 39

THE NEXT MORNING I was walking to school and my whole body felt like lead. I felt like I had just run out of steam. I missed Dad and the wonderful life we had on the ranch. Things seemed to run so smoothly back in that other life. I was tired.

I was tired of the principal calling me in without justification and Beth's anger. I was tired of Jennifer's rudeness. I was tired of having to talk to the sheriff. I was tired of having to watch behind me. I was tired of feeling like a prisoner. I was tired of fear. I was tired of my schedule of constant school, homework, and taking care of Hero. I was tired of the anger I felt toward Mom, especially when she wanted to send me away. I turned off my phone as the ultimate sign of my mutiny.

As I was thinking these things I suddenly realized my feet were no longer taking me toward the school. Somehow they had taken me to the stable. Beth had fed Hero and he was just finishing his breakfast.

I went into his stall and sat down in the corner. With my head on my knees I felt like I had just quit. I didn't want to try being nice to Jennifer. I didn't want to have straight A's so I could be a vet. I didn't want a sweet boyfriend. I didn't want an understanding Mom.

I felt like something was terribly wrong with me. I knew I should want all those things, but I just didn't feel like I had the strength to keep going anymore.

I wanted my dad back. He would make things right. I cried like I hadn't cried in months. The sobs rolled out of me like waves on the ocean. What was the matter with me?

Hero finished his food and came to see what the strange person in his stall was doing. It was a puzzle for him too. It wasn't long until he went outside in his run. I thought, oh God, even Hero has abandoned me.

When I heard Beth coming down the barn to turn horses out, I left the stall and walked around the corner. I didn't want her to see me.

I began walking back toward home. There would be no school for me today. I wasn't going. As soon as I made the decision a great feeling of rebellion against everything that hurt came over me.

I walked a few blocks to downtown and spent the day wandering around. I had lunch at the ice cream shop, spent time in the library, and walked to the park to take a nap in the sun. I felt free, and wicked. I refused to let myself think that Dad was watching me.

When I had wasted the whole day, I walked back to the stable and fed Hero. Then, with my feet dragging on the pavement, I walked home.

Then I saw Mom's car in the drive. Uh oh, I thought. Why is she home already?

I went into the house.

"Where have you been? I have been worried sick. The school called to see if you were sick. I came home right away to see what was going on. I thought you had been kidnapped or something. I've talked to the sheriff and they've been looking for you. What have you been doing?" Mom ranted.

"I decided not to go to school today. I'm tired of it," I said, knowing that would not be enough explanation.

"What do you mean you got tired of it?" Mom said as she slammed her fist on the table. "Emily this is not you. I've always been able to count on you. You are an exemplary student."

"Yeah, well that is what I'm tired of being, exemplary. I'm tired of Dad being gone. I'm tired of missing the ranch. I'm tired of defending myself at school or at the stable. I'm tired of being alone," I yelled. I started toward my room, but it wasn't going to be that easy.

"Whoa. Whoa. Where do you think you are going?" Mom demanded.

I sat down at the table and put my head down on my hands. I felt overwhelmed with the anger in me and I could see that Mom felt the same way. She paced back and forth. And then I heard her put the tea kettle on the stove. Always it was the 'hot drinks' to calm us.

Mom made me a hot chocolate. She put our drinks on the table and sat down.

"Okay, young lady, explain yourself," Mom said in a much more calm tone of voice.

"I don't know how to explain anything. I just started to school and never got there. I was downtown and in the park all day. I also checked on Hero and fed him. I was just too tired of everything from missing Dad to trying to get along with Jennifer. I was just too tired," I tried to make some sense.

"Well, skipping school is not the answer, nor is scaring me to death. I guess I better call the sheriff and tell him the crisis is under control," Mom said.

When Mom returned she laid her hand on my shoulder. "I'm sorry Emily. I know you've had too much to bear. But you need to talk to me about how you feel."

"Mom, you are always so busy and tired after working all day. I get home from feeding and do my homework and life just seems like a grind. I miss Dad and the ranch so much," I said.

"I know. I miss them too. I suppose we are bound to feel the grief overtake us from time to time. I think that is what happened to you today. I certainly understand. But, please, you must understand that disappearing is not the answer. Especially with my concerns for your safety now," she said.

"I know. I agree," I said.

"I think we need to set aside some time for each other on a regular basis," Mom decided. "I need to be in better touch with how you are feeling. You have been so strong that I've probably lost touch with how much you are hurting. I promise to do better," Mom said. "I'll tell you what. Let's treat ourselves to a night out with dinner at The Cloverleaf and we'll rent a movie on the way home. I guess you don't have any homework since you didn't go to school," Mom laughed. "I want you to know that my time with you is the most important time I have. I don't tell you that enough."

"Thanks Mom. I guess I have some making up to do at school. Next time I feel like running away to Montana, I'll try to talk to you about it," I said, though I wasn't sure I could keep that promise. I did feel relieved.

CHAPTER 40

A COUPLE NIGHTS later I was feeling more like my old positive self. As I lay in bed trying to go to sleep the rustler issue kept going through my mind. The thought that maybe there was more I could do to solve our problem nagged at me.

The sheriff's words kept going through my mind. Could Robert Donaldson know one or more of the rustlers? Could he know them from a chance meeting without knowing they were bad men? Could he be friends with one or more of these bad guys? Could he know they are the people who have threatened me? Maybe the meanness I saw in him was the tip of the iceberg.

I began to wonder if there was any way I could talk to him and try to find some clues to his knowledge without putting myself at risk. It was a scary thought, but maybe there would be a way. Maybe I need to meet him in a group where I could talk to him within the sight of others. Was there any way I could use Brenda to get near him?

I decided I needed to talk to Luke about this. He is the only person that I can trust and who would help me.

The next morning I managed to run into Luke before school began.

"Hi, Luke. How you doin'?" I greeted him in an upbeat fashion.

"Hey, good to see you. I haven't seen you in forever. Well, it seems like forever," he laughed.

"Don't suppose you would have some time after football practice to give a sweet girl a ride home, would you?" I inquired innocently.

"No problem. I can give a sweet girl a ride anytime. Do you know of any sweet girl who needs a ride?" he asked. I can count on Luke!

"Well, actually, I've been very stressed and I have to stay after school to study in the library about the extinction of frogs, so I'm sure I'll be feeling sweet and feeble by then," I tried to sway him to my wants.

"Well, okay, you've talked me into it. We should be done by five o'clock today. I'll be scruffy, sweaty, dirty, and undesirable. But of course a sweet girl can't be choosy. What is the reason for this feebleness today, besides stress and study?" Luke asked.

"Actually it is confidential. I will be swearing you to undying secrecy, even to a point of endangering yourself, to serve me, my knight," I replied.

"Sounds right up my alley, until we get to that endangering part. Danger seems to stalk you these days and the other boys have been warning me to stay far away from you. Of course, I shun their cowardly reserve. They have no idea of the rewards of serving as your knight in shining armor," he expounded grandly.

I was saved by the warning bell.

"Get thee on to your class you lug. See you about five. And don't forget me," I said as I headed to my first class.

"I shan't forget," he called back as he went the other way.

After school I called Mom and told her Luke would bring me home at five and that we might go by the ice cream parlor on the way. I didn't want her to worry and everything I did these days that wasn't routine seemed to provide worry. Love that cell phone.

At five I went to Luke's truck where he parks by the practice field and he soon came out.

"I can't wait to hear about this great secret," he said in way of greeting.

I hopped into the truck and suggested a stop at the ice cream parlor to gain time to talk to him. He thought that was an excellent idea as he is always hungry after practice.

On the way to the shop I told him about what Sheriff Martinez had told us about Robert.

"I'm not surprised," Luke said. "My parents have known his parents since about the time they moved here, but they haven't spent a lot of time together. I wish we had never introduced you to them. His parents are nice, but I think Robert may have fallen in with some bad influences. We know he doesn't know how to respect a lady."

When we sat down with my ice cream cone and Luke's hamburger, I began my plotting.

"I think the hunt, for what is presumed to be the connection between the rustlers moving in from Wyoming and the threats to both of us, is heating up with several sheriff's departments in Wyoming and Colorado. But they don't seem to have many leads yet. This connection with Robert seems to, maybe, have promise. I have no idea whether he is connected or just met one of these guys in a bar," I said trying to ease into my idea.

"So do you have an idea?" Luke asked somewhat suspiciously.

"Glad you asked. First, I must say that I've had some thoughts about how to help get more information that would lead to arrests, but I'm only speaking to you about this because I trust you. You are smart and anything we come up with that you agree to, I believe will be sensible. We dare not let anyone else know what we are talking about," I said. "I'm not even going to ask you to swear to secrecy because I already trust you and your judgment."

"I'm glad, I think, but I'm beginning to feel more and more uneasy about what your brain has concocted," Luke said. "But you know I'm with you. Do or die."

"I've just been wondering about a way that we could talk to Robert, get near him, and do it safely. Since Sheriff Adams has talked to him it will probably be hard to draw him out, but maybe we should try," I plotted.

"Oh, yeah. We are two of his favorite people right now. You want me to waltz up to him and say 'I'm sorry I beat the crap out of you and could we talk about the interview you had with Officer Adams!'" Luke laughed. He could always see the ridiculous side of things.

"Well, I don't see it exactly like that. I've been trying to imagine how we could get him in a relaxed situation where he might forget his distrust when he wants to be the big man. Maybe we could ask your parents to have a barbeque after the football season to celebrate and they could invite Robert and Brenda. After all, they won't know about Robert being questioned by the sheriff," I suggested.

"Hmm, maybe that would work," Luke said thoughtfully. "If we had a big group you should be safe from him doing anything nasty. I would have to apologize to him for our 'misunderstanding' and suggest we let bygones be bygones."

"We can't serve alcohol, but he will probably come with a hidden flask. If he drinks a little I might get him to say something that would give us a clue to what he knows," I said feeling excited that this might work. "Could you ask your parents to do this without lying to them?"

"No, I would have to talk to Dad honestly about what is going on, but he might want to be helpful," Luke said. "I wouldn't put them in a bad place, but my dad can decide what he tells my mom."

"Good," I agreed.

"Is there a better plan B?" Luke wondered.

"I thought about having my mom do a smaller barbeque in our yard, but my friends wouldn't provide as much protection, in the way of beef, as your football buddies would, if anything got out of hand. Plus she couldn't help us like your dad could," I decided.

We had finished our food and headed out for Luke to take me home. I still had to go look after Hero.

"Let's mull this around and see if we find any faults with the plan," Luke said. "I'll talk to my parents about maybe throwing a party to feel them out that far. See if you hear anything more from Sheriff Martinez. And in the meantime you keep alert."

"Not to worry," I told him. "I'm operating like a Seal or ninja these days."

"Oww, bad simile," Luke laughed.

We agreed to talk again in a couple days.

Chapter 41

A COUPLE DAYS later Luke picked me up on the way to school.

"I wanted to let you know that I talked to my dad about the barbeque and why we wanted to have it. At first he said I was nuts and I should forget it. But the more I talked to him I think I may have convinced him that a party for the football team would be nice whether we invite Robert and Brenda or not. He agreed with that and he's talking to my mom about a date," Luke told me.

"But what good will it do if Robert isn't there?" I asked.

"One bridge at a time. I told him I would approach Robert with the idea of including him at the party as an apology. If he has Brenda with him, he'll be less likely to misbehave. Dad is thinking about that," he explained further.

"If it did work so we got Robert there, I've been wondering how we would approach him," I said.

"Yeah, we would need a good plan. We might get him into a situation where he just wants to brag or act tough. I suppose he might get me aside and threaten me," Luke pondered.

"Well, that doesn't sound good. What if we just talked about the murder and the danger of these men being in the area? I could mention that the sheriff thinks maybe they are afraid I could identify one of them, though I can't. A lot of people probably don't know about the attempt they made on our ranch. Who knows how he might react or what he might say," I speculated.

"I hate to say this, but I think we'll have to use you as bait to get him to come. Maybe you would even have to do the inviting or we could do it together. We'll have to be careful to not make him suspicious of anything," Luke added.

"I can be the bait if you and your dad make sure one of you is always around. I sure don't want to be alone with him. I admit, he scares me," I warned.

As we arrived at school Luke said he would let me know what his dad decided and then we could make plans. We would probably end up with a football barbeque either way. Luke and I agreed that we needed to think more about the details of how to approach Robert.

After I got home that night from caring for Hero, I talked to Mom about the idea of the barbeque.

"That sounds like fun for the football team, but you aren't on the football team. Why will you be there?" she asked.

"I guess Luke and I are sort of dating. We haven't talked about it, but I think it is getting so everyone assumes we are. We spend time together and Luke sort of looks after me. Please don't complicate things by asking me about what I'm not sure of myself," I told Mom.

She laughed. "Let me know when you get it worked out. I can take you to the party if they decide to have it. I know Luke has been a special friend and he is a nice boy. I don't have any problem with you 'dating' him, if you are," Mom assured me.

The next time I got to talk to Luke at school he told me, "Mom and Dad have agreed to the barbeque. We set on a date in two weeks on Saturday night. I suggested to Mom and Dad that you might like to bring Sandi, Jennifer, and Becky so you would have some of your friends. Some of the guys may want to bring dates. It can be like we're throwing the party together and that will make sense for us both to call Robert and Brenda. What do you think?" Luke suggested.

"That sounds good except for the Jennifer part," I told him. "It is hard being around her but she seems to be part of the stable gang. I'll ask them."

"Okay, go ahead and ask them and their dates. I'll invite the team after practice tonight. Guess we're in for a dollar," Luke said.

"By the way, Mom asked me if we are dating," I stated out of the clear blue.

"What did you tell her?" he asked, smiling with amusement at my discomfort.

"I told her we are good friends and that I think people assume we are dating. Maybe with Robert around it would be good to leave that impression," I avoided the real issue.

"I'm officially asking you now," he said. "Will you be my steady, despite being only a freshman?"

"Wow, what a romantic! That sounds like the offer every girl holds her breath for," I said.

"Okay, I'll make my request formal and appropriate at a better time than in the school hall. So be prepared with an appropriate answer that, of course, won't disappoint me," he prompted me. "See you later.

Well, I won't be distracted in my first class! Ugh!

At lunch I talked to Sandi, Jennifer, and Becky and they were pleased at the prospect of a barbeque with dates. I told them my mom could take any one who needed a ride out to Luke's ranch and deliver them home.

"I'm going to ask Jimmy Tucker. He's on the team, but he drives and I want to go as his date. And his dad owns the lumber yard and drives a Cadillac. He winked at me the other day. I think he finds me irresistible," Jennifer flaunted.

"Oh right," Sandi said. "You think all the boys are just bonkers over you."

"Well, look at me. I'm the prettiest girl in the school," Jennifer said as she flipped her long blond hair.

"Yeah, you can't get Luke. You wanted him, but he's devoted to Emily," Sandi taunted Jennifer.

"Stop it you two. I'll un-invite you if you can't be pleasant. And by the way, Luke has asked me to be his steady," I told them.

"What! When were you going to tell me?" Sandi gasped.

"I guess I didn't think it was too big a deal. It was just this morning and I'm telling you now. Did you want me to make an announcement on the public address system?" I chided her.

"Well, it is a big deal," she said.

"Did you agree?" Jennifer asked harshly.

"Not exactly," I replied. "We're going to talk about it. We've been such good friends for so long that it doesn't really seem like much of a change in what we'll do together. My plans for vet school are so long term that even dating sounds sort of dumb to me."

"You're an idiot. All the girls like Luke," Jennifer said, surprisingly calm. I hoped she wasn't scheming. I had a feeling Jennifer would think of more ways to make me miserable since Luke wanted to go with me. She's a puzzle.

"I like Peter from the Nerd Club. I'll ask him," Becky said, to my relief changing the subject.

"I guess I'll ask Tony Burton," Sandi said grudgingly. "Jennifer broke up with him so I'll be able to help him mend his broken heart."

"I'm going to ask Brenda and her brother from the Bar 2 ranch. They are friends of the Winslows and we should include them, I guess," I said.

"Wait, isn't her brother the guy who tried to force you into his car?" Sandi charged.

"Yes, but because their families are friends, Luke and I decided to include them and apologize for our misunderstanding," I tried to justify as if it were perfectly natural.

"Well, that's pretty forgiving," Sandi pressed. "I thought he and Luke were really on the outs."

"We're going to try to fix that. Okay. Do we have a plan?" I changed the subject.

They chorused that they were pleased and would ask their preferences for dates right away.

That evening I called Mrs. Winslow to thank her for planning such a big shindig for us. She was her usual gracious self and said it would be fun to end the football season with a blowout. I asked if I could bring anything, but she already had her menu planned and said she would have all that was needed.

"I'm glad you and Luke are including Robert and Brenda. Their parents have been friends of ours since they bought the Bar 2. I know Robert is a year older than Luke and thinks well of himself, but many boys go through that as they begin thinking of themselves as men. It is a decent thing you are doing," she told me.

After we hung up I had a guilty feeling because Luke and I had ulterior motives for inviting the Donaldsons which we were hiding from Mrs. Winslow. Apparently Mr. Winslow hadn't told her about all of Luke's discussion with him. I had to focus on the importance of finding any clues we might get from Robert about the rustlers.

Chapter 42

Since I wasn't able to ride Hero far from the stables on the trails, I decided to start refining his training a little. He had put on weight and muscled up so that to look at him no one would know what he looked like when I got him. I felt Dad would be very proud of what Hero and I, as a team, have accomplished.

After school I groomed him and saddled him. I took him to the round pen with his saddle, but no bridle. The round pen is sixty feet in diameter with a solid wall.

Inside I took his halter off and turned him loose. With the lead rope off the halter, I walked to the center of the pen. Hero was exploring the bits of grass that grew along the edges of the wall when I called to him. At the same time I stepped toward his rear and with the rope in that hand swung it a little while my other arm pointed in the direction that I wanted him to go. It was sort of like gently driving him in that direction at a walk. If he tried to stop or turn, I would step toward his rear and drive him forward by swinging the lead rope.

When I wanted him to stop I took a few steps to move in front of him and he stopped. Then I changed his direction by changing the hand that held the rope, stepping toward his rear driving him the other way, and pointed with my other arm in the opposite direction.

He soon picked up on the idea. If his mind wondered I would swing the rope and keep a strong signal going to him so that his attention was drawn to me. The idea was to get the horse to "hook on" which means to keep his attention on me and have him doing what I directed, not wandering around on a whim. The trainer must establish who is boss. Soon I moved him into working at a trot. I gave verbal cues to him each time I asked for a change so he'd learn the sound of the commands, too.

We worked on that for about twenty minutes. As usual Hero was an attentive student. When I would tell him to stop he was soon stopping and turning to stand and watch me for his next cue.

Then I put his bridle on, mounted him, and worked a little more on his gaits. In this smaller space he would be forced into more collection in his gaits and better balance. It would continue to help him in developing his muscles.

At the end I let him walk out on a loose rein in a good forward walk to extend and relax as he cooled out. It was a very satisfactory lesson. When I was done I got off and loosened his cinch and then gave him a carrot. He loves his rewards. As I walked to the gate he followed me, which is a good indication of "hooking on."

I tried to work with him like that three times a week. By the time we could ride the trails again, he would be improved in his strength, balance, and suppleness. I was pleased that Hero was reaching his potential, despite the bad treatment he survived.

Over dinner that evening I brought Mom up to date on Hero's progress, our party plans, and Luke's request to go steady.

"You're pretty young for that," Mom said. "Just what does going steady mean to you?"

"Well, I guess it means that other boys won't ask me out on dates. That is fine with me since I don't want to go out with any of them. Luke and I pretty much do everything together anyway. On the ranch there really weren't other friends close for me. Sometimes having friends feels like an alternate reality. But Luke is still my best friend. I feel like he treats me right," I explained.

"If he feels the same way, I guess there is no harm in it," Mom said hesitantly. "Just make sure you keep focused on your studies. With Hero, you have a lot on your plate."

"I know. Luke won't make any difference in my studies or activities. He's pretty busy too. I think I would like Robert to know I'm dating someone," I said, hinting at part of my motive. "That should discourage him from asking me out anymore."

"That is a good idea," Mom said emphatically.

"If Luke raises the question with me again, I'll at least know it is okay with you. Thanks," I said. Then I faced evening homework.

CHAPTER 43

WITH A COUPLE weeks until the barbeque, I was able to focus on some deadlines at school.

On Wednesday we had to be present at the Science Fair booth on environment. Our Nerd Club project was not in any competition, but since it was an extra circular project, we had to explain to the judges what we had discovered in our research. Peter, Morton, Levy, Shauna, and I had to each present some of the information.

After we had made our presentations they awarded us each with a certificate of outstanding accomplishment. That would be nice to add to my college applications. One of the judges, from Colorado State, lingered near me and, as things broke up, she approached me and said, "Are you any relation of Colin Campbell?"

"Yes I am. He's... was my father," I stammered.

"I'm sorry. Was?" she asked.

"My father was killed this summer in a fall with a horse. Did you know him?" I asked.

"Yes, I did long ago. I'm sorry to hear that he was killed. We were classmates in college. I see you are an outstanding student like your father was. He was a fine young man. Do you have other family?" she asked.

"No siblings. My mother is my family now," I explained.

"My name is Carol Neuminski. I teach at Colorado State in the vet program," she said.

"That's a coincidence. I hope to go to vet school to study Equine Medicine. That is my lifelong dream," I told her.

"Well, our meeting is a coincidence; almost like fate. You should consider our intern program for the summer following your junior year in high school. We are always looking for dedicated students," she said in a kindly manner.

"Thank you. That sounds exciting. Next summer I'm going to work at a breeding and showing operation near Denver. They bought one of our foals and assured me I could go and work with her next summer," I said with pride.

"It sounds like you are on the right track. I remember Colin dating a girl who was in the med school. Any idea how that worked out, if I might ask," she did ask.

"That would be my mom, Anna. They married and moved to the Campbell Ranch. My dad had an outfitting business," I explained.

"That sounds right. Your dad was quite an outdoorsman. I'm glad I met you Emily. You should keep in touch and I'll provide any help I can in explaining anything about our program. You certainly shouldn't have any trouble getting into a good school," she said as her group moved away.

"Thanks. Nice meeting you," I said.

As we left the science event Peter pulled me aside. "Becky Osgood has asked me to go with her to a barbeque at Luke Winslow's home. She said you are sort of the co-hostess," he said as though it was a secret.

"Yes, that's true. The football team will be there celebrating the end of the season and some of my friends are coming too. I hope you will come," I told him.

"My parents don't want me to go because they remember reading in the paper about you and Luke being shot at. They think you might be disreputable," he said.

Well, that was just great, I thought. Now they think I'm some kind of gangster.

"I can assure you, Peter, I'm not a gangster. Your parents might not know my parents because until this fall I lived on a ranch and, even though I went to school here in Alton, we lived sort of isolated. Your mom would be welcome to talk to Mrs. Winslow or my mom to see if she would feel reassured. It will be well chaperoned. In fact, if your parents want to chaperone, they would be welcome, I'm sure," I told him.

I had never anticipated this issue and I hoped I could alter my reputation! I wouldn't tell Luke about this. I would never live it down.

"Did you tell them I've worked with you on our environmental project?" I asked.

"No. I guess I should mention that. I'll talk to them. I'm glad Becky asked me. Thanks," he said.

As Dolly Parton would say, "Isn't that a fine fix." I had my work cut out for me. One minute I was commended by a Professor from Colorado State and the next I discovered a classmate who thought I was a shady character.

When I told Mom about meeting Professor Neuminski she suggested I start a file with my Certificate of Achievement and notes on meeting Professor Neuminski. She said I should start keeping a good record of my student qualifications, including grades, for when it is time to start submitting applications.

Sometimes I wonder if at fifteen I think too much about college. I have plenty of time yet to enjoy high school. I guess it is just good to know my goal.

Chapter 44

On Wednesday after school Luke gave me a ride home and came into the house with me. We wanted to call Brenda to extend our invitation for next week. We still weren't sure how to extend the invitation successfully, so I just jumped right in. I put our land line on speaker and dialed their number. Luckily Brenda answered. I took a deep breath.

"Brenda, this is Emily Campbell. How are you?" I asked.

"I'm fine. I haven't heard from you in a long time. How are you doing in your new home?" she asked. I was surprised she sounded so friendly.

"It's been a hard adjustment. I really miss the ranch and all my horses. And my dad, of course. I'm learning to be a townie who walks to school and the stable where I'm keeping one horse," I said hoping I didn't sound as nervous as I felt.

"I know I hated moving five years ago, but I didn't have nearly as much to cope with as you have. I enjoyed our ride on the Fourth of July at the Winslows' barbeque. We should do something like that again," she said.

"Well, that fits right in with why I'm calling. You know Luke Winslow plays football and we are dating now, so he has invited me and some of my friends to his end-of- the-season barbeque for the team. We thought of you and Robert and wondered if you would want to come. It's next week on Saturday," I jumped on the opening she presented to me.

"That sounds great. I'm sure we'd love to come. Robert isn't here now to speak for himself, but I'll accept for both of us. He is spending a lot of time with some guys he met recently who are out of school. I think he might be doing some work for them," she explained.

I paused for a second to absorb that and plunged in again. "I don't know if you know or not, but Luke and Robert had a disagreement a few weeks ago when they ran into each. Luke wants to extend an offer to Robert to let 'by- gones be by- gones.' Hopefully it was just a mis-understanding. You know how hot tempered guys can be," I smoothly ad-libbed.

"I haven't heard Robert speak of it. I hope they will make up. Robert has been sort of touchy lately. Mom says he's going through a stage, but I say at seventeen he should be more in control of himself. Ugh! Brothers. You're lucky to not have that problem," she blew off steam.

"I'm sure I am lucky that way," I commiserated as I stuck my tongue out at Luke who was making an abused gesture. "Any way, we'll look forward to visiting. You'll get to meet a lot of the kids from our school. Mr. and Mrs. Winslow are planning a big get together and, as you know, they are very generous hosts. Just call me if there is any change of plans."

"Thanks. I'll do that. See you Saturday of next week," she said and then hung up.

"You should be a Thespian! What a performance. Now we'll just have to see how Robert reacts to the invitation," Luke said. "And did you pick up on the things she said about Robert's friends?"

"I did. I think we are already gaining clues. I hope I can be as cool when I actually see him, though I didn't feel cool today. This whole undertaking feels risky. But I guess we're committed now. I hope we can pull it off," I said, slumping down with the release of tension. "That wasn't as easy as I apparently made it look. My heart is still pounding. Brenda seems innocent of your fight."

"Yeah. I hope that's true. She seems very different from her brother. I guess Robert wouldn't run home and relate that he was in a fight with me. You're going to handle this very well. All I'll have to do is stand around looking handsome and making it known that you belong to me," Luke said with his usual mockery.

"Oh brother! Here we go again with the belonging thing. Remember I'm just going steady with you for the purpose of our undercover work," I reminded him.

"So, then we are going steady. I never got to go through my formal request. It was going to be magnificent. By the way, you very subtlety got that message to Brenda. She can break the news to Robert," he mused with a smile.

"I want to get the news out. It will relieve me of the constant need to fight off all the upper classmen. It's been a burden. Since you are my hero, I think I can bear up under the burden of you," I said shoving him toward the door. "You must go home and I must go take care of Hero. We are on our way to solving the mystery of the identity of the murderers."

"Yes, but now that we are going steady, we should think about when I should kiss you," Luke said, posing in a pompous, thoughtful stance.

I laughed and shoved him again toward the door. "Get out."

Chapter 45

THE NEXT DAY I got a letter in the mail with a return address from Black Diamond at Golden Gate Canyon Quarter Horses. I had to laugh when the envelope indicated the letter was from Black Diamond. I excitedly tore it open. Two pictures were included. One showed Black Diamond from the side and I could see how beautifully she was developing. The other was of her running with another foal and she was mid buck high in the air. Here is what it said:

Dear Emily,

I miss you and wanted to let you know that I haven't forgotten you. I'm doing fine and making new friends. Sometimes Magpie gets miffed at me for running with the other foals, but I beat them all, so I keep doing it. The lessons you gave me about leading make me feel very grown up and I prance when they take me out. I am growing so fast that I'm one of the biggest foals.

I'll see you next summer, if not before.

Love,

Black Diamond

As written by Jessica

Well, that was a cute surprise. Jessica was the last person I would have thought would be so thoughtful. She must have had more feeling for my losses than I would ever have given her credit for. It just goes to show that you have to get to know someone before deciding whether they are friend material or not.

I sat down to write a grateful note back to Jessica. This is what I wrote:

> *Dear Jessica,*
>
> *It was so thoughtful of you to write to me for Black Diamond. I have really missed her and sometimes feel sorry for myself for not getting to have more time with her. It really helps to know she is doing well and that you and your father appreciate her. I hope the opportunity you guys have offered me for next summer is one that I'll be able to take advantage of.*
>
> *With very best wishes to you and your father. Thank you so much.*
>
> *Regards,*
>
> *Emily Campbell*
>
> *PS I hope to hear from Diamond again.*

Finding that note in the mail went a long way to cheering me up. It had been a bad day at school. In history class the teacher had called on me to answer a question and my mind was a million miles away. It was really embarrassing and certainly out of character for me. My mind was on the coming confrontation with Robert.

I had really hoped I would never see him again and now I have initiated the circumstance where I would have to talk to him with my apprehensions hidden. I'd have to appear normal and relaxed while all my instincts would be telling me to stay away from him.

I hoped Luke and I could determine whether there was any reason to think Robert knew anything about the location of my archenemy, the shooter. I'd be trying to use my antagonist to locate my archenemy.

What a crazy situation. I was exercising my brain on word games when I should have been thinking about the causes of the Civil War.

After class, Mr. Kidder asked me why I wasn't prepared today.

"I'm sorry, Mr. Kidder," I said. "I'm afraid my mind wandered."

"I know you've had some distractions in your life lately. Can I help in any way?" he asked kindly.

"Oh no. Thanks. I just need to focus. Things are really going well for me now," I tried to ease his curiosity and get away.

"Well, don't hesitate to call on any of your teachers if you want to talk about anything," he said.

I thanked him and hurried to my next class. I'll pay better attention in this hour.

Chapter 46

Finally, the dreaded Saturday arrived. Mom had to work in the morning so I went to the stable to do my cleaning and feeding chores. I have been really distracted that week, anxious about what had to be accomplished tonight. I sure hoped I was doing the right thing and that it would work.

I worked Hero in the round pen and rode him close to the stables. Sandi on Tonto and Becky on Sky joined me.

"I'm excited about tonight. I guess we should dress sort of 'ranchy?'" Sandi asked.

"Sure, that would be fine. I'm assuming you mean casual. Dress like a fall picnic. The evening may get cool," I told her. Sandi's concerns were never too deep.

"I hope I can visit okay with Peter," Becky said. "I haven't dated much and I know he's very smart. I might bore him."

I laughed. "Becky you are one of the smartest girls in the high school. You'll do just fine. Just be yourself."

"Geez, Emily has been going steady for what, a week? Already she is giving dating advice," Sandi said.

We all laughed. "Let's face it. None of us knows what we are doing. But it will be fun. There will be lots of people there and Mr. and Mrs. Winslow are hosts who will make everyone comfortable," I tried to assure them while knowing I was the most nervous of all.

"Did Robert agree to come?" Sandi asked.

I hated to get on that subject, but I didn't think I could duck it. "I don't know. I talked to his sister but I haven't heard back about whether he is coming. There will be an edge on things if he comes until we find out how he reacts to Luke. Luke will take a 'forget and forgive' approach. I don't know how Robert will react. Maybe he won't come," I explained.

After an hour of riding I was glad to make my excuses and head for home. I needed to go home and prepare myself for the coming encounter.

When I got home the phone was ringing. It was Brenda.

"Hi Emily. I just wanted to let you know that Robert won't be coming to the barbeque tonight, but I would still like to come," Brenda said.

"Of course, we'll look forward to seeing you. Robert will still be welcome if he changes his mind," I told her.

When we hung up the disappointment washed over me. Luke and I have worked so hard to set this up with our ulterior motives. However, I knew it would still be a great party and that I could just relax and have fun. Poor Mrs. Winslow had no doubt, done a lot of work to prepare and they wanted to do this for the team, so it would still work out well.

The tension drained out of me and now I could do my homework and get ready to go in a much more enjoyable attitude. I was surprised at the level of my relief despite the disappointment for our detective work.

After my homework was done I had a couple hours to make myself lovely. That was always a challenging undertaking. I washed and dried my hair and Mom got home in time to help me fix it. She used the curling iron and made it look like she had before the dance. My wardrobe was simple, but perfect for a barbeque. Most of our occasions were very informal. I planned to wear jeans, my favorite boots, and a pretty new blouse Mom bought for school, but I hadn't worn yet.

Mom and I headed for the ranch somewhat early to see if they needed any last minute help. All the other girls had rides with their dates. I assumed Brenda's parents would drop her off.

As we drove in Luke was on the veranda and came to greet us. "Hello, Mrs. Campbell. Thanks for bringing Emily out. I can bring her home after the party if you want me to. It won't be very late," Luke offered.

"That would be nice. Thanks, Luke. Does your mom need any help?" she asked.

"I don't think so. Everything seems ready," Luke seemed anxious for Mom to leave.

"I'll just stick my head in and saw hello," Mom said as she headed for the house.

When she was out of ear shot I blurted, "Luke, I have bad news. Brenda called about noon and said she is coming, but Robert isn't. Can you believe that after all our scheming?"

"You're kidding! Geez, I was geared up for this. Darn!" he said. After a pause to absorb the news, he added, "I guess we just have to enjoy the get together and come up with another plan. I'm sorry."

"I'm sorry too. I really appreciate the work you and your parents have done. I guess we'll survive. Thanks for offering to take me home. I think we are going to need that kind of time to debrief and make a new plan," I said.

"I'm not going to ask where you came up with this lingo, like 'debrief,'" he laughed.

"I read military and spy novels. Where else?" I laughed with him.

Soon the other guests started arriving and we had a mob of people. Mr. Winslow had a great barbeque pit and Mrs. Winslow had everything set up buffet style so we could feed everyone at once. I could tell the Winslows liked to entertain.

Sandi, Becky, and Jennifer all at some point got me aside to tell me how much they were enjoying themselves. The dating thing was a big deal. I thought Becky and Peter especially had a lot in common.

Sandi and Tony were doing a lot of laughing so they seemed well suited. Jimmy Tucker seemed smitten by Jennifer so she was happy. The Winslows had even invited the coaches and the football team seemed to mingle around them. It was a splendid dinner.

Brenda's parents brought her as we started eating. I welcomed her and went with her through the line to fill our plates.

"How do you like high school?" she asked.

"It was a bit of adjustment at first, but I think I'm getting things figured out," I told her. "I still have a horse with me so I don't have time after school to participate in many activities, but I've made new friends at the stable," I explained.

"I've had sort of a rough time. Robert has turned into something of a trouble maker and that seems to alienate the kind of kids I want to be friends with. My grades haven't been too good, but I think I'm beginning to get them up," she confided.

I sensed that Brenda wanted a friend and that she had only come here tonight because she already knew Luke and me.

"Well, I'm glad we know each other. Even though we go to different schools we can confide in each other about how we feel. Let me get Jennifer, Sandi, and Becky over here to meet you. They are fun," I said.

I went and told them to come meet another one of my friends. It wasn't long until Brenda was laughing and talking with them in a somewhat shy manner, but one that seemed to say she was enjoying herself. Maybe it was easier to make friends away from where Robert had an influence. When Luke called me into the house I left a happy group chatting.

"Come help me carry out some more meat for Dad to get going for second helpings," Luke called.

I went inside and Luke asked how it was going with Brenda. "I think she needs some friends," I told him. "It seems that Robert has become something of a trouble maker in the school and that makes it hard for her. She really is a sweet girl."

"Too bad that Robert is such a rotten apple in that family," he sympathized.

As we walked back out with platters of meat and buns, to our surprise, Robert walked onto the veranda. Luke about dropped the meat. We walked to Robert and Luke said, "Hi Robert. I'm glad you could make it after all. Come on in and make yourself at home. Get a plate and load it up at the barbeque pit and at the buffet table. I'll introduce you around."

Luke and I delivered our platters and Luke waited for Robert to get some food. When he had a chance Luke extended his hand to Robert and said, "I'm glad we can put our misunderstanding behind us."

They shook hands and Robert said, "Yeah, that was a bad day. I'm glad you invited Brenda and me tonight. How'd your season end?"

"Well, we didn't win any championships, but we ended up 5–3. We're still building and had a lot of sophomores on the team. Coach says we'll be tough next year. But I suppose coaches always say that," Luke responded.

Robert laughed. "I'll bet they do."

"You been doing any hunting," Luke asked.

"Yeah, as a matter of fact I have. I've spent a lot of time hunting deer. I've made some friends who hunt," Robert said.

"Is that right? Are they from your school?" Luke asked.

"No. They're mostly a little older. They like to camp and drink beer. I find the high school crowd very boring. I'm ready to move on from that scene," Robert bragged.

"Let's sit with Brenda and Emily," Luke suggested and they came to join us at a picnic table somewhat to the side of the main crowd.

"So Emily, Brenda says you are going steady with this loser Luke," Robert said in the way of greeting. He pulled out a pack of cigarettes and lit one.

"Yes, I'm very lucky. All the girls want Luke, but his poor vision has led him to picking me. He says it's the sound of my lilting voice that attracts him," I replied lightly, covering my instant tension.

"Do you have to smoke, Robert? You don't have to impress anyone here," Brenda put him down.

"Ah, what fun it is to have a little sister," Robert said, ignoring her.

Their rift made me uncomfortable. I went to get a drink and asked Jennifer, Becky, and Sandi to bring their dates to meet Robert and visit more with Brenda. I hoped it would distract Robert and Brenda from bickering. I also wanted to get my friends impression of Robert.

The evening was fun and about 10:00 it started breaking up. As everyone dispersed Brenda left with her mom, but Robert seemed to linger till last. I walked Jennifer, Sandi, and Becky, with their dates, to their cars.

"Thanks for coming, you guys. I enjoyed having you here. It would have been a long evening with just me and the football team," I told them.

"It's been fun. I'm glad you asked us," Sandi said.

"Are you going to ride tomorrow?" Becky asked.

"Yeah. Probably about 10:00. Shall we all meet at the stable?" I asked.

"I have ballet in the morning and I'll be busy," Jennifer said. Sandi and Becky agreed to meet. As the boys were talking cars, Sandi said, "I think we'll need to dissect the evening." Everyone agreed with a laugh.

As I turned to go back up to the veranda Robert moved out of the bushes to block my path. My heart leaped. I had thought I had avoided a confrontation, but here he was.

"What's up, Robert?" I asked happily, covering my anxiety.

"Nuthin' really. I just wondered why you decided to hook up with that loser Luke," he said.

"Luke is anything, but a loser. He is fun and we've known each other a long time. I like the way he treats me," I countered. "But let's not talk about Luke. What have you been doing?"

"Funny. Luke asked me the same thing," he said stepping closer.

To move further from him I stepped to the side of the walk way and sat down on a large rock. I hoped Luke would soon notice my absence.

"Well, we haven't seen you. Why wouldn't we ask," I inquired.

"I don't know. Maybe Brenda was saying stuff to you," he said belligerently. He sat down beside the rock. "Now you are behaving more civilly," he said.

"I've always behaved civilly, Robert. As I recall, it was you who have stepped over the civility line," I said.

"What, because I wanted to get you out of the coming rain and take you to get ice cream?" he said innocently.

"No. And you know better than that. You were not a gentleman and you didn't respect that no means no," I told him. "What have you been doing? Isn't that a civil thing to ask?" I said, feeling like I was holding my own with him.

"I've been making friends with older guys. High school kids are boring. I like to smoke and drink a little beer. These babies on the football team don't know what it is to be a man," he growled.

"So what does it take to be a man?" I led him on, hoping to keep him engaged until Luke came.

"For one thing, not being intimidated by anyone, including that stupid Sheriff Adams. He really pisses me off. Swaggerin' around and asking questions," he continued.

"What kind of questions would he ask you? Have you been in trouble?" I pushed.

"He wanted to know about my friends. They are tough guys so he wants to challenge them," he said.

"What makes them tough guys," I asked.

"I think they've been moving some cattle," he said.

"What do you mean moving cattle? You mean like rustling? It was in the news that a rancher got killed by some rustlers," I said.

"Nah, that wasn't them. Couldn'a been. Enough talk about me. If you'd let me kiss you, you would find out that I'm a much more interesting guy to be around than goody, goody Luke," he said taking a firm hold of my arm.

I pulled away and stood up. "Don't start that again, Robert. Luke and I invited you here tonight to show that we want to be friends, but I think you should know that I'm not interested in you that way," I said as my anxiety level hit a high point.

Robert spit on the side walk and looked off into the distance. "You know I could just stuff you in my car and take what I want, don't you?" he said belligerently.

"That would be rape, Robert, and you would go to jail. You should try to straighten out your life before you ruin it for yourself and your family," I told him.

To my great relief I saw Luke coming down the walk looking for me. "Hey, you two, what are you doing out here in the dark?" Luke said jovially.

"I was seeing Jennifer, Sandi, and Becky off," I said. "Robert just came along to visit as I was coming up."

I met Luke and took hold of his hand squeezing it hard. I wanted to send an urgent message of 'where have you been.' He looked down at me knowingly and his eyes apologized.

"Well, Robert, I'm glad you could come tonight. We all enjoy Brenda, too. She is a sweet girl," Luke said. I sensed some menace in him that belied his words.

"Yeah, I'll be going," Robert said and he stomped off toward his car.

After we watched him leave Luke said, "Do you have some things to talk to Sheriff Martinez about?"

"Yes, I think so," I said, leaning against him. "That was scary. I would never make it as a law enforcement officer."

CHAPTER 47

EVEN THOUGH IT was Sunday, Luke came to our house the next morning and with Mom joining us, we called Sheriff Martinez.

"Sheriff Martinez here," he answered.

"Sheriff Martinez, I'm sorry to bother you on Sunday, but Luke and I may have some information that would be helpful to you," I told him.

"Say no more. I'll be right over," the Sheriff said.

In about a half hour he was at our door. Mom invited him into the kitchen and we all sat at the kitchen table. Mom had prepared coffee for herself and the Sheriff. I made hot chocolates for Luke and me.

That sounds really wholesome, but I hate coffee. I told Luke I didn't want to offer it to him because it might stunt his growth. He just laughed. "I love hot chocolate," he smiled.

Then the Sheriff launched into an update, "Since the foreman at the Bar K Bar ranch was killed, the state's issue with rustlers coming across the border from Wyoming is even getting the FBI's attention. Tell me about what you've heard," Sheriff Martinez said.

"Luke and his parents had a barbeque for the football team last night. Some of my friends and I went to the party. Robert Donaldson had declined an invitation, but he showed up late. His sister Brenda was there too, but she came on her own. Luke offered to "bury the hatchet" with Robert and let 'by-gones by by-gones.' We hoped that Robert might say something that would be a clue for us as to where the rustlers might be, something he hadn't shared with Sheriff Adams," I explained.

"As it turned out he said quite a bit to Emily. Brenda had mentioned to Emily that Robert was getting the reputation of a trouble maker and she thought it had to do with the older men he was running around with," Luke picked up the story.

I continued, "At the end of the party Robert followed me to the parking lot and blocked my path as I was returning to the house. I tried to engage him in conversation. We learned that he has been spending a lot of time with a gang of tough older men. He said he is bored with high schoolers. He even mentioned that they may have been 'running some cattle' before he quickly changed the subject. He didn't indicate that he was with them, but he seemed to know a lot about what they do. He said he likes to smoke and drink beer and he does it with them."

"That is very interesting," the sheriff said thoughtfully. "It corroborates our suspicions. Robert must have a good idea of where to find these guys, or at least where they hang out. I wonder how he would communicate with them, if that's the case," the sheriff speculated. "I'm surprised that after your run in with Robert and Luke putting the hit on him that he even came to the party."

"He had said to Brenda that he wouldn't come, but came later with his own car. He hit on Emily in the parking lot and tried to talk her into wanting a real man, instead of a loser, goodie, goodie high school sophomore, like marvelous me. I suppose that's why he didn't want to be sharing a ride with his sister," Luke explained. "It sounds to me like he knows these guys who killed the rancher."

"I believe you may be right. I'm glad you kids managed to talk to him in a place where he couldn't start too much trouble. This could have been dangerous, especially to Emily," the Sheriff chastised us somewhat gently in front of my Mother.

"I was just thinking about how crazy this was for these two kids to be anywhere near that guy," my mom joined in. I could see the growing anger in her eyes.

"Mom we were at a party hosted by Mr. and Mrs. Winslow. They were with us all the time and the team coaches were there. When Robert stopped me I made it clear that no still means no, and I knew Luke would be looking for me soon. Robert seemed angry at the rejection when he left, but we kept everything as civil as we could," I tried to paint a complete picture for my mom.

"All in all, you did a good job. I'm going to call Sheriff Adams. I think he needs to pick up Robert and question him more about where he finds these guys. It sounds like Robert's machismo led him to say more than he would have if he were any kind of experienced bad guy. Sounds like he's a 'wantabe,' a bully, and a bad egg. Good work. Emily I want you to continue staying in town. Luke you should be careful too, driving back and forth. I'll keep you posted."

We thanked Sheriff Martinez for coming over so promptly on Sunday and he left.

"I don't mind telling you two that as far as I'm concerned you, Emily, are grounded. Luke you have lost a lot of credibility with me, despite what the sheriff says. I question both of your judgement for being anywhere near Robert. The only place Emily will be going until these men are caught is to care for Hero. Now Luke, you should go," Mom expressed the anger I had seen in her eyes.

"I'm sorry, Mrs. Campbell," Luke said. "Emily was never in any danger with me and my dad keeping an eye on things. She was only with him for a couple minutes alone and she kept him talking with much poise."

"Alright, Luke. Run along now," was all Mom said.

Chapter 48

On Thursday, Sheriff Martinez came by our house right after I got home from school. Though Mom wasn't home yet, she would be soon. I invited him in.

"I wanted to talk to you before the news breaks. Sheriff Adams has arrested eight men in Garfield County. I drove up there on Monday and told him about you and Luke's discussions with Robert. He went and talked to Robert's dad right away and the two of them confronted Robert for information. Robert folded and it turns out he knew in what area these guys had a camp. Sheriff Adams and all his deputies, the FBI, and some state troopers moved into the area to encircle the camp. Then they had a helicopter pinpoint the men and were able to arrest all of them," he told me with such enthusiasm that he was short of breath. "I seem to recall Robert's dad mentioning a future for him in military school. He needs some discipline."

"That is great! I thank you so much," I said and on an impulse I put a big hug on the sheriff. He had an "aw shucks moment." I told him that I hadn't realized how intense life had become until this very moment when I felt such relief flow through me.

"We owe it all to you and Luke figuring out how to get the information out of Robert. I have a feeling he was beginning to realize he was aiding and abetting some pretty bad guys. We don't know yet which one shot the rancher, but we'll get it figured out. The FBI took over the prisoners and they really know how to do their work to establish a case. They may ask you to look at a line-up at some point," the sheriff said. I could see he was very happy to have his usual quiet, law abiding county free of these outlaws.

Just then Mom arrived. "I saw your car outside Sheriff. Is there something the matter?" Mom said as she rushed in.

"Just the opposite," I whooped. "They caught the rustlers!"

Mom sat down in a chair heavily. "Oh my lord. I've been so worried. I didn't want to make a prisoner of Emily, but every time she was out of my sight I could hardly stand it. It was a shock to have my teenage daughter shot at."

"I know, Mrs. Campbell," Sheriff Martinez said as he patted Mom's shoulder. "You've had way too much to deal with this year."

Just then both Maria and Miguel came running in without pausing. They had heard on the news about the rustlers being caught and saw the sheriff's car outside.

"We are so happy to hear that you have caught those really bad men," Maria gushed to the sheriff.

Miguel just shook the sheriff's hand over and over. He is a man of few words, especially when he feels emotional.

"I better call Luke. He should be home by now," I said. When I got hold of Luke I explained everything. I told him the sheriff had credited us with helping to get the information from Robert that broke the case.

"That is great," Luke said. "Now you'll have your freedom back to ride the trails and come out and ride in the mountains. You've been very brave through this ordeal, Emily."

"Thanks Luke. We did this as a team," I said. He said he needed to go tell his parents and we hung up.

When I returned Mom was thanking the Sheriff for his diligence and thoughtfulness through this ordeal.

Then the sheriff, Miguel, and Maria left us to absorb the glorious feeling of relief. Mom and I surrendered ourselves to the sofa. For some reason we just started laughing in unison.

"Honey, I can't imagine that the world will ever be able to throw more stress at us than it has this summer and fall. You have handled things like an adult. You are no longer grounded, but that doesn't mean I forgive you and Luke for taking on Robert like you did," Mom told me.

"Fair enough. But now we can just relax into a normal life and look forward to the Thanksgiving celebration that we promised to have with Miguel and Maria," I said.

"I had forgotten," Mom said sitting up in perky anticipation. "You are right. That will be in about six weeks. How time flies," she said laughing a laugh that expressed so much.

Chapter 49

When I saw Luke at school on Monday I literally let my pent up need for a ride in the mountains engulf him.

"Hi Luke. I need a long ride in the mountains. Are you free next Saturday?" I bubbled.

He laughed. "I don't know. I'll have to check. We had talked of packing into the mountains again for a few days before it gets too cold. I'm sure we could make room for one more."

"Oh, that would be the nuts. Will we miss some school days?" I wondered.

"Yes, we will leave early Friday morning and return late Tuesday. My brother, Ed, will be home on leave from the Army and we're going at his request," Luke said.

"I've not seen Ed since I was in middle school," I recalled.

"He's been in the Army for over two years," Luke reminded me.

"I never really knew him because of the age difference. Do you think he or your parents would mind? You should check with them," I said, trying to control my excitement. "I don't want to interfere with family time."

"I think they will be glad to have you. The principal is usually pretty good about absences this time of year because some of the kids are bringing in cattle from summer pasture or hunting with their dads. I was going to ride Star but I can ride a less fine steed," Luke pouted.

"I would be glad to have you ride Star. I could ride any horse. What kind of gear would I need?" I asked, covering my disappointment about Star.

"All you would need to bring would be your sleeping bag and whatever clothes you want. I know all your dad's gear went to the guy who bought your horse string. What if I brought the horse trailer to school on Thursday and took Hero on out to the ranch. Then you would have him there to ride on Friday," Luke said with eyes widening at his own genius.

"Fantastic! Hero is ready to try some real trail riding and it would be good for him. He even knows Star so he would fit right in. Do you tie or hobble at night?" I worried about what else I needed to train Hero to do.

"We usually run a high line picket among the trees and tie the horses at night. He'll get used to it pretty quick if we tie him with another horse he knows, like Star," Luke assured.

Just then the bell rang.

"I'll tie him at night this week several times so he gets the idea. Gotta run. I'm excited," I said as I headed for class.

"I can see that," Luke laughed again. "Talk to your mom and I'll talk to my parents."

I was so excited that I had trouble thinking about school. I decided not to say anything to anyone until this was set up for sure.

I was so ready to go on a pack trip with Dad in June. Now maybe I'll get a chance to go out in the mountains the way he and I had talked of doing during the summer. Things sure didn't work out as we had planned.

I'm glad Dad taught me so much about packing and I was glad to introduce Hero to such an adventure. I thought he'd take right to it.

When Mom came through the door after work, I was ready for her. "Mom, you'll never guess what I want to do this weekend," I exclaimed without even greeting her.

"Well, let me guess. Do you want to go clothes shopping and take a trip to the beauty parlor? We could have a girls' day out," Mom said with a grin.

"Oh, Mom. Don't be disappointed," I said, totally missing her joke. "I would love to do that with you the next Saturday. We have earned it.

But Luke is asking his parents if I could go with them on their family packing trip Friday through Tuesday. Luke will trailer Hero to the ranch so I can ride him. The rustlers kept us out of the mountains all summer, but now they are in jail and we have our freedom back," I said, employing all the persuasion I could conjure up.

With a chill I saw Mom's face slide into her old expression of fear that I saw so often after the shooting. She pulled out a chair and sat down.

"Mom, I'm sorry. What is the matter? What are you thinking?" I asked as I sat down beside her.

"You know my feelings about horses and mountains. This summer hasn't given me any confidence in my loved ones riding in lonely places. Your dad might not have died if he had gotten to a hospital sooner. And then you were shot at. I don't think I'm ready to have you go up there again," Mom said hesitantly. She seemed shaky.

"Mom, you know I love riding out in the wilderness. It isn't something I want to give up. My first thought was that this would have to be the trip that Dad and I planned to take together. I'll be safe," I said gently. I realized that maybe this was just too soon for Mom.

"I know it isn't something you will want to give up. You just took me by surprise. Let me think about this and try to get used to the idea," Mom said. She got up and put the tea kettle on. A hot drink was always the answer for her when she was afraid and needed to think.

"Mom, I'll be with Mr. and Mrs. Winslow, Luke, and Luke's brother Ed who is home on leave. I guess Ed requested that the family do this together. He has been away for a couple years," I explained realizing that, in my excitement, I hadn't given Mom any of these reassuring details. "I think Luke's dad often takes some of their ranch hands along too. And Luke said the principal is lenient about letting students off a few days of school this time of the year."

"Well, three days is quite a bit of time off school. I guess if we decide to do this you should try to get some of your assignments ahead this week," Mom gave me hope as she seemed to be thinking more positively.

"I'll have to work on tying Hero for longer periods this week, so he'll tie all night okay with the other horses," I eased into this additional requirement. "I'll have to take a sleeping bag and some clothes. They have all the camping equipment that we'll need."

I had studied many of the videos of Warwick Schiller training horses on YouTube. He is a very good trainer from Australia who trains gently, but by teaching the horse to accept the rider as the boss. That was where I learned about "hooking on."

I knew I could use his methods and have Hero comfortable with the tying. I've tied him a lot, but never overnight before. So I left for the barn to give Hero a lesson and to let Mom think about how much I deserve this trip.

The next morning Luke drove by the house early to pick me up and to give me the exciting news.

"Mom and Dad would welcome you on our trip. They said they wondered why they hadn't thought of it. Mom said she would be happy to have another female along for a change. I think a couple of the ranch hands are going, so we'll be seven. Dad said I could bring the trailer in on Thursday to get Hero after school. You could just ride out then and spend the night at our place. I'll bring you and Hero back then on Tuesday. Have I made your dreams come true?" Luke said while Mom sat at the breakfast table and took this all in.

"I have to tell you Luke, I'm uneasy about Emily riding in the mountains again. I guess I'm sort of shell shocked on that score," Mom said immovably.

Luke looked contrite. "I'm sorry Mrs. Campbell. I guess none of us thought of that. We should have been more sensitive. But Emily had assured me that this wouldn't be a done deal unless you agreed. Maybe it is too soon."

"I guess you are right. I am a bit super protective now. I know I shouldn't be unreasonable and that I shouldn't squelch all Emily's fun. I don't want to be a wet blanket. It's so soon after losing Colin," Mom seemed to be thinking out loud. "You are two energetic and talented teenagers who really thrive in the outdoors and with your horses. It's not that I'm ungrateful for that and for your family's willingness to include Emily."

"Do you want me to have my mom call you?" Luke asked.

"No. This is something I need to work out on my own. Let me think about it for a day or so," Mom said, standing to get ready for work.

I assured Mom that I really wanted to go, but I would respect her feelings and her decision. I wanted to remind her of my lost trip with Dad, but decided it wasn't the right time to revisit that again. Luke and I headed for school feeling a little hang-dog.

The next evening, after caring for Hero and eating dinner, Mom asked me to sit with her for a few minutes. I was really worried that she was going to tell me I couldn't go. I remembered my disappointment in the summer and hoped I didn't have to act all "mature" again.

"Emily," she said, "I know I have some fears now that don't seem too rational. I'm aware of that. So I went and talked to a psychologist at the hospital and explained to her our situation and asked her advice. She assured me that as hard as it might be for me to let you go, I'm going to have to let your world expand beyond my control and not feel fear. I trust in your skills and certainly in the judgement of Luke's parents. I'm going to let you go on this trip with them and I think you will have a wonderful time. That is what is most important to me."

"Oh thanks, Mom, I gushed. "I will be very careful. I understand where you are coming from and I appreciate your willingness to let me go. I'm very excited about it. I remember all the trips I made with Dad into the mountains. They're some of my best memories," I told her.

I called Luke to let him know I could go. I felt like I was going back to where I came from before Dad died, back to my happy place and my freedom.

Chapter 50

Luke came by the house after school on Thursday. I was all packed and ready to go. Mom wasn't home yet, so I left a note saying good-bye, that I would be careful and that I loved her. I worried about her being lonely while I was gone, so I had called Maria to tell her what was going on. She said she would spend the evening with Mom to soften the transition. We've hardly ever spent nights separated.

Luke and I went to the stable and loaded Hero and my tack into Luke's horse trailer. We were like two kids heading for vacation. It only took about thirty minutes to get to Luke's ranch.

We unloaded Hero and put him in a corral with the horses we would be using so they could all get to know each other. There was the usual squealing and kicking for a few minutes until everyone settled down. Luke's dad suggested we should use a high line picket to tie the horses tonight so Hero could get used to being tied that way with the other horses, but first we would leave them free for a while to settle.

When we went into the ranch house, Mrs. Winslow was busy packing food and making sure we had all the supplies we would need.

"Emily, I'm so glad you are going with us. You have no idea how glad I am to have another lady along," she greeted me.

"I'm excited out of my mind to be here," I told her. "Mrs. Winslow, I'm pretty good around a camp fire, so you should tell me anything you want me to do to help."

"I think, under the circumstances it would be fine for you to call me Betsy. We are almost like family. Your mom is certainly my best friend," she said.

"And Luke is my best friend, Betsy," I said trying it out. We both laughed.

After a nice dinner, Luke, Mr. Winslow, and I went out to put the horses on the high line picket. We watered them first and then tied them. Their horses were used to this and were quiet. Hero paced in a circle for a few minutes trying to figure out why he couldn't walk away, but soon he accepted this new circumstance. We tied him on the end with Star against him because that way one of the strange horses couldn't kick him.

Back at the house we sat on the porch and visited for a while. It was decided we would turn in early and be ready to go to work at 5:00 AM. Luke and I walked down one more time to check the horses on the picket.

They were behaving like seasoned trail horses, though Hero was less relaxed than the others. After a long days ride tomorrow, he'd probably be happy to spend time on the picket line by evening.

As we walked back to the house, Luke took my hand. We were both quiet. I was a little uncomfortable with this new level of intimacy between us. I had never before slept over night at his place or been so close a part of his family. And this was all new going on an adventure without my dad. He was much on my mind. I wanted to prove my worth as a contributing member.

"You okay?" Luke asked.

"Oh yes," I told him.

"You seem kind of quiet," he pressed.

"I just want to be able to prove a good person to have along on a trip like this. I've never actually lived with another family before," I tried to explain.

"You'll do fine. You know about all that has to be done. Just remember, most of the time we will just be riding and having fun," Luke comforted. "Since your dad's last trip ended so tragically, are you uneasy about the similarity to what we are doing?"

"That is a good question that I hadn't thought about. How about you? You had a real bad experience on that trip," I questioned.

"Well, I returned to the mountains with my family just before school started for a couple days. I'm fine. But you've jumped into this without thinking about some of the underlying anxiety. Should we talk to my mom and dad about it?" he asked.

"No, I don't think so. We don't want to do anything that ruins everyone's excitement about going, especially Ed's enjoyment. This hadn't even surfaced for me until you expressed it. You are probably right; it is in the back of my mind. Let's enjoy ourselves and agree to talk between us about any uneasiness that comes up. Okay?" I requested.

"Sure. That is a good plan. We'll enjoy our freedom from the threat that has hung over us and focus on loving the mountains," he agreed.

Now, for some reason, I began to feel better. Maybe I was feeling some anxiety, but I felt better now realizing what was nagging at me. Once again I had to appreciate Luke as a friend.

When we got back to the house, Mrs. Winslow, Betsy, walked me to their small guest room to make sure I had everything I needed. She gave me a hug good night, which startled me, but I liked it. Then she left and closed the door. I was soon asleep.

CHAPTER 51

THE NEXT MORNING we were all busy by 5:00. Luke and I ran to the barn to feed the horses that would be going on the trip. They had all done fine through the night on the high line picket. We put them in a corral and fed them and made sure of their water supply.

Then we had a fast breakfast and Luke, Ed, and Mr. Winslow went to load the pack saddles. Betsy and I finished packing some of the final packs of food. We each had our personal saddle bag and slicker, just as Dad had provided to our guests back in in the spring.

By 8:00 o'clock we were ready to ride. It was a beautiful morning, somewhat cold, but that just felt refreshing. We all wore jackets that we would tie onto our saddles later in the morning.

As we rode away from the ranch Mr. Winslow took the lead, Luke and Ed each led a pack horse, and Betsy and I rode along visiting at the tail end. It was a beautiful sight to see these lovely horses with a background of the looming mountains and the blue sky. I could only have been happier if Dad had been with us. Mr. Winslow had decided not to take any ranch hands. He said we had plenty of experienced help.

We rode steadily all morning, stopping only to water the horses when we crossed streams. We each had our canteen for quenching our thirst from the saddle.

Hero settled into a nice stride that matched Betsy's horse. He seemed to like getting out beyond the confines of the stable. Hero was proving to be a good trail horse as he watched his footing and took in all that was around him. It did often seem like he was drawing from some deep genetic mustang harmony with the land around. It reminded me of when Tom Norton said some distant mustang blood might be why Hero had survived hunger.

We took a mid-morning break and dismounted to eat snacks from our saddle bags while the horses grazed for a while. I felt so lazy in the warm sunshine lying in the grass and holding on to Hero's reins. Luke joined me and I also enjoyed seeing Star thriving in this natural state. Horse and man, or woman, equals a special bond.

"How ya' doin'," Luke asked as he sat near me.

"I'm in heaven. There is just no other way to express it. Your family is so nice to include me. I'm bringing Dad with me as though this was the trip we had planned to have together. Nothing will ever be able to take that away from me," I expressed dreamily.

"I'm glad you are here. I suppose that sounds trite, but I am glad, but I can't wax poetic like you do. I would just sound too mushy. But you say things that get right to the bone and meaning of a thing. Are you sure you don't want to be a writer," Luke grinned at me.

"Actually today I think I would love to be a writer. I feel the beauty of nature just bubbling inside me. This is bliss," I laughed.

Betsy left her horse with Mr. Winslow and came to join us. "What are you too sounding so serious and deep about?" she asked.

"I was just telling Luke about how joyous I feel being out here like this and how grateful I am to you and Mr. Winslow," I explained.

Betsy sat down beside me and I sat up to receive her hug. "You are the daughter I dreamed of when I ended up with these two cowboys," she teased.

"Hey, Mom, you can't talk about your football hero son like that," Luke said, posturing like a big football star. "When I win a scholarship to college based on my brute strength and lion like courage, you will be so glad for such a formidable son."

"You are right," Betsy agreed. "You are my lion and your brother my soldier champion." Then she rejoined Mr. Winslow.

Ed soon came to join us. He is sort of quiet, but I hope to draw him out some as we get to know each other better.

"Are you enjoying the ride?" I asked.

"You'll never know how much," he said, smiling and turning, with his arm raised to the heavens, in a three hundred and sixty degree circle paying homage to the heavens. "This trip is at my request, you know."

"Good choice. I hope you don't mind a stranger tagging along," I sort of apologized.

"Stranger than what?" he said laughing. I began to feel that his personality was a lot like Luke's, but he was just less outgoing.

"How long will you be on leave?" I inquired.

"I have a month and then I'll be transferred to Germany for a year. I'll probably get out of the Army at the end of that year and head back to the Rockies. I really miss this place," he warmed to the conversation.

Just then Mr. Winslow called out, "Time to mount up if we want to reach our destination, set up camp, and eat before dark. Riders up!"

We made sure we had everything picked up. The men checked the pack horses' cinches to make sure they were tight. We all tightened our saddles again and mounted up.

As I sat on Hero ready to go I was proud as I looked at Star and saw how fine he looked. Luke looked just right on him. I was proud, too, of Hero. He felt willing and not tired at all. He was moving in unison with me as though he was tuned into my leg pressures and weight shifts. Taking a long ride like this gave us a good chance to learn the feel of each other as the demands of the trail shift and change. Dad did a great job of picking Star and we were lucky to fall into having Hero. Once again I felt that Hero was saving me, just as I had saved him.

We had a long ride that day to reach a high lake where the men wanted to fish tomorrow. I had fun riding with each member of the group and visiting with them. I got to know both Ed and Mr. Winslow better than I had before. Luke and I rode together most of the morning. We liked ranging somewhat away from the group when we weren't confined to a narrow trail, as when crossing a high valley.

Mr. Winslow and Ed seemed content to lead the pack horses. They've done this so much that exploring doesn't seem to tempt them. Betsy is happy to follow along on the trail.

I had chances to ride alone, too. I wanted to have time to separate Hero from the other horses so he didn't feel dependent on being with them. Horses are herd animals and some horses get so they are frightened of being away from the group. Hero seemed very independent and he liked wandering around.

Sometimes I wanted to feel how he was moving when he wasn't required to keep pace with the others. He isn't as conditioned as the other horses because of the set back of malnutrition. I needed to tune into whether he was tiring. But he seemed relaxed. His stride was still long and ground covering. He didn't seem worse for the wear.

I also enjoyed riding where I didn't have to talk. I liked to hear the nature around me. The sound of the breeze in the leaves, the birds and the squirrels, the impact of the horses' hooves on the rocks or dirt, the sounds of running water, all spoke to me. I also wanted to sense when any of those sounds got quiet and I heard a foreign sound. All these things were part of tuning in to the nature around me. Riding with my friends wasn't noisy or intrusive, but I wondered sometimes if I might miss a message from nature.

A little later we had a pleasant lunch break sitting on a high spot with a magnificent view. I liked the high places better than the deep, dark valleys. We made sure the horses got to graze and drink.

Tonight we would hobble the Winslow's horses when we got into camp so they could wander and graze. They were all trained to hobbles. We would tie Hero to Star so he could follow Star and get used to travel within the confines of the hobbles. Mr. Winslow would then put some hobbles on Hero to let him get used to them. Then on the other days he too could move around camp to graze more freely before the string was tied for the night.

About four o'clock we arrived at the lake and set up camp. As we sat around our campfire that evening, after a dinner prepared with teamwork, we had a quiet conversation that reflected the healthy fatigue that a long day on horseback creates.

"When I was on the trip with Emily's dad, we sang around the fire at night. Emily had warned me that Andy couldn't sing, but that it didn't dampen his enthusiasm. She was sure right. I could see the guests giving each other secret smiles at his efforts. He was truly enthused with hearty singing," Luke told everyone.

Before we settled in to sleep, we brought the horses in and put them on the picket line. Soon their heads were hanging low and some of them dozed. Always one or two stayed more alert to watch over the group.

The men crawled into their tent and Betsy and I got into our tent. It was tempting to sleep outside, but the nights were getting very cold and we were all glad for the shelter. The camp grew very quiet very quickly. I fell asleep listening to the forlorn howl of a coyote.

CHAPTER 52

THE NEXT MORNING we were all out of our sleeping bags early. There was just something about smelling early morning coffee brewing while watching the sun rise over the peaks. It was jacket temperature and we danced around waiting for the fire to boil the water.

After lingering near the warming fire we tended to some tasks. Betsy was busy seeing to the preparation for breakfast, Mr. Winslow was caretaker of the fire, Ed searched for more fire wood. Luke and I went to release the horses from the picket with their hobbles on so they too could get breakfast and get a drink at the stream.

Soon we all gathered again around the fire. We sipped our coffee or hot chocolate (the preference for Luke and me). Betsy started cooking a skillet of bacon, which really smelled good. Mr. Winslow tended to the flap jacks (also known as pancakes). I assisted Betsy with a second pair of willing hands.

We sat around the fire on logs we dragged up last night and the conversation picked up as we were now feeling awake and anxious to start our day.

"Emily, the boys and I are going to fish the lake. You want to join us?" Mr. Winslow asked.

"Hmm. I'm not much of a fisherman. It seems like a very smelly sport," I told him. "I think I'll spend some time exploring the area on Hero."

"You just can't get enough of riding, can you?" Luke commented on my passion.

"No, I sure can't," I replied. "I need to make up for the time I was grounded."

"I'm going to take advantage of the beautiful surroundings and do some sketching," Betsy chimed in. "I get so few days when I can just sit down and take it all in. Why don't you each take what you want from our lunch supplies and carry them to wherever you are when hunger strikes you mid-day."

"That sounds like a good idea," Mr. Winslow agreed. "Ed thinks he can catch the biggest trout, but he doesn't understand the tremendous advantage of my years of experience knowing where those beasties like to lounge about."

"Well, now the challenge is on the table," Ed said. He soon gathered his fishing gear and prepared to head for the lake with his lunch slung over his shoulder.

"Well, I'm tempted to explore with Emily, but I feel the family honor must be carried forward by the youngest fisherman, who will carry the honors into the next generation. I better take up the gauntlet and meet the challenge that has been thrown at my feet," Luke declared. "After I've caught the biggest trout, I'll ride with Emily tomorrow."

"What makes you think you will be the one to represent us to the next generation?" Ed asked Luke.

"Shoot. You don't even have a girlfriend and I've captured the heart of the prettiest girl in Colorado," Luke responded.

Ed gave Luke a playful slug and the two of them headed off toward the lake. I helped Betsy clean the breakfast dishes and repack the supplies. She pulled her sketch pad from her saddle bag and ambled to a nearby rock to sit and study her subject.

After visiting for a while with Star, I caught Hero who was trying to nose into where I was giving Star attention. Hero needed conditioning more than Star did, but maybe I'd take a ride on Star tomorrow, depending on what Luke did.

I brushed Hero good and checked his shoes. Then I put my tack on him and started wandering along the valley floor. Since I was in no hurry, I didn't mount Hero, but just led him along in a leisurely stroll. Periodically I let him graze where there was especially nice grass. I searched the woods around me to try to spot the activities of any wildlife.

After a while I mounted and continued moving up the valley. I wanted to work on Hero's muscles by doing some climbing, so we headed up the trail toward the pass above us. I spotted birds, squirrels, a fox, and some coyotes. I saw a lot of deer tracks and even once I spotted some elk tracks.

I felt so at peace. My mind wandered to a review of all that had happened to me this past summer. So much in such a short time had certainly changed my life. I felt relief that I'd survived without a major breakdown of courage. It had really all fallen on Mom to hold things together for us. I hoped I would learn to be as strong a woman as she was.

When Hero seemed to notice the steep grade, I gave him a breather. The morning passed fleetingly as I dreamed my way up the mountain. When my stomach reminded me of the hours since breakfast, I got off and led Hero until I found a level spot with some big rocks to sit on and nice grass for him.

I didn't think Hero would run off, but I slipped the hobbles on him just in case. I sure didn't want to have to walk back. It would give him more chance to get used to them, though he seemed to have figured them out pretty quickly. I pulled my saddle off and put it by the rock where I could lean back on it while I ate and I took in the view.

It was so peaceful here that I drowsed a little after eating. In a while Hero hopped close to me as though he was ready to get those darn impediments off his front legs. I packed everything back into my saddle bags and, just as I got ready to saddle him, I saw a hiker coming up the trail.

He looked like a really seasoned hiker with a small day bag on his back. His steady strides up the hill told me this was a man who was in good condition for the mountains. I threw Hero's saddle on and tightened the girth. Then I took the hobbles off and tied them to the saddle.

"Hello," the hiker said as he arrived at my resting spot. "Nice looking horse. You're smart to ride rather than walk up this brute of a mountain."

"I couldn't agree more," I replied. "Let the horse build the muscles."

He laughed and dropped his day bag to take out his water and have a drink.

"Nice country up here. You ride it a lot?" he asked.

"Every chance I get," I told him.

"You must know the country well," he said.

"Been here all my life. My dad was a packer until he was killed and he taught me all he knew about the wilderness," I told him as he repacked his water and came over to sit on a rock.

"I'm from up near Cheyenne, but I think I heard about a packer having a fatal accident down this way. That your dad?" he asked.

"I'm afraid so," I replied. I policed my area again to make sure I hadn't left any trash and moved to mount Hero. As I did this guy moved over to me and took hold of my arm, pulling me away from Hero.

"I believe I know just who you are," he said assertively pushing his face to mine. My heart leaped. Who was this and what was happening! The rustlers were in jail and I didn't know anyone else that would threaten me.

I tried to pull away but he shoved me down. "What do you want?" I yelled at him. "Just who do you think you are?"

"I'll tell you who I am," he spat in my face. "You're the little lady who got my men put in jail and you're going to be their ticket to freedom."

"What are you talking about?" I cried.

"That stupid sheriff in Garfield County put it out that he caught all the rustlers. I got news for you. He didn't get the brains of the outfit. I thought that was you riding up the trail yesterday with a group. But now you have verified that you are that little bitch who got stupid Robert to talk. Well, you're going to pay now."

He jerked me to my feet and I tried to fight him off, but he was too strong for me. He pulled out some zip ties and tied my hands in front of me. While he was doing that he noticed my cell phone in my pocket. He took it and threw it as far as he could.

"Why'd you do that? My mom gave me that phone. There isn't any reception here anyway," I complained to him.

"Yeah, there's no reception but phones can be traced. You think I'm dumb? Till that one is traced we'll be long gone from here," he growled.

Boy, was I scared. I thought all this fear thing was behind me. I was angry, too. My first thought was of Mom and how she would worry if I didn't come back on time. She would blame herself for whatever this was that was happening to me.

He walked over to Hero and lengthened my stirrup leathers to his legs. Damn, I thought, he is going to take Hero. Hero snorted and backed away from the guy. My captor jerked the reins and violently backed Hero to punish him. Hero snorted again, but didn't fight the guy. Poor Hero. I was so glad he behaved compliantly so the guy wouldn't rough him up any more.

"What do you think you are doing?" I asserted myself again. "I'm with a party that will soon be looking for me."

"They won't find you where I'm taking you, so shut up," he spoke very roughly, but hadn't hurt me.

I ran for the trees, but he soon overtook me and tackled me. Man it hurt when I hit the ground with him on top of me. He jerked me up and dragged me back to Hero. He tied his back pack onto my saddle and untied Hero's lead rope from the saddle. He hooked the rope through my zip ties. Then he mounted Hero.

"Okay, now I ride and you walk," He growled. He started up the trail forcing me to walk along beside Hero. Soon he had both Hero and me puffing. I fell a couple times when he jerked the rope. Fortunately, he stopped long enough for me to regain my feet and then on we went.

Though I was feeling numb and scared out of my wits, I tried to keep thinking and paying attention to where we were going. As we neared the top of the pass, I realized for the first time that if we crossed over we would be near where Luke and I were shot at. Our ranch was down the other side.

This must be where the sheriff thought they were scaring us away from their hideout and where the sheriff and the helicopter had searched.

Truly this guy must be part of the rustler gang. From what he had said, I assumed he was going to hold me to bargain for his men. That didn't sound good to me at all. The sheriff wouldn't release his men. That was absurd. I knew I was in deep trouble.

I also knew that it wouldn't be long until the Winslows realized I should be back to camp. I guessed that they would assume I might have fallen or been hurt and they would try to track Hero. They knew I was going to explore the valley and they would be able to pick up Hero's tracks.

However, they would have to go for help when they realized that I was really gone and that would take hours. Surely they would split up and some search, while others went for help. This sure was a bad year for camping in these mountains with Wyoming thieves in residence, I thought. I was sure the sheriffs had relaxed their vigilance now that they thought they'd caught all the bad guys.

Geez, I knew I was really in for it.

CHAPTER 53

I DIDN'T KNOW how many hours passed, but the sun was getting low on the horizon. We had crossed the top of the pass, and moved northeastward higher into the mountains. I had lost count of the times we had climbed and descended.

All I knew was that I couldn't go on much longer. I was so tired. Though we stopped at several small streams to drink hastily, I was constantly thirsty. I was hungry. And I was scared more than I had ever been before in my life. I also knew I had to keep my wits about me. I reasoned that if he was going to try to use me to get his cohorts out of jail, it wouldn't make sense for him to kill me.

We had turned from any trail some time ago and were climbing to the base of some cliffs. Finally, he stopped and dismounted. He led Hero to the base of the cliff.

Poor Hero looked exhausted. This wasn't the conditioning I had in mind for him.

Our captor went to some bushes and started pulling on them. To my surprise a door swung open. He had hidden a cave opening with bushes nailed to the door. He pulled me forward and pushed me ahead of him through the door. Behind the door was a fairly large cave. It was even big enough for Hero. He led Hero in and he lit some torches. Then he pulled the door closed.

No wonder the helicopter couldn't find their hideout!

There was a pool of water to the rear of the cave with fresh water trickling in from above. He led Hero to the water and Hero took a long drink. Then he pulled Hero's tack off and turned him loose. There was nowhere for Hero to run away to. There were some bales of hay stacked to the side and he fed Hero some hay. I was relieved he was taking care of Hero.

He saw me observing this as I sat leaning on a wall of the cave. "Might as well care for this horse. He'll bring a better price if his ribs aren't stickin' out when I sell 'im."

So he planned to steal Hero and sell him. I can't let that happen, but I could only sit quiet and see how this was going to play out. I decided it was best to be cooperative and friendly to see if he relaxed his guard. I had to figure out what his plan was.

"You goina' feed and water me too? I'm mighty hungry after being drug up and down the mountains all afternoon," I said.

"Just shut up. You'll find out soon enough what I'm going to do with you. We got a truck comin' to move a batch of cattle near here tomorrow. I'm goin' to ride this nag out tomorrow and put him on that truck. Then I'll head out of here. I'll leave you here to starve or be exchanged. If the damn sheriff doesn't want to cooperate Mother Nature will take care of you in time. You've been nothin' but a pain in my ass since the first day I saw you checking the fence at your ranch. We got run off by some traffic on that road, but we was goin' to go back and git your horses."

Geez, just like that he had given me the plan. I didn't expect it to be so easy. I was relieved that he didn't seem to be planning to kill me, at least for now.

Eventually someone would track into these mountains looking for me. Our trail from today would be very hard to follow since we spent so much time traveling across rock shelves, but Hero's shoes probably left some sign. I had tried to break some branches on bushes as we traveled. Surely a good tracker could find me. The first rule of survival had taught me that I must remain calm.

"What's your name?" I asked. "If I want to speak to you, I need to know your name."

"You don't need to be talkin' to me. Just shut up," he growled.

"But sir," I said, looking panicky. "I need to go to the bathroom."

"Yeah, I guess it's been a long time. Just go back in that dark corner over there. I'll not be lookin' at you. Call me Shifty if you think you just have to open your trap," he directed.

Fortunately, he took the cuffs off my wrists which were rubbed raw. I guessed that meant there was no way I could escape the cave. As I moved into the dark corner I tried to take in every aspect of the cave to familiarize myself. It was cold and damp and with my fatigue I could already feel my muscles stiffening up.

There was a dipper by the pool. I dipped some water and rinsed my hands and wrists. I also splashed some of the cool water on my face and took a long drink from the dipper.

"Well, ain't you the fussy one," Shifty grunted as I returned to my chosen sitting place. He was starting a fire and I would be close enough to ward off the chill. I was glad for that.

My fatigue and hunger were making it hard to focus on anything else. In the cave's sanctuary I was beginning to feel my fear relax, but I reminded myself to try to keep alert.

Shifty opened a big can of beans and a can of beer. He began to heat the beans over the fire. The fire was small enough that the cave would absorb the smoke and it wouldn't escape outside to draw attention. Too bad.

I ate the plate of beans Shifty gave me. I enjoyed watching Hero eat contentedly. That horse was sure unflappable. He seemed to be accepting his transformation to 'cave horse' as long as there was good hay. His shoes were noisy on the cave floor, so it would be easy to keep track of where he was from the sounds, even in the dark. I was becoming more alert to different sensory inputs that I would need when it was dark, as it would be when the torches burned out.

After I ate I began to fall asleep. Soon Shifty went to his supplies and pulled out a blanket he threw to me. Then he put the cuffs back on me and looped a chain through my cuffs and clipped it into a ring in the wall high enough that I couldn't reach it. I guessed that would keep me from escaping through the night. Shifty seemed to have no worries as he sat by the fire smoking. Neither Hero nor I would be able to get out of this cave.

I slept fitfully through the night. When I would waken due to the cold it was really dark and scary. I thought at least once I could hear something moving in the cave and decided there might be an opening where some bats had come in. At least an opening would provide fresh air.

I soon realized that Hero was standing near me. I could feel his warm breath so I knew he had his head hanging above me. My heart warmed to that horse. I had to think we would get out of this whole mess without either of us hurt. I knew I was in a dangerous situation, but I couldn't let myself think anything, but that Hero and I would be okay. I knew by now the Winslow family would be in rescue mode. I hoped someone rode for the sheriff and others had tried to track me.

I hoped Betsy had gone to be with my mother. I just couldn't let myself think about my mother right now. It was just too sad to think of her going through something like this. I knew she would be in terrible pain. She was probably afraid something like what happened to Dad had happened to me. I knew she would blame herself. I was so sorry. I tried to think positive thoughts about my safety and send them over the miles to her.

Once Shifty woke up and he built the fire up enough to help warm me. I decided he wasn't all bad.

Early in the morning I awakened to see Shifty putting out some hay for Hero again. Hero went to the water and drank. Then he went right to his hay. That horse would always appreciate food.

"I guess you need to go to the back of the cave again," Shifty said as he unchained me from the wall and removed the cuffs again. I took advantage to get some pressing bladder relief. I drank at the pool again and splashed my face.

Shifty wasn't paying any attention to me so I wandered around the cave. I noticed where some light was coming in around the door and through an opening high above in the roof of the cave. The water that trickled into the pool was draining in a small stream on down deeper into the cave system, so the water was fresh. There was hay and supplies for several people and their horses to stay in the cave for some time. No doubt this had been the place where some of the rustlers had stayed while they were watching the area for livestock to steal and apparently keeping some track of me from time to time.

I looked back on that day when I found the tampered fence and almost wished I had never taken that ride. Fate seemed to have tied me to the rustlers that day when they guessed I had reported the fence damage, and again when I got so close to their hiding place with Luke.

I still felt that Shifty wasn't going to have a reason to kill me, so I knew that somehow I would get out of this fix. I just hoped that he wouldn't sell and ship Hero to some distant place where I could never find him.

Shifty seemed to be preparing to leave. I would soon find out what my fate was to be. He saddled Hero and packed up some of the things around the cave.

"I'm going to ride out of here now. We'll ship the cattle and this horse tonight. I'll contact Sheriff Adams and offer him our deal to get the release of my boys. If he lets them go, I'll tell him where to find you. If not, I'll be long gone and those boys can rot in jail, while you rot here from starvation," he told me.

I bit my tongue. I didn't want to say anything to antagonize him, so I just stared at him.

"I'll chain this door shut from the outside so you can't get out of here. No need for cuffs. There is plenty of water and enough food for you to survive for a week. There is enough wood stacked over there to keep you warm at night. If you've eaten all the food you'll know that the sheriff didn't cooperate and this will be your tomb. Doesn't matter to me either way what happens to you," he said.

I went to Hero and patted his neck. I whispered to him, "I'll find you Hero. I promise I'll find you."

Shifty came over and tied some things on the saddle and then he jerked Hero's bridle and led him to the opening. When he led Hero out,

I moved to the door and noticed the blue sky and sunshine for possibly the last time. Shifty slammed the door closed and I could hear him chaining the door shut.

The fear slammed into me as I heard Hero's footsteps recede. I felt buried alive. It was very dark. The pain I felt for losing Hero and the fear I felt for my mom were devastating. I lay down on my sleeping pallet and cried until I could cry no more. What a strange way for a fifteen year old to die. I had such wonderful anticipation for my life and I sure felt sad to think it might end in this lonely cave.

Chapter 54

As soon as my tears dried, I went to the supplies in the cave. I found a flashlight, but wouldn't use it unless I was really scared. I wanted to preserve the batteries. The food supply "for a week" looked pretty meager. It was all canned goods, so I would have to eat some cold to preserve my wood supply. Thank goodness for the good water supply which shouldn't fail. I put all the blankets I could find on my pallet anticipating cold nights. I'd have to use them despite their bad smell.

I tried to focus on the things I'd need to do to survive. Working on something helped to avoid dark thoughts and panic. Pushing, pulling, and beating on the door revealed no weakness there. Searching the cave I found no other outlet.

I sat down and ate half a can of beans cold. Boy, I'll be sick of beans. There was some soup and I could add water and heat that when I really needed something warm. I sure would miss my morning hot chocolate.

Missing something brought Mom to mind again. I just couldn't let myself think about her. It was too painful. I wondered about Luke, too. What must he be doing and what must he think? I knew it was Sunday and I felt sure the Winslow family would have initiated a search for me.

I imagined how things were going with the search. The search would follow my trail as long as possible, but might be lost in the rocks. However, they would at least know what direction I went. Hopefully, they'd be able to follow my tracks at least to the point where Shifty rode Hero and I walked. They would be able to see that I was okay to there, but was forced by someone to walk as a captive.

Maybe Sheriff Adams would question the jail birds and find out they had a leader at large. Or, of course, Sheriff Adams would soon hear from Shifty about the deal he wanted. I hoped that was the case because that would surely spark a large search for both him and me. I guessed Shifty could get out of state pretty fast. That made me hope the searchers concentrated on the mountains where I disappeared first. I sure hoped that would be the case.

Bottom line, I knew I'd be found, but how long would it take.

It was a long day sitting and pacing in the gloomy cave. Little light filtered in, but it was enough that I could see what I was doing. I used a stone to make scratches on the cave wall to mark the number of days after Shifty left. Well, it was only day one, so one mark. I wished I had my homework or a book, but I knew I couldn't waste the flashlight.

I found myself worrying more and more about my mom. I thought about all my friends. I bet many of them would soon be out searching for me. I pictured Luke and Sandi riding to my rescue, as they somehow would find this cave.

I really felt hungry and knew I was going to have to discipline myself to not eat the food too fast. I rummaged through Shifty's supplies once again to see if I had missed anything and I did find an unopened box of cereal. Hoorah! Variety in my diet. I poured a big bowl and put water on it. That was lunch. There was also some instant coffee that I'd save for tomorrow morning if I had a fire then to keep warm. There was no hot chocolate.

The day seemed endless until I noticed that my little bit of light was fast fading. Oh, how I dreaded the hours of deep darkness. With nothing to do I could only lie in my blankets and think.

I thought this must be like a torture for jail prisoners. I wondered how Hero was fairing and I worried about him. I hoped he didn't end up again in an abusive situation. I regretted that I would lose my saddle, breastplate, and bridle from Mom and Dad, but it was more painful to lose Hero. I thought I was getting depressed by thoughts of my losses. I should be thinking positive things.

So I started listing all the people I'd met since moving to town who have contributed to my quality of life. There was Sandi, Becky, and Beth at the stable. I thought about Miss Baker, Morton, Peter, Shauna, and Levy and our science project success. Of course, I knew Maria and Miguel would be standing by Mom and helping her. Hopefully, Sheriff Martinez and the State Police would be helping in the search for me. Luke was in my thoughts all the time. I guess the effect was like counting sheep because the next thing I knew I had awakened in the dark.

Small noises now and then in the cave told me I had the company of a small animal or two. It was probably mice. I heard the dripping water. To my relief I did not hear anything that caused me alarm. I was pretty safe in my cave jail.

There were bears and mountain lions in these mountains, but there wasn't any reason for them to have any interest in me, plus they couldn't get to me. I thought about the deer that would be wandering around outside and my mouth watered at the thoughts of a deer steak. It was warm enough under all my blankets so I just lay there until I dozed off again.

The next time I awoke I could see light beginning to filter in around the door and from the hole in the roof. I thought I could hear some birds singing. Morning was welcome. Deciding to build a fire, I got some of the wood and stacked it in a tent shape. I rummaged in the supplies for matches, but alas, Shifty hadn't left me anything to light a fire. It would be all cold food and no instant coffee. I refused to let thoughts of when the food ran out and winter started to settle in invade my mind. I couldn't think about that yet.

I hoped Sheriff Adams had a rescue organized so I didn't have to spend a whole week in this tomb, as Shifty called it.

The next two days were repeats of the first day I spent in this depressing jail. I felt so hungry that once I ate a whole can of beans. Discipline seemed to be weakening as I lost weight and struggled more and more with fear. I knew what I must do to endure this torture and survive, but it was getting harder and harder. I tried to recall all the things my dad had ever said to me about courage and determination. I hoped I had what it would take.

Then Wednesday evening I heard new sounds outside the cave. It sounded like a horse walking around. Oh, the relief! My rescuers had arrived! I started calling for help as loud as I could hoping they wouldn't ride by, not seeing the cave entrance. I yelled and yelled, but when I listened I didn't seem to be having any effect.

Finally, I slumped down onto my pallet exhausted. If there was someone out there they had ridden past. Or maybe I was beginning to imagine things. I cried myself to sleep.

The next morning I tried to keep distracted with my routine of getting breakfast, marking the wall to count the days, and remembering happy memories from when I was free. It was like becoming a convict who was dulled to a narrow existence.

Once I thought I could hear a horse again, but this time I didn't respond. I knew it must be my imagination. The sounds of shuffling footsteps and a snort or two had to be in my head.

I was beginning to spend a lot of time on my pallet in a stupor. By my calculation this was the fifth day of my captivity. I had to wonder if Shifty was having any luck making a deal. I hoped he would honestly tell the sheriff where I was, but then I would realize that the sheriff would never make a deal with him.

My hope had to rest with my friends, family, and Sheriff Martinez searching for me with the State Police. Search and rescue was probably involved, too. They're the best. I tried to imagine what would ever take searchers so far from where I was known to have been. Then I realized I might just starve to death in this cave. Damn! It made me mad.

I tried working on the door again. I thought maybe I could dig under it, but soon found the hard dirt only led to bed rock. I worked on the hinges, but they were heavy and strong. I had no tools.

Then about mid-day, according to my calculation, I thought I heard voices. I stood with my head to the door and again thought I heard something. It also sounded like I could hear the stamping of horses.

I started yelling for help again. This time I knew for certain that I had heard something pretty close. I kept yelling and yelling for help. Then I knew I heard Luke's voice.

"Emily is that you? Keep yelling. Where are you?" he was calling. Soon other voices joined his.

"I'm in a cave. The opening is covered with bushes. It's at the base of the cliff," I yelled.

"Keep calling. You are sounding louder," he called to me again.

"I'm in a cave at the base of the cliff. The opening is behind the bushes," I called again.

"Emily, I've found the opening. It is chained. Hang on. I think some of the search and rescue people may have a cutter. Hang on," Luke sounded like he was right outside now.

"Oh, Luke, is that really you. I need your help so bad," I mumbled.

"Keep talking to me," Luke said. "Are you okay?"

"I'm awfully hungry," I called to him. "Otherwise I'm okay."

I heard Luke's wonderful laugh. "Stand tall. We have food," he said to me.

"Emily, this is Sandi. Are you okay? We've been so worried about you," Sandi called to me.

"I'm okay. It is so wonderful to hear your voice. I've been locked in this cave," I told her.

"Luke said you are hungry so we're getting a fire going. When we get you out of there we'll have hot food," she said. "It is so good to hear you want to eat."

I slumped down by the door suddenly very exhausted. I realized that I have not really relaxed since I ran into Shifty. I said a hearty thanks to Dad for being with me. In my darkest hours I could hear his voice encouraging me as he had always done. And I was so grateful to hear my friends' voices. My trust in them was justified.

"Emily, the rescue team is bringing up some cutters. We'll have you out of there in about an hour," Luke had come back to update me on progress.

"I'm so tired, Luke. I'm right by the door and I'm listening to your voice even if I can't talk," I told him.

"That's okay. We are all right here," Luke said in his gentle assuring way.

"Luke, how's my mom?" I said softly.

"She's been very worried, but she knows there have been many volunteers looking for you and that you would be found. She'll be so happy to see you," Luke explained.

True to his word, after about an hour I could hear men working on the door chain. It was dark now, but they said they had plenty of flashlights. When I heard the crack of the chain giving I was overwhelmed with relief. The door moved slowly and there stood Luke, Sandi, and Becky with the search and rescue guys.

Luke stepped in and sat down beside me and put his arms around me. I think I might have briefly passed out, because the next thing I knew the rescue team was carrying me to the side of the fire and putting me down on some sleeping bags.

Sandi brought me a hot drink. The men urged me to sip it slowly. Their EMT member checked my heart and questioned me to determine my state of mind.

When he was done he said, "She'll be alright. She is just exhausted. We should all camp here tonight before trying to move her down the mountain. We'll have an ambulance at the road."

It wasn't long until Becky came by with some hot cereal they had made. It was like eating paste, but it seemed delicious to me. They made me eat slowly to give my system a chance to recover. They were like hens watching over me.

There must have been fifteen people gathered around me preparing to camp for the night. I felt so safe again and so thankful to all these people. They had radioed that I was found and through the night other small groups, who had been searching in the area, gathered in our camp.

Later in the evening I was feeling so much better. I was so happy and could hardly wait to get home. A long hot shower came to mind. I knew I must look bad and smell worse, but I didn't care.

"Sheriff Martinez will be at the ambulance tomorrow when we get there," Luke told me. "He'll want you to tell him all about how you managed to get yourself locked into a cave far away in the mountains." Luke was able to make me laugh again.

"I'll tell him all about it, but I don't want to think about it tonight," I told him. "I just want to be warm, fed, and safe among friends."

"Understandable," Luke said, "but I have one friend that wants to come over here to greet you." Luke got up and walked away into the darkness.

That's very mysterious, I thought. Haven't all my friends been right here beside me?

Then Luke came out of the dark leading Hero!

"Hero," I yelled. "How did you find him? He was stolen. I thought I'd never see him again."

I stood up and went to Hero and threw my arms around his neck. "Oh Hero, I was so worried. I thought you were gone forever. How did you find him?" I asked.

"This morning we were searching about ten miles from here when he came down the trail. It was as though he was headed home. He had your tack on him, so we thought you had fallen. We followed his tracks back to here," Luke explained.

"You're kidding. I thought I heard a horse outside the cave a couple times. I thought searchers were riding by and missing the cave. I called out and got no answer. He must have come back here looking for me. Oh Hero, you have truly saved me," I said. I felt such intense love and gratitude for this horse as I lay my head on his. Hero nickered softly.

CHAPTER 55

THE NEXT MORNING I was given a hearty breakfast and everyone camped around me was attentive to my every need. I walked among all my rescuers and thanked them for all their efforts and for saving my life.

"You can thank your horse too," the lady in charge of the search and rescue team communications said. "Following his trail brought us into this area far from the valley you started from. We hadn't been looking this far from where you disappeared. It was a couple days before we ran into Hero coming back toward home. It sure was important that we finally spotted your horse. Incidentally, word has been relayed to your mom that you are doing fine. We'll be anxious to hear your story, but you must talk to the sheriff first."

I gave her a hug with tears running down my cheeks. These people had so much love to give in the efforts they made to save others. I would always feel gratitude for search and rescue organizations.

I felt good enough that the idea of going to the closest road to ride home in an ambulance didn't appeal. I went to the man in charge of the group, Jim Lourdes, and, after thanking him, pleaded my case.

"I feel really much better this morning. Is there any chance that instead of going home in an ambulance I could ride out to the Winslow ranch where I started this trip? My friends have to take their horses back there because they had trailered to Luke's place to help. Hero has to go back there, too," I hoped I had convinced him.

"Well, that is not a normal procedure in a case like this. Let me radio the sheriff and see what he says," Jim said.

I went to Luke and the girls and told them about my request.

"If you are really up to it we would have fun doing that. We'll have to camp one night on the way back, but we can do that. Most of these guys have their trailers at our place and they will have to go that way and camp too," Luke said. The girls grinned and agreed. They all looked so tired, but as happy as I felt.

"I didn't realize how far away from your place we are. I guess I should have remembered. The trip here is sort of a blur," I said. "I really do feel fine though."

"What about your mom?" Becky said. "She will be so anxious to see you."

"I know. I'll ask them to radio and ask her, too, about me coming home without an ambulance," I faltered thinking how she would feel about this plan.

As camp was packed up Jim Lourdes came to me. "The sheriff says he'll meet you at the Winslow place. He's glad you are doing well. He said your mom about flipped out, but after he talked to her she agreed to you having a couple days to recover on the trail. It will be a bit of a zoo when you get back, with press and all. I convinced her that the time to decompress would be good for you and that you would be well looked after with so many rescuers."

"Oh dear, you're right," I said. "I will need a couple days to sort all this out before meeting the press. I didn't realize this would be such a big deal. Thanks."

"We are all going to be going back the same way anyway. We'll just take you back to the Winslow ranch," he smiled as he gave me this gift of a couple days.

The ride back gave me so much time to think and try to gather myself before facing Mom and school. I needed to get back to a normal life. I thought about Thanksgiving with Mom, Miguel, and Maria. That anticipation of something normal took on a great deal of importance.

I also visited with Luke and the girls. They questioned me about the days in the cave and how I got there. I was somewhat reticent because I knew that as a story got retold, person to person, it would tend to change. I felt I needed to talk first to Sheriff Martinez.

Shifty was still at large and that worried me some, though I felt very safe in this crowd. I also had time to thank each of my rescuers. That was very important to me. A couple days riding on Hero would go a long ways toward recovery from this trauma.

CHAPTER 56

WE ARRIVED AT the Winslow ranch late in the afternoon. As our group rode into the barn lot I saw Mom come running from the house. I jumped off of Hero and into her arms. She hugged me so tight that I felt like I couldn't breathe. I expected us to cry buckets of tears with the relief, but instead I found us both smiling ear to ear. The joy was overwhelming. We just held each other.

Luke had jumped off his horse and he took Hero toward the barn. "Don't worry about our horse hero. I'll take good care of him," he said as he put his hand on my shoulder and winked at me. On the ride home Luke and I had shared some laughs and he told me about their search for me. I knew he was my hero once again. On the return trip I realized this experience had given me many heroes and I was grateful.

The rescue party loaded their horses in their trailers and headed for home. They were weary and ready to declare "mission accomplished." Sandi and Becky were anxious to get home too and we said our good-byes. I, of course, repeated my thanks many times. Mr. Brenton was there to take them and their horses home. My need now was to be with my mom to make sure she was okay.

Mom escorted me to the house where Mr. Winslow and Betsy showered me with more hugs. Everyone was over joyed and full of gratitude. There was going to be a fine celebration.

But I saw Sheriff Martinez standing across the kitchen and I knew I had business with him first. I was anxious to get him on the trail of Shifty by providing all the information that I could. I pulled away from the hugging crowd and walked to him.

"Welcome home," he said. "It is a great relief to have you safe. You had us all pretty worried."

"I know. I'm sorry," I said. "But I really didn't have any choice. I'm ready to tell you all about what happened."

Mr. Winslow escorted us into his office. Mom and a couple deputies followed us. Mr. Winslow closed the door. Mom sat with me on the leather sofa while the sheriff and his deputies took seats around the room. Mr. Winslow also stayed, I assumed as a witness.

Sheriff Martinez began. "First of all I want to put your mind at rest about one thing. Sheriff Adams had a surveillance operation on a pen of cattle that had been found in his county. They observed trucks and men gathering there and knew something was going down. A known felon named Walter Dumler showed up on your horse. The surveillance saw him arrive. When he dismounted from your horse he slapped the horse with his reins on the face. Your horse reared up and struck him in the head. When Dumler went down the officers moved in and arrested him and the other men working with him. It was soon discovered through law enforcement in Wyoming that he was suspected of being the gang leader."

"In all the excitement Hero ran off, apparently in the direction he had come from. He must have been headed toward home, which took him back past the cave. The rescue party found him coming down the trail they were tracking," Sheriff Martinez filled in the last blank for me.

Sheriff Martinez paused. I needed a few moments to take all this in. So Shifty was Walter Dumler and he was the rustlers' leader. And Hero had reared up and struck Dumler. I had to assume Dumler had been pretty rough with Hero more than once because Hero didn't normally behave that way. And then Hero headed back to where I was.

"So you caught Shifty?" I asked with relief. "He had jumped me when I rode out of camp on Saturday. He rode Hero and made me walk all day to his hideout. He left me there locked in a cave and that is where the rescue party found me. He said if he couldn't cut a deal to release his men that I could just stay there and starve." I was beginning to get the big picture of all that had been happening. "And when I heard the sounds of a horse outside the cave it was Hero and then he headed down the trail and met the rescuers."

"I guess Shifty was the name you put on him, but it was Dumler. Only he could have had your horse," the sheriff explained. "When we questioned him, he would not tell us where he had left you or how he had gotten your horse. We all refused to do anything but search for you until you were found. Your mom, your friends, and the Winslows were as determined, as the various law enforcement departments, to find you. I guess we owe it to Hero that we found you in that cave."

"So let me get this straight. You have captured all the gang for sure. Because of Hero running off I was found. And this nightmare is all over?" I asked incredulously.

"Yes, I would say that is true. You will probably be asked to testify at Dumler's trial, but I think you can handle that," Sheriff Martinez assured me.

I turned to Mom and for the first time the tears of relief rolled. I couldn't believe this whole nightmare was actually over.

"Your perseverance during your days in captivity is a testament to your strength and courage, Emily. We're proud of you," the sheriff told me. Everyone in the room joined in with a "hear, hear."

We rejoined the Winslow family in the kitchen where everyone was gathered around a big table. Betsy said, "We have a welcome home dinner for you. They had radioed that you would be here this evening."

"Awesome. I'm starved!" I exclaimed and they all laughed at my enthusiasm.

Everyone joined me in a huge feast of steak, baked potatoes, fresh salad and strawberries from the garden. I ate and drank like I was famished, which I was. Mom and I couldn't be separated. Luke sat on my other side during dinner and we communicated our pleasure with our eyes.

CHAPTER 57

THERE WAS A lot of hoopla for a while after my rescue and the arrest of the rustlers. There was plenty of credit to go around. The FBI honored our Sheriff Martinez and Sheriff Adams from Garfield County for their diligence in finding the rustlers. Our two sheriffs had worked closely together. There was even one TV interview of Robert who claimed to have offered the first tip on where to find these guys. I wrote to our search and rescue team to thank them again.

Of course, at school Luke, Sandi, and Becky were famous for their devoted efforts to rescue me. They had ridden out every day until I was found. I did an interview with the lady TV anchor from Denver. Most of that interview was about my time in captivity in the cave. I tried to emphasize the story of how I had saved Hero and about how he had saved me in return, but the anchor was more interested in the horrors of being stuck in a cave to starve. I guess that made better news.

Mom and I weathered the storm just hoping that things would soon quiet down, and they did. We got back to our routine of Mom working at the hospital and me going to school and caring for Hero. It was a busy time and I didn't see Luke for a while.

Hero seemed to like the role of hero at the stable. My stable mates kept coming around offering him treats. He had lived up to his name

Beth told me, "I think it is marvelous the way you tried to tell the story of Hero and to give him the attention and credit that you did. I believe an editor I know at *Western Horse* magazine wants to tell that story. He believes your story will heighten awareness about abused horses. Hero may end up an ambassador!"

I liked that and I agreed to the interview. I was sort of liking being famous.

My teachers were helpful to me and my rescue team to catch up at school. Now I can look forward with anticipation to finishing my school year and then going to work with Diamond. I have so much to look forward to. I'm sure glad I didn't end my life at fifteen in a cave.

Finally I saw Luke about a week later at school.

"Sorry, Luke, I haven't had much time to see you. You know my gratitude to you and your family is overwhelming. Things are beginning to quiet down. Getting back to normal may allow us to go riding again, right?" I asked hoping he would forgive me.

"Of course. I know all the attention has been pretty disruptive. I'm just grateful that you are okay. My family wants to make up for the disastrous packing trip this year by planning another trip in the mountains in the spring, but we will keep you tethered to one of us at all times," Luke said, giving me a wonderful smile.

Then he asked me to go with him to a movie Saturday evening and to have something to eat afterwards.

Mom agreed to our first official date since the dance. It seemed that since my rescue Luke had regained his favored place in her estimation.

Thankfully Mom never blamed the Winslows for my being kidnapped. When I talked to her about the day Walter Dumler, alias Shifty, captured me, she said, "You were each in your group doing exactly what would be expected on a packing trip—fishing, sketching, and riding. We all thought the bad guys were in jail. I saw the efforts that the Winslows went on your behalf and I can only judge them to be the best of friends."

So on Saturday evening Luke came by and picked me up. We went to a movie, but I wasn't impressed with what was playing. It was just nice spending time with my friend. After the movie we went to our only real, local restaurant, The Cloverleaf, and had hamburgers and sundaes.

"We have been going steady for some time now, though I'm not sure you are acknowledging that yet," Luke said as we ate our ice cream. "You are my best friend and I was really scared when we couldn't find you. Dad wanted me to ride for the sheriff, but I told him, 'Send Ed,' because I was going to start looking for you. It was a rough five days. I sure didn't sleep much."

"Luke, I just don't have enough words to tell you how I feel about your devotion. You have just been the best friend in the world. And they were right. I have avoided talking about going steady, though we used the idea to persuade Robert to come to the barbeque. And I did tell my friends that we were going steady. And Mom agreed to it. I was just afraid of the commitment at this stage," I tried to explain myself. "I guess I have only avoided saying to you, 'Yes, I want to go steady.'"

"Emily, we have been going steady for several weeks and nothing horrible has happened to you because of it. Don't make too big a deal out of this. We're not getting married, after all. I just want to date you exclusively. I want to keep the less deserving boys away from you. I don't have a class ring yet to give you, but I have this," Luke said as he pulled out a jewelry box. "My mom helped me pick it out."

"Oh Luke, it's beautiful and so thoughtful. Thank you," I said as I pulled out a beautiful charm bracelet. On the bracelet were a horse, a cowboy, a camp fire, a saddle, and the vet caduceus. "I will wear this with pride and it will represent that we've agreed to date exclusively. I'm very proud to be seen as your girlfriend."

Luke had a big smile. "I'm so relieved that you are finally succumbing to my charms. And Ed told me I was too dumb for you. You don't even mind me being a dumb cowboy."

"That's because there is nothing dumb about you," I declared. "You are a fine upstanding young man, admired by all the girls, and destined to succeed in all that you do."

"That is well deserved praise," he beamed. "Let's go tell your mom." And we did.

CHAPTER 58

NOW THAT I have allowed myself to revisit the events of this past year, a year of terrible losses and of finding friendships and love, I believe that revisiting all that has happened has given me, if not closure, at least a positive outlook. Next Wednesday, June 1, will be my big sixteenth. The Big Sweet Sixteen. The year that brings a driver's license. I'm sorry Dad won't be with me for my sixteenth, but looking back has freed me to look ahead.

I had a wonderful Thanksgiving with Miguel and Maria, who are very special to me. I've just completed my freshman year in high school. I was able to get the good grades that I worried about. I was able to settle with Mom and Hero into a new life. I gained many new friends and maintained old ones. I've adjusted to living as a 'townie,' not a goal I anticipated.

Most importantly, my mom and I have grown closer and have learned to successfully lean on each other. Ours is a love forged by her in giving me the freedom to be who I am. This past year our love and respect for each other has been strengthened by our mutual determination to survive. The successes that Mom and I have shared have been due to the kind of man Dad was and the influence he had on us. She is the best mother and I tell her that regularly.

Mom has finally agreed to let me go to Denver this summer and Mr. Butler has renewed his invitation to me to work as an intern. I'm anticipating spending the summer at the Golden Gate Canyon Quarter Horse stables helping to work with Diamond and getting some practical experience learning about doctoring horses. Luke has graciously agreed to keep Hero on the ranch for me.

I've had communications with Professor Neuminski and she continues to encourage me to pursue my interest in being a horse vet. She thinks my summer internship will look really good on my college application.

Not a day goes by that I don't spend time with Dad. He is always with me and I'm grateful for the courage I've been able to tap into because of the things he taught me. He left me with a course for my life that came from his own love of nature, animals, home, and family. He will always be that handsome forty-two year old cowboy who waved goodbye from horseback. I'm determined to, throughout my life, do the things that would have made him proud.

As Luke and I both go through high school and travel the path that will be each of our journeys, our friendship may grow into something permanent. But if it doesn't, I will always have him as a friend I can count on and he will have me.

When I look back at how we took Hero into our hearts and gave him a second chance at life, I can't help but realize that he has returned the favor many times. Not only was he instrumental in getting me out of that horrible cave, but he has been invaluable in helping me to adjust to the loss of the ranch. I guess we rescued each other. I'm sure glad I named him Hero.

The future looks exciting.

ABOUT THE AUTHOR

©Orlando Diaz

Former pilot, stockbroker, horse trainer, and forever Mom, Camilla Kattell has had the privilege, in retirement, of indulging her passion for writing. Living in Santa Fe, New Mexico, she has had an outlet for both her love of horses and for the mountainous beauty of New Mexico and its history. "Cam" has written several books for young adults, including *Youth on the Santa Fe Trail*, an anthology about young people who traveled the Santa Fe Trail in the 19th Century. In *Hero, the Horse That Rescued Me* she writes a beautiful story about a young girl dealing with adversity and prevailing with inspirational courage.

CPSIA information can be obtained
at www.ICGtesting.com
Printed in the USA
BVHW031512120919
558309BV00001B/40/P

9 780996 675468